"Not too many folks move to Maine in February."

He laughed and shrugged one shoulder. "Not the sane ones. Figured I might as well see what I was up against right off." Shadow returned with the stick and gave a quick bark of impatience. "Good boy." Bear ruffled the dog's ear, gathered the stick, and threw it even farther. "Go get it." He looked back at her. "Didn't catch your name."

Kay watched the dog. "I didn't throw it. Fetch isn't really my game." She collected the sketchpad and shoved it back into her bag. "Thanks for retrieving my towel, however."

"You're not going to tell me who you are?"

She shook her head and started back toward the stairs leading to the cottage.

"What if I promise to keep Shadow on his leash from now on?" he called. "What would you say then?"

She glanced back over one shoulder. Bear and Shadow stood watching. The dog dropped his stick and looked a bit disappointed. So did his owner.

"I'd say, *Good boy.*"

I0680597

Against the Wall

by

Lisa A. Olech

Stoddard Art School Series

Against the Wall

Cover Art by *Angela Anderson*

The Wild Rose Press, Inc.
PO Box 708
Adams Basin, NY 14410-0708
Visit us at www.thewildrosepress.com

Publishing History
First Champagne Rose Edition, 2016
Print ISBN 978-1-5092-0980-4
Digital ISBN 978-1-5092-0981-1

Stoddard Art School Series
Published in the United States of America

Dedication

To Jennifer A.
An artist who brings color to the world
one perfect stitch at a time.

Chapter One

The bells over the door announced her as they had a thousand times before. Kay Winston breathed in the familiar scents of the gift shop called Polka Dots. Candles, soaps, saltwater taffy. Rows of gift cards, souvenirs, and a tall rack of tiny Maine license plate key chains, arranged alphabetically by name. Kay picked up an ugly red ceramic lobster with the words Bell Harbor, Maine, printed across its tail in gold. She was home.

"Be right with you!" a cheerful voice called from the back. "We just got a new shipment of lovely placemats. Matching napkins. Buy one, get one at half price."

The bargain placemats sat prominently on the end cap with an artistic arrangement of hand-dipped candles, a bottle of local wine, and a dried flower display.

"I love them," Kay called back. "I'll take them all. How much for the whole lot?"

Dottie Polk rushed through the curtained doorway leading to the back office. "Did I hear you say the whole—*Kay?* Kay!" The older woman pulled her in for a tight embrace. "What a wonderful surprise. What are you doing here? We weren't to see you 'til July." Dottie pulled back and cupped Kay's cheek. "It's great to see you." A frown marred her soft face. "What's wrong?

Are you okay?"

Kay grinned down into Dottie's gentle brown eyes and felt a catch in her heart. *Damn.* "Nothing's wrong. I'm great."

"Don't you be fibbing to me. You couldn't get away with it when you were five and sneaking candy coins, and you sure as hell can't be doing it now."

Kay never could get anything by Dottie. Didn't mean she couldn't try. "I'm fine," Kay insisted, averting her eyes. "How are *you?*" She glanced toward the back room. "Where's Walter?"

"He's out being a pain in the ass. Don't try to change the subject." Dottie smoothed the length of Kay's hair. "Everything okay in Stoddard? Things all right at school?"

"Stoddard is Stoddard. School is great. The end-of-semester show is running at the Bruce Gallery in Boston, and I've three pieces on display this year. Quite the coup. By this time next year, I'll have my MFA. Can you believe it?"

"You've a helluva future headed your way."

Kay smirked. "Let's hope so."

"Don't worry, I've enough faith for the both of us." Dottie patted her arm and led her to the office. "Come on out back, and sit. There's a pot of tea steeping. Probably strong as sock dye by now." She grinned over one shoulder and winked. "Just the way I like it."

Kay followed into the quaint little office, Dottie's private sanctuary. Kay used to play here on rainy summer days. The kneehole in Dottie's desk was her pirate cave. It was a great place to hide away and nibble on foil-wrapped chocolate coins pretending they were her buried treasure.

She stopped in the doorway and smoothed her hand over the penciled scores that ran the length of the painted wood. Every summer when she came to Bell Harbor with her mother and stepfather to visit, Dottie's husband, Walter, measured her height on the doorframe. The marks were still there. Proof she'd grown up right on this very spot.

Dottie poured them each a cup of tea. "Ahhh," she sighed. Kay smiled into her cup. Dottie always sighed with her first sip of tea as if it were the finest wine she'd ever drunk. Now she'd say—

"That's the ticket."

Thank goodness, some things never changed.

"Not that I'm complaining, mind ya, but why are you here so early in the season? What's going on with you, or shall we spend the afternoon dancing around this?"

Kay shrugged. "I decided instead of one week at the cottage this year, I'll spend my summer break here. Things in Stoddard are...kind of complicated right now."

"What kind of complicated?"

"I didn't get the internship I wanted. My summer class cancelled."

"And? What about Todd?"

"Todd is over."

"What's he done?"

Kay sipped her tea. She wasn't about to tell Dot all the gory details. Wouldn't tell her how she found Todd and Gwen going at it like two sex-starved howler monkeys in their bed. Or the ugly screaming match that followed. She swallowed the painful lump in her throat. "He went back to his ex."

"Slimy bastard." Dotty clicked her tongue, "*Tsk, tsk.* Well, I'm sorry about the internship and your class." She raised an eyebrow. "As for the other, I won't lie, I'm not unhappy you're rid of that Johnny Come Lately."

"Johnny Come Lately? Who talks like you?" Kay shook her head. "She can have him. I packed what I could fit into my car, and took off. I figured I could use the cottage to clear my head for a bit. I've enough savings to live for a couple months if I don't eat much, and if you'll let me sell some sketches here like last year, I should make it through August. Where I'll live come the fall semester, I have no idea, but I'll cross that bridge when I get there."

"Of course I'll take your sketches. All you can give me. They sell great, but you can't live on that. Walter and I could—"

"No."

"But, Kay…"

"We've been over this before. I'm not taking your money."

Dottie pursed her lips and gave Kay *the stare*. "Do your folks know you're at camp?"

"Not yet." *Not ever if I can get away with it.* "I doubt they'd care. I'm the only one who uses the place, anyway. I'll tell them. Eventually. Maybe."

Dottie gave her the stare again. The door to the storeroom slammed.

"It's colder than a witch's tit out they-ah! It's May, but I swear I'm smelling snow, Dottie. Yessah. Do ya know what the weather's gonna be?" Walter hollered as he moved through the boxes of stock. "Yogi got back from down in Beantown. You should see the pile he

4

brought with 'im. Got some wicked cool stuff."

"Yogi?" Kay whispered.

Dottie shook her head and flipped her hand to dismiss his rambling. "You know how he makes up names."

Kay understood. Walter had a nickname for everyone.

"I'm chilled clear to my woolies! Be a luv, put on the kettle." He stopped to hang his coat on the top corner of the office door. When he saw Kay, he lit up. "Special Kay!" He pulled her out of her seat into his arms and gave her a great bear hug. "How's my girl?"

"I'm great, Walter, how are you?"

"Well, I've been bettah, but it's cost me more." He patted the belly of his overalls while keeping an arm wrapped around her shoulders. "Did you know she was comin'?"

Dottie shook her head.

"You don't usually get here 'til flatlander season. How long you stayin'?"

"How about all summer?"

"Well, I'm tickled pinker than Aunt Fanny's pig. Did ya hear, Dottie Dot? All summer."

"I heard." Dottie's grin didn't mask the concern in her eyes.

Kay kissed Walter's cheek. She hated to worry Dot. Given time, she'd tell her everything, but for now, she wanted to feel safe and loved and cherished. She found all those things with Dottie and Walter. It was good to be home.

"I should get myself over to the cottage and move my stuff in before dark. I stopped here first." She smiled at Dottie. "Had to make sure Polka Dots was still the same."

"Nothing much changes 'round he-ah. Ya know that." Walter gave another squeeze.

"I do. Why do you think I keep coming back?"

Dottie rose and grasped her hand. "You want any help moving your things?"

"No, I packed for a speedy getaway. It won't take me long to unload." Kay gave Dottie's fingers a reassuring squeeze. "I'll pop in when I come back into town for supplies."

"If you need anything, you know where to find us. Get yourself settled. Then you're coming to dinner. Tomorrow night. I'll make pot roast just the way you like it."

"I love your pot roast. It's a date."

Stopping by the penny candy counter on their way out, Walter scooped a handful of foil wrapped gold coin chocolates into a small white bag. "Your favorites."

"They are." Kay laid a kiss on his lined cheek. "And so are you."

****

Gravel popped and crunched beneath the tires of her Mini as she pulled into the parking spot. The "camp" sat low on the slope heading down to the rocky shore of Abbott's Cove, one of the many inlets in Bell Harbor. From the gravel pad, a worn set of stone steps led to her charming cottage by the sea.

Correction, it wasn't hers. Not yet. It was still her parents', at least until they could find the optimum time in the ever-changing real estate market to make a handsome profit on the place.

Kay had spent every summer here from the time she was four years old. Her mother, Claire, married

Charles the week Kay turned three. Charles thought Claire's simple background growing up in Maine had been quaint. They found this place on Abbott's Cove. With Dottie being Claire's best friend all through school, Bell Harbor had been the perfect place to get away and visit old friends.

But things changed. Her mother changed. She'd gone from being a poor, single mother struggling to keep shoes on her daughter's growing feet and enough food on the table, to a woman who played bridge on Thursday afternoons with the women from the club. Maine's quaintness had soured in her mouth. She changed how she spoke, forcing her accent away. She started telling people she was from New England, not from Maine. She became a snob.

That hadn't stopped Kay from loving Bell Harbor. When her parents decided summer vacations in the Hamptons were preferable to the coast of Maine, she begged them to send her to Dottie and Walter's. She hadn't needed to beg. They were glad to see her leave.

Bell Harbor became her escape. Her refuge. She still ran here when life became unbearable. It continued to be her soft place to land. But this time, the fall had broken her. Damn near killed her.

She and Todd had planned to come here for two weeks in July to announce to Dottie and Walter that they were getting married. He'd asked her on Valentine's Day. He'd brought home two bottles of cheap champagne and a convenience store rose and taken her to bed. The rose he'd stripped as naked as the two of them and showered her and the bed with the crushed red petals. After they'd made love, he'd asked her if she wanted "to get hitched." He'd joked afterward that it had been the champagne talking. He'd gotten carried away in the moment, but "what the hell, why not?" They were already living together.

It wasn't the proposal of every girl's dream, but he swore he loved her. And she loved him. So what if he didn't get down on one knee and present a little black velvet box with a stunning diamond ring nestled inside. That was only for cheesy romantic movies. She was much more pragmatic.

Kay ran a thumb over the tender tip of her finger. Over the sensitive spot where the rose's thorn had drawn blood. When she'd found Todd and Gwen in bed three days ago. He'd pulled all the petals from a cheap, convenience store red rose and sprinkled them in the sheets. Kay found the stripped stem on the hallway rug moments before she heard them. Saw them.

Crushing it in her fist, its thorns stabbed deep into her finger. Deep into her heart. She never felt it. She was numb.

Damn, I should have thanked Gwen—once she'd climbed down off Todd's penis, of course. The girl saved her a boatload of misery. Just think, she could have married the dog. Rephrase that. It gave dogs a bad name; she loved dogs.

Stepping out of her car, Kay pulled the heavenly combination of rich pine scent and the crisp tang of the ocean deep into her lungs. She closed her eyes and listened to the hushed rhythm of the waves kissing the beach. It called her name.

Unloading could wait. The draw of the surf was too great. Rushing down the stairs, Kay stepped out onto the pebbled beach that welcomed her like an old friend. The water sat high, but the tide had turned. Smoothed stones glistened in the waning light. The sky, streaked with peach, danced on the tips of the waves.

Tears filled her eyes as a familiar peace settled on her. Was there a more beautiful place on earth? Not to her. It was perfect. Well, almost.

Kay closed her right eye. There, now it was perfect.

She shook her head and laughed at herself. It was silly. She headed back up the steep stairs to her car and retrieved her suitcase. Completely childish. But when you're twelve and arrive in your personal, *private* playground only to discover someone else in your sandbox, you get to do silly things.

It had been the worst summer. Claire and Charles decided it would be their last vacation here, and it was breaking Kay's heart. Claire and Dottie argued and stopped speaking for the first time in their friendship, and to put a cherry on top, someone dropped a house on the point like twister residue from *The Wizard of Oz*.

Modern and sleek—it was the ugliest thing she'd ever seen. With stark lines and oversized gaping windows, it was cold and lifeless. In all the years she'd been coming here, she'd never spotted a soul out there. Dottie said the couple who owned it didn't come up until the last few weeks of August, which is why she never saw them. They were nice according to her, but Kay never even asked their names.

They'd invaded her territory. Her best *thinking spot* sat out there beyond the house, at the tip of the point. How was she supposed to think out there with that…that icebox of a house hogging all the space?

Kay dropped the last carton onto the painted wood floor and pushed the hair out of her face. She'd started a small fire to take the months of chill from the place. After pulling all the dust covers off the faded hodgepodge of furniture, she lugged her paints and supplies up the narrow flight of stairs to her studio. The second bedroom originally, it still had the single iron bed set along the back wall, but now it served as her work area when she was here. Set on the seaward side of the house, the morning light shone brilliantly, and the view of the cove was magnificent. As long as she closed her eye.

Kay raised the window and pushed aside the sheer curtains that danced on the evening's breeze. The sun set, pulling the last of the peach-tinged sky with it. The soft navy blue of night settled in to blanket the darkening sea. She blinked. Both eyes.

Were there lights in the point house?

Chapter Two

Kay woke and stretched beneath the snuggly warmth of the homespun quilt. The only sounds were the breeze whispering through the treetops and the regular cadence of the waves. She sighed. It had been the first decent sleep she'd had since…since the howler monkey incident.

She shook her head and squeezed her eyes tight against the image burned into her mind's eye. No, no, no. She wouldn't let Todd ruin her peace. Not here.

Downstairs, Kay rummaged through the kitchen's near-empty cupboards. A dusty jar sat in a back corner. *Thank you, God! Instant coffee!* "I'm saved!"

While the kettle did what kettles do, she jotted a short list of what she'd need to survive on her shoestring budget. Coffee had to be first on the list. Caffeine was an absolute essential.

A dozen picture frames were number two. Dottie had agreed to take on some of her sketches. Not much income, but every little bit helped. When she went into town later for a few groceries, she'd swing over to the consignment shop and see about the frames. She'd stop by the copy store as well.

Leafing through her things as she unpacked last night, she'd found six charcoal drawings that would make great gift cards sets. Copies, envelopes, and a little ribbon, and she'd be in business.

She took a tentative sip of the coffee. Covered her mouth as she grimaced. *Damn!* It tasted like someone ran a dead brown crayon through hot water. Eeew! Could coffee go bad? Ick! She stuck out her tongue. Where was a Dunkins when you needed one! Dumping her mug into the sink, she underlined coffee on the list. Three times.

After rinsing out the cup, Kay twisted her long hair into a loose knot and secured it with a clip. The beach was calling. Coffee would have to wait. She loaded a tote and grabbed a towel from the tiny hall closet.

The wide deck running along the back and up one side of the cottage was cool, and moss edged beneath the tower of pine trees that guarded the house. Granite steps led through the thick underbrush. They were chilled and damp against her bare feet.

Bleached white and tumbled by generations of surf, the beach stones were blinding as she stepped out into the morning's sunshine. They warmed her chilled toes. She dropped her things and headed to the water's edge. The constant pounding of waves crushed the beach into a coarse, wet sand. Kay dug her heels into the cool rasp. She sighed gazing out to where the sky and the sea blended into one. Gorgeous.

From there the Atlantic stretched clear to Europe. Above, gulls dipped across a perfect blue sky and screeched at one another. Lifting her arms over her head, she reached for that perfect blue and stretched in the sunshine. The crisp bite of salt air filled her lungs.

The morning tide was rising. Each wave reached a few inches closer until its icy fingers tickled Kay's toes. She shivered. The water was frigid. This was Maine after all. Even in August, the water would numb her

feet, and you didn't stay in long. It took a brave soul—
or a foolish one—to swim in the glacial temps in May.

Kay moved back up the beach. The waves
wouldn't reach this far, and the pebbles were smooth,
dry, and blissfully warm. She pulled the sketchpad out
of her bag and bent to spread out her towel.

The bark of a dog startled her, and she
straightened. A large, black Labrador retriever barreled
down the beach. He didn't appear fierce as he raced
straight toward her. He almost seemed to be smiling, if
dogs indeed smiled. A large pink tongue lolled to one
side of its mouth. Still, strange dog, tearing at her full
speed. She yelped and held the towel in front of her like
a baby-blue terrycloth matador's cape.

The dog stopped inches away, danced a bit, and
then lowered its head to its front paws while leaving its
butt waving in the air. Its entire body wagged. It gave a
quick, low *woof*, snatched the towel from her grasp, and
raced past.

"Hey!"

The dog stopped and assumed the same position as
before—this time holding its prize just out of reach.
When she stepped toward it, the dog leaped backward
and shook her towel as it growled playfully.

"You brat. Give that back." Kay laughed.

"Shadow! No! Drop it!" the dog's human shouted
as he chased up the beach. He was a big man, wide
shoulders, strong legs. He wore a red plaid flannel shirt
over a navy T-shirt, both untucked from the waist of
dark jeans. Dark brown hair that curled slightly on the
ends, morning scruff of a beard. He didn't look
threatening, still—strange man racing in her direction,
and she'd already lost her protective cape.

"I'm so sorry," he huffed. "He bolted as soon as he saw you." Holding up an empty collar and leash, he shook his head. "He's a big goof. Won't hurt you. He just wants to play."

"Tug o' war?"

"Yeah, we play tug a lot." He motioned to the dog that crouched staring at them both expectantly. He gave a quick scan of the area. "If I grab it, he'll pull and shred your towel." The man walked a few feet, picked up a bit of driftwood, and held it aloft. "Good thing he's easily distracted." The quick flip of his eyebrows and the mischievous glint in his light brown eyes confirmed he was as *goofy* as his dog.

Holding the stick high, he jerked it as if to throw it. The dog dropped the towel and froze. Eyes locked on the prized stick, its body a coiled spring waiting to launch in whichever direction the stick flew.

"Get the stick." The dog's owner hurled the bit of driftwood backhanded down the beach. The dog took off like a bullet. Kay followed the impressive arc of the toss as Shadow's owner snatched her towel off the stones.

"Nice throw." She reached for the towel from his outstretched hand. He was standing close enough to see that his eyes were more green than brown, and that beneath all that scruff, the man had a gentle cleft in his chin. *Goofy* wasn't the right word to describe him either. Relaxed? Easy-going? Sexy as hell?

"It's got a little dog drool." He didn't let go. Did he mean to play tug too? "I could clean it and return it later."

"Not necessary." When he released it, Kay stuffed the slobbered towel back into her bag as Shadow cheerfully dropped the stick at his owner's feet.

He picked it up and flung it away again. Wiping his hands on his jeans, he offered her his hand. "I'm Bear." He jerked his head in the direction of the racing dog. "He's Shadow. We're out on the point." He took her hand in his.

His fingers engulfed hers. His hands were large and rough, but warm and gentle. Her lady parts whispered their approval. "*You* live on the point?"

"Yep, I bought the place last winter. Been here since February."

"Not too many folks move to Maine in February."

He laughed and shrugged one shoulder. "Not the sane ones. Figured I might as well see what I was up against right off." Shadow returned with the stick and gave a quick bark of impatience. "Good boy." Bear ruffled the dog's ear, gathered the stick, and threw it even farther. "Go get it." He looked back at her. "Didn't catch your name."

Kay watched the dog. "I didn't throw it. Fetch isn't really my game." She collected the sketchpad and shoved it back into her bag. "Thanks for retrieving my towel, however."

"You're not going to tell me who you are?"

She shook her head and started back toward the stairs leading to the cottage.

"What if I promise to keep Shadow on his leash from now on?" he called. "What would you say then?"

She glanced back over one shoulder. Bear and Shadow stood watching. The dog dropped his stick and looked a bit disappointed. So did his owner.

"I'd say, *Good boy.*"

****

"These are wonderful." Dottie perused the stack of greeting cards and prints while Kay set the table for dinner.

"The cards came out great, didn't they? Pete at The Copy Corral suggested using the same image in packs of six rather than a mixed set. Made sense. I'll finish framing the rest of my stuff. You'll have them by the weekend."

"The customers are going to love these."

"Let's hope," Kay joked. "I've grown pretty fond of eating." She slipped a polka dot napkin next to each dinner plate. "Speaking of which, everything smells incredible. I can't tell you the last time I ate a home cooked meal."

"You know, if things are that tight for you—"

"I'm not taking any of your money. It's bad enough you're not charging me commission on the things I'm putting in the shop." Kay finished laying the silverware.

"Maybe if you talked to your folks—"

Kay snorted. "No."

"If they understood the situation, I'm sure—"

"No." Dottie wasn't the only one who'd mastered *the stare*.

"There's no shame in—"

"Dottie." Kay took hold of her hands and held her gaze. "No."

"You're a very stubborn young lady, do you know that?"

"Yep. But you love me." She kissed Dottie's hands and found some candles to add to the table. Rummaging through the kitchen's junk drawer, she unearthed a box of blue-tip matches.

"Of course I love you, but I don't see the difference between staying in their cottage and asking them for help."

Kay struck the match. The puff of smoke stung her nose as she lit each taper. "They know I come up here on vacation, so my vacation is a little bit longer this summer. I'm paying the water and electric direct, so it's not like I'm sticking them with the bill." She blew out the match and tossed it into the sink. "I've been the one keeping the place up, taking care of things. How many years has it been since they came here? They care about that cottage about as much as they care about me."

"That's not true. They love you. If they knew you were struggling—"

"They'd be the first ones to say, I told you so."

"Kay." Dottie gave her that pitying look Kay hated.

"You of all people know what they're like." Kay stopped herself from heading down that long, winding road filled with parental potholes. "I don't want to talk about them anymore. I'm fine. Everything is fine. I'm here now. With you...and Walter." She gave Dottie her brightest smile. "That makes everything perfect." Kay stirred the gravy. "Speaking of Walter, where is he?"

Dottie checked the clock. "I told him to be home by now. He's no doubt making a pest out of himself at the inn."

"I saw all the construction going on over there earlier. Someone's actually fixing up the old place?"

"Sure 'nough. A nice fella bought the inn last winter. He stopped by the shop not too long after, asking Walt who he'd recommend hiring to do some of the work. Didn't figure once he'd asked Walter for his opinion, he'd get such a buttinsky. The man has an opinion on just about everything, don't ya know."

"Walter likes to help."

"At least him being over there keeps him out of my hair for a bit." Dottie pulled a pie out of the oven, browned and bubbling, and set it aside to cool.

Kay gasped. "You made me lucky pie?" Her mouth watered.

"Sure did."

Dottie's blueberry pie was legendary for making wishes come true. Kay requested it every year in place of a birthday cake. "But my birthday isn't for weeks."

"Still had some blueberries in the freezer from last season. So you'll get an extra wish this year."

"Sorry, I'm late, sorry, sorry." Walter burst through the kitchen doorway and ducked as if he expected Dottie to take a swing at him. "I got chewing the fat with—"

"I told you to be home a half hour ago." Dottie fussed at him.

He pulled a business card out of his breast pocket. "When ya hear what I got to tell ya, you'll be happy I'm late." He handed the card to Kay. "Have your ears been burning?"

"What have you been up to now?" Dottie planted her hands on her hips.

"Just singing Kay's praises."

Kay read the warm, cream-colored card pinstriped with a gold border.

BELL HARBOR INN
Barrett Coulter, Owner

Walter jabbed at the card with his finger. "He's needin' someone to paint a mural in the lobby. 'I know a wicked good artist,' I said. Told him all about that fancy school you're going to. You were in town for the summer, too. He wants to meet with ya. I don't know any of the particulars. We didn't talk money, but he's not cuttin' any corners on fixing things up. Wait till ya see. Place is turnin' out real nice." He plucked a bit of pot roast off the serving platter and popped it into his mouth giving them both a smug look. "Now, it ain't a definite, mind ya, but if ya stop in tomorra, 'bout two, he'd like to talk to ya."

"A mural job? That would be fantastic!" Kay hugged Walter around his middle and peeked over her shoulder at Dottie. "Can we eat our pie first? I think I know what I'll wish for."

Chapter Three

Kay dropped her cell phone into her purse. She'd happily let the damn thing die, but because Walter gave it to Mr. Coulter as a contact number, Kay charged it overnight. She found eight messages when she checked this morning. None from Coulter. Good. None from Todd. Even better. Eight from Madeline Sullivan, the art director from the Stoddard School of Art.

Cell phone reception at the cottage was nonexistent, and the landline had been disconnected years ago. She'd wait until she returned to town to retrieve them.

Eight messages from Madeline could only mean really, really good news...or really, really bad. She'd listen to them *after* her meeting.

She ran nervous fingers through her hair as she walked up the sidewalk toward the Bell Harbor Inn. Switching her portfolio from one hand to the next, she brushed a bit of lint off her black sweater. She wanted this job. Who was she kidding, she needed this job. Sketch work was great, but her real passion was murals.

Kay loved working large scale. There was something daring about standing in front of a blank wall with a brush full of paint in your hand. That first stroke. Color against white. It was like jumping into a deep pool and hitting cold water. Part exhilarating and part terrifying. But once in, she would begin to swim...or fly might be the better word. Filling the space. Creating just the right feel to match the room's purpose. Color upon color. Layer upon layer. From the largest detail to the smallest until she'd filled the wall. Or the ceiling, or the floor, or all of the above.

As Kay approached the hundred-year-old inn, she could see it was receiving a much-needed facelift. New windows, fresh paint, stunning new landscaping. It already looked 100% better than it had. Bright colors and a cheerful street presence made it feel welcoming. A newly painted sign glistened in the afternoon sun. Golden accents complemented the royal blue lettering on a rich cream background. New evergreen shrubs flanked each post. Accent gardens lay tilled and waiting next to the foundation and along the walkway.

Up an impressive set of granite steps, a wide porch led visitors to tall doors wearing a fresh coat of matching royal blue. In true painted-lady style, accent colors of forest green and a touch of deep, rich purple highlighted the dentil moldings and gilded starburst pediments over each window.

A screened porch swept off to the right encompassing the idyllic view of the harbor inlet. Kay could envision guests lounging out there with their glasses of wine to watch the lobster boats coming in after a long day of hauling their traps. Lovely. If this were any indication to the attention to detail inside, the inn would be spectacular.

Before she could knock, a dog barked. Its nails clicked against the floorboards as it came around the corner. Kay recognized the sleek black dog with the goofy grin.

"Shadow?" The dog danced at her feet. Kay

laughed as she patted him. "Hey there, boy, what are you doing here? You didn't run away from the beach, did you? I bet you're helping with the gardening?" Giving a quick glance around, she expected to find Bear. "Where's your handsome owner?" The dog's tail thumped against the floorboards in reply. "I saw you two out running the beach last night. You sure love racing through the water."

She'd first caught a glimpse of them from her studio window vantage point. The day had been warm, and Bear ran shirtless. *Holy moly!* The man's shoulders went on for a week. A week and a half if you added the ink decorating the top of his left arm. He'd been too far away to make out the design. What could it be? Maybe a bear? Or a rose with Mom? Or the name of his girlfriend?

She shook her head. Why was she even interested? She had more important things to do. Kay ruffled the dog's ear before checking her watch. It was two. "Wish me luck, Shadow."

Kay tapped lightly on the door and entered. The smell of fresh paint and varnish was strong in the lobby. Ladders and tarps were the only decoration, but the space was impressive. Large marble tiles made up the floor with a compass rose pattern inlaid in cobalt blue gracing its center. A wide curving staircase swept up the left side. Its oak banister gleamed under a glossy new coat of finish.

The sound of a saw filtered down from one of the upper floors. Muffled music drifted in from somewhere on the first floor. An antique oak desk peeked out from under a canvas tarp. One corner sat bare to hold notes, files, and what appeared to be architect's drawings. Kay lifted a page to sneak a look.

"Can I help you?"

"Oh." Kay spun around. Her heart kicked from zero to sixty at being caught.

Bear stood, paintbrush in one hand, gallon can of polyurethane in the other. *Damn!* He was a mountain of a man. *Bear* suited him. Kay wasn't tiny, but he towered over her. The broad shoulders she'd been dreaming...er, thinking about moments ago filled out the olive drab T-shirt. Its short sleeves looked painted on where they hugged his biceps. A sprinkling of dark hair along his strong forearms only accentuated the play of veins along those muscles. *Double damn!* Teddy *Bear* he wasn't. He looked about a cuddly as a steamroller.

"Hey, it's beach girl."

"Bear." She fought the urge to reach out and test the firmness of his arms. "I thought I might find you here."

He raised an eyebrow and shot her a smile that had her rethinking that warm, fuzzy idea. "You were looking for me?"

"Don't get any ideas." She gave him a coy smile in return. "Shadow met me outside." Kay glanced past him while she pulled the business card from her pocket. Holding it between two fingers, she waved it at him. "I'm here to meet with the owner, Mr. Coulter."

Bear gave a snort. "Why are you meeting him?"

"You sure do ask a lot of questions." Kay checked her watch again.

"You sure do like to avoid answers." The corners of his eyes crinkled when he smiled.

Kay shrugged. "What can I say; I'm a woman of

mystery."

He laughed. "Most women are a mystery to me."

"We're a very hush-hush society. There's even a secret handshake." She smiled. "But if I showed you—"

"You'd have to kill me."

"Exactly." She glanced around again. "So where can I find Barrett Coulter?"

Bear swept his arms wide. "You found him."

"You're Barrett Coulter?" She shook her head and scoffed. "You are not. Quit kidding around. I have an appointment."

"How can I prove it to you? I've got my hands full, but my license is in my wallet." He turned his hip and offered her his butt. "You're welcome to fish it out."

She eyed him suspiciously. He was mocking her. Did he think she wouldn't dig into his back pocket? She stepped closer and reached behind him. "You just want me to grab your ass. Getting back at me for not telling you my name? Fine, I'll play your little game."

This close, she needed to lift her gaze to see the bemused expression on his face. She could smell the soap he used. Mixed with polyurethane it made her a bit lightheaded. She plucked the wallet from his pocket and hopped back.

Giving him her best, eyebrow raised, sassy, *I have you now* smirk, she flipped open the billfold and pulled his license from the warm, worn leather. Reading the thick laminated card made her stomach dropped. "Damn and crap…"

"What's it say?"

She closed her eyes tight. "It says your name is Barrett Coulter, you're six foot five, and you're an organ donor."

"That would make *you* Kay Winston."

"Double crap. On a cracker."

****

Color flooded Kay Winston's cheeks. God, she was cute when she blushed.

Even with her eyes still shut tight, Bear remembered their deep blue color. When she opened them, she kept her gaze on the floor. "Turn around, please." She made the circle motion with her finger. He obliged, and she stuffed his wallet back into his pocket. "Shortest interview on record," she mumbled behind him. "Sorry to bother you."

He turned back to find her heading away with her portfolio. "Hold on. Don't run off. Let's not get ahead of ourselves. Why don't you hit the kitchen and help yourself to some coffee, and we can start over." He held up the brush. "I'll go clean this."

She gave him a side glance. "I don't think—" She shook her head.

"Do you want the job, or don't you?"

"I do." She was quick to reply.

"See, answering a question doesn't have to be so difficult."

She ran a hand through her hair. The other morning on the beach, she'd had it twisted up off her neck. He liked it better down. It fell past her shoulders and curled at the ends. Was it as soft as it looked? Not many women kept their hair long these days. He liked long. And the dark, honey-blonde color was working for him too. She tucked it behind an ear. A hammered silver star hung from her earlobe. It caught the light.

She took a deep breath and squared her shoulders. "Okay, let's start over."

"Good." He jerked his chin in the direction of the kitchen. "Door's that way. Watch your step, there's a ton of supplies out there. Can't miss the coffeemaker. Give me a minute, and I'll meet you in the dining room. Swinging doors with porthole windows. Right side. Can't miss it."

Five minutes later, he'd grabbed a cup of coffee for himself and sat with her at one of the square tables scattered about the dining room.

"This is wonderful. Cozy, intimate." Her gaze traveled around the space. "The view is spectacular, and the colors are great. Rich, yet muted."

"This was the first room to be finished, paint wise. The linens are due next week."

"I can picture couples eating here. Holding hands. Staring into each other's eyes over the rim of their wineglasses. Celebrating anniversaries, having first dates, maybe lovers from out of town who come here once a year to have their affair."

"You get all that from some muted paint and new drapes?" he teased, yet he was enjoying seeing the room through her eyes. With all the details and scheduling and grunt work, sometimes it was hard for him to appreciate what others might think of the place.

"Sure, where's your imagination?"

"Oh, I have plenty of imagination. I'm imagining a kitchen staff that knocks out something other than boiled lobster. I'm imagining all the business I'm losing by not opening in time for tourist season. And I'm imagining the day I can stand back and say, 'There, it's done.' "

"You'll finish it. So you miss this summer. Maybe you'll be open to catch the fall foliage people. Bell

Harbor is stunning in the fall and beautiful in the winter, too." Her dark eyes met his over the rim of her coffee mug.

"I agree." He wished he had her optimism. "I fell in love with this place when my wife and I vacationed here several years ago."

She set her coffee aside. "So, you're married."

"Not anymore. Diane and I split. Not too long after that vacation, actually. We own—owned an architectural design firm in Los Angeles. She thrived on the constant push and pressure. Me, not so much. We met in college. Got married. Moved to LA."

"She's still in California?"

"Yep. We talk. It ended amicably as soon as I signed over the business to her. But no regrets. It wasn't the life for me." He shook his head. "How did we get from drapes to my divorce?"

"Hey, Bear." A workman stood at the doorway of the dining room. "Sorry to bother you." He jerked his chin toward Kay. "Hey."

She grinned back. "Hi."

"Did you need something, Skippy? Or just coming to say, hey?"

"No, no. Which molding you want for the cap on the wainscoting? Up on four. The bullnose?"

"No. Match the hall trim."

"Yessah." Skippy saluted Bear with the hammer he held and left. Kay winced.

Bear huffed out a breath. "I hate when he does that. One of these days, he's going to bean himself in the head. 'Course that's better than when he scratches his ear with his screwdriver."

Kay bit her lip to keep from laughing.

"Okay, where were we?"

"Drapes to divorce." She shook her head. "I'm sorry, I shouldn't have pried."

He waved it away and took a swallow of coffee. Opening his planner, Bear checked through his notes. "Back to the interview. What is this, start over two or three? I've lost track."

"If you count me making an idiot out of myself, this would be number three."

He shrugged one shoulder. "I set you up. Walt described you perfectly. I knew who you were when you walked in. When you turned out to be beach girl, I couldn't help myself."

"Walter calls you Yogi." Kay pointed at him.

"Has since the first day we met. I kinda like it now."

She shook her head. "I should have put two and two together. Bear...Yogi..."

"Quite the character, that Walt. He raves about you being a *wicked good* artist."

She shifted in her chair and sipped at her coffee. "He's prejudiced. He loves me."

"It's obvious. He's showed me a few of your pen and ink sketches. I liked them a lot. There's something so familiar in them. Comforting. You capture this area so well. Not just visually, but it's like you understand the spirit of the place."

"Thank you." Her cheeks pinked again and she dropped her gaze. "Bell Harbor's my home away from home. I've always liked the feel here. The ease of things. Even when it's packed with tourists, they're happy and relaxed."

He grinned. "Sometimes too relaxed, like when

you're trying to get an inn open."

Her eyes met his. "Folks here don't like to move too quickly."

"Nothing like LA."

"No, I would say Bell Harbor, Maine, is the exact opposite of Los Angeles," she agreed, looking sympathetic. "I don't work at LA speed either, but I do work rather quickly. Tell me what you're envisioning for the lobby project. I'm assuming you'd like the back wall done."

"Yep, that and all the rest. I'd like all four walls painted."

Her eyes widened. "That's quite the job."

"Would you be able to handle that?"

"Of course. I've done jobs this size before." The sparkle in Kay's eye made him smile. She slid her portfolio onto the table and unzipped the case. "These are my murals." She pulled out conceptual sketches as well as finished photographs. "I've done several full-room commissions." She laid examples across the table. Her enthusiasm was contagious.

"Your work is very diverse."

"Each job is different. I try to meet the client's wishes while at the same time bringing my own artistic voice to the project." She pulled a listing out of the back of the portfolio. "Here are my references. Clients, professors, etc."

Bear took the offered sheet. "Impressive." He examined the photographs again. Even though each mural captured their settings perfectly, her paintings all carried a unique styling.

Why did her work feel so familiar? It was as if they'd met before, but he sure as hell wouldn't have forgotten her. "What if the client doesn't know what they want?"

Kay smiled as if this wasn't an unusual occurrence. "I ask a lot of questions, listen to what their plans are for the space, and come up with some ideas that I think will fit."

No, he would have remembered her smile. She leaned to pull a small spiral notebook out of her bag giving him a ring-side view of creamy cleavage within the V of her black sweater. He was wrong. Cute didn't describe her at all. Blushing or not, she was beautiful. Refined, understated, with a definite hint of daring. He'd have to keep on his toes with her around. Why did he all of a sudden envision being swept off his feet? "I'd like to hear your ideas for my lobby."

"Well, I'm already getting a sense for the style you're going with. Antiqued, yet elegant. Four walls, soft colors..." She tucked her hair behind each ear. Wait, her earrings didn't match. A silver star paired with the crescent moon. Tapping the end of her pen, she glanced toward the front of the inn. "You don't want anything too bold when you first walk in." She scribbled a few notes. "Seasons, possibly. With the compass rose—four winds, perhaps...hmmm... vignettes, could work. A bit of trompe l'oeil possibly." She jotted one idea after another into her notebook. Bear sat back in amused silence. She was captivating to watch.

"I'd need to take some measurements, but I could sketch out a few things for you along with an estimate, say by Friday?" Kay pulled a thirty-foot tape measure out of her purse.

A woman with a tape measure? Be still my heart.

"Friday would be great. I've got the room's specs. I can give you a copy of the blueprints."

"Perfect." Her smile lit her face and slammed him in the chest.

Yep, damn near perfect.

Chapter Four

Kay almost ran down the sidewalk toward her car. Through her nervousness, the familiar bubbling of excitement filtered to the surface. The full lobby of the inn? Her mind was already reeling with possible designs. Slipping into the warm car, she thawed her chilled hands on the steering wheel.

Bear Coulter owned the inn? Hunky Bear Coulter? Hunky, please-let-me-see-your-tattoo Coulter? Kay let out a shaky breath. She hadn't seen his tattoo, but she'd felt his ass! Her head was spinning at how the interview had gone from mortifying to *When can you start?* If she wanted to keep from making a total fool out of herself, she needed to remember the golden rule. This was a job. He was a customer. And you should *never* feel the ass of your customers. Not twice, anyway.

But then he shook her hand good-bye, that big paw of his engulfed her fingers. It sent lovely electric shimmers up her arm...and straight to her knees. He walked her to the door, his hand resting casually on the small of her back... That small touch had shot more than shimmers to a place slightly north of her knees.

He's a client. He's a client. He's a client!

Watching the charming bustle of the small village of Bell Harbor through her windshield, Kay came up with an inspired idea for the mural. She could picture the whole scene in her mind. She had to get it all down on paper. A visit to the library would be necessary. They closed early on Wednesdays, however, so she'd go there first thing in the morning.

Kay pushed her keys into the ignition when her phone vibrated in her bag. Hearing the low hum, she dug past blueprints and her portfolio and scrambled to find her cell at the bottom of her purse.

"Kay Winston."

"Thank God. Kay, where are you?" Madeline Sullivan's husky voice screamed at her from the receiver. "I've the whole town of Stoddard searching for you."

"Calm down, Madeline. I'm in Maine."

"Why the hell are you in Maine?"

Kay wasn't about to get into the particulars about her escape from Stoddard. She reloaded her purse and ran a hand over the blueprints. "I've found a mural job over here in Bell Harbor. I'm staying at my folk's place."

"I've been trying to reach you for days."

"I noticed your messages, all eight of them. I was going to call you after my client meeting. What's so urgent?"

"I have news. Good news."

"That's the best kind. What's up?" Kay turned the key in the ignition enough to open some windows. The warmth of the afternoon was heating up her car."

"Two things. First, I got you into Luc Girard's class for the fall semester."

"Wow." Luc Girard was a Stoddard alumnus. His blown glasswork was brilliant. "Everybody wanted that class. Wasn't there a waiting list?"

"There was, but grad students got pushed to the

top. I worked a little magic."

Kay smiled. Madeline was famous for her *magic.* "That's wonderful."

"So I moved your Tuesday and Thursday schedule around a bit, but you're in."

Kay didn't know where she'd be eating and sleeping come the new semester, but at least she knew what she'd be doing on Tuesdays and Thursdays. "That's great, thanks."

"And even better…are you sitting down?"

"I'm sitting." Kay shook her head. Madeline was also famous for her theatrics. Kay fumbled for her water bottle.

"Your painting. The lighthouse one. What was it called?" Papers rustled in the background. Kay pictured Madeline in her cluttered office. Every flat place piled high with artwork, paperwork, a half-eaten sandwich, and a bobble head Andy Warhol… "*Point of Light.* One of your Bruce Gallery pieces."

"Yes?" A flush of optimism raced through Kay as she found the bottle of water she was searching for under the passenger seat.

"It sold."

"Honest?" The *Point of Light* piece was special to Kay. She had a momentary twinge of sadness at the news. It had been the star of her portfolio when she'd interviewed for the graduate program at Stoddard School of Art, but she'd loved it long enough. It was time to sell it.

"Yep, it caused quite a ruckus. Two parties wanted it. Bad. It went into a bidding war."

"You're kidding." Kay uncapped the water, took a sip, and grimaced. It was warm and tasted like plastic, but it was wet.

"Nope. Some woman from Cape Cod, and a guy. I forget where he was from, but his pockets were deep and he wanted that painting. No ifs, ands, or buts about it. Daniel Bruce was thrilled, to say the least."

"That's awesome. I'm flattered."

"How's six grand for flattery?"

Kay choked. "I'm sorry, I could have sworn you said six grand."

"I did. Six thousand, seven hundred and twenty dollars. I have the Bruce Gallery check right here. That's eight thousand minus sixteen percent commission. Daniel only charges students half."

Eight thousand? Kay's mouth opened and closed like a dying fish. She had no words. Screaming might work, but words? Nope.

"Kay? Did you hear me?"

"Ahhh…yeah, I heard you. I'm waiting to wake up now."

"You're not dreaming. Check your hands."

"Hands? What?" Her brain was jumbled, and Madeline was giving her whiplash.

"They say if you look at your hands in your dreams, they're all weird."

What? Kay examined her fingers. Ten normal-looking fingers. "Shit, I'm not dreaming."

"Told you. Congratulations."

Kay let out a screech and frightened two elderly women who were passing on the sidewalk. "Sorry. Sorry." She waved to them. "Oh my God, Madeline, I…this is unbelievable."

"Highest sale in the whole show. You should be very proud."

"I am. Add stunned. Thrilled. Oh my God!"

"So I guess you can't swing by and get this check."

For a second, Kay actually considered driving the three hours back to Stoddard. "I'm not exactly in *swing by* territory."

"Okay, let me find a pen. I'll pop it in the mail. Where are you?"

Kay gave Madeline the address for Polka Dots. "Send it in care of Dorothy Polk."

"Got it. I'll post it today. You should have it in a couple of days. Do me a favor and let me know when you get it. And don't fall off the face of the earth again. You had me worried."

"Don't worry, Maddie, I'll let you know the minute I get it."

"Good. Congratulations, Kay."

Kay checked for little old ladies before she screeched again. "Ahhhhhhhh!" She moved to uncap her water, sobered, and tossed it over one shoulder into the backseat with a wicked grin. Snatching her purse, she jumped out of the car and headed at a half run down the block.

With a bottle of the best champagne she could find at Fred's Shop Hop, and two dozen deep purple Japanese irises (Dottie's favorites) that she purchased at Seaside Floral Fantasy, Kay sent the bells clanging as she rushed into Polka Dots.

Dottie dropped the carton of beeswax lip gloss she was stocking and slapped a hand to her chest. "Kay, for goodness s—"

"What the *hell* do you put in that pie?"

****

Kay stretched her arms high over her head as she

stepped out onto the back deck. The sky was beginning to lighten. She zipped her hoodie against the damp chill of the morning and leaned her elbows on the railing easing the stiffness in her back.

So excited when she returned home from Dottie's, she'd worked through the night laying out her idea for the inn's mural. Her mind had been too busy to consider trying to sleep, but the work was good. She hoped Bear would like her suggestions.

Most of the time, her ability to *read* a job was spot on. Visiting the location of the mural would give the feel of the space, the owner's favorite colors, their vision for the piece. Of course, there were those handful of times when she was dead wrong about a painting. She'd been asked to create a desert sunset once and came back to the client with a lovely sketch in soft pastels. Nope. The client envisioned something more striking. Bright purple for the mesas, deep teal for the cactus, and orange with fuchsia swirls for the sky. They wanted bold. Bold is what they got.

A rustling in the underbrush to the left of the deck caught Kay's attention. Chipmunk. But then the chipmunk...mewed? A dirty, raggedy kitten pushed past the leaves to sit on one of the lower stairs. It scratched itself with a hind leg. Hard to tell in the dim light what color it was. Palest orange, or filthy white. One ear dipped lower than the rest and bore a nick in its edge. The poor thing's ribs and hip bones stuck out.

"Hey, little one." At the sound of Kay's voice, the cat shot back into the bushes. "No, no, I won't hurt you." She moved down a few stairs. "Here, kitty, kitty." No amount of coaxing could lure the kitten from its hiding space.

Kay went back and rummaged through the cabinets. Minutes later, she brought out a can of tuna and a bowl of fresh water. She placed them on the stairs. "I'll just leave these here. You must be hungry. This is the good people tuna. Don't get too used to the high life, not yet anyway. If you'd like to stick around, keep me company, I promise I'll keep you in kibble. When Daniel Bruce's check arrives, it will be premium kibble at that." Wide green eyes stared at her from under a fern. Seemed fear overruled hunger. "Okay, I'll leave you be and hope for the best."

The sun was just swimming to the surface of the horizon. Kay continued down the short path and stepped out onto the beach. Brilliant golden pinks and lavenders swept the sky. The sea was at low tide, the waves tipped to match the sky. She sat to watch the sunrise and greet the day, or say farewell to the night, she couldn't decide which.

She should be exhausted given the whole no-sleep thing, but she was still riding the high off yesterday's good news. Be it Dottie's magic pie, or just this place, to Kay it meant that she'd walked away from the bad into something that could be great. She'd done the right thing by coming here.

The sun blazed over the horizon. Kay closed her eyes and let the first light of day bathe her face. A familiar bark had her shading her eyes and welcoming Shadows exuberant greeting. Bear soon joined them.

"Morning." He wore black running pants and a gray sweatshirt with the sleeves pushed back to his elbows. His strong veined forearms and rugged hands made her wish she were a sculptor...or he was and she'd be the clay.

Dammit, he's a client!

"Morning." She ruffled Shadow under his jowls. "It's a beautiful day." She tipped her chin toward the bright disk of the sun.

"It sure is starting out nice." He smiled. "We don't usually have the pleasure of seeing you out here this early. Getting a head start?"

"No, more like a wind down. It was a long night. I'm not much for keeping normal hours." Shadow sat next to her bumping her arm if she slowed her pats. "And you don't keep promises."

"Promises?"

"I'm not seeing a leash," she teased. "You're obviously not a good boy."

Bear laughed and held out both hands palms-up. "That wasn't an actual promise. That was a definite *what if.* There was no formal promise made, and hell, once we learned who you were, Shadow argued that there was really no need to negotiate any further."

"I see." Kay spoke to Shadow. "You're lucky I'm a sucker for big brown eyes and doggy breath." She earned a wet kiss. She got to her feet, brushing off her behind. "I'll let you get back to your run."

"You should come with us sometime," Bear suggested.

"I'm not much of a jogger. I'm a better swimmer, but I'll wait until the water warms some."

"Not me." He stared back toward the waves. "The sea and I aren't the best of friends."

Kay frowned trying to make sense of what he said. "But you live on the point. You're practically surrounded."

Bear shrugged. "I didn't say it wasn't beautiful to

look at. It's perfect. But me *in* the water? Not so perfect. I sink like a stone. I'm an expert wader, though. When I first visited, I achieved knee depth. It was quite the accomplishment."

Kay laughed. "So no skinny dipping for you. Got it."

"No, not me. Out there? Hell no, not me. That water would freeze the balls off a brass monkey." He looked back at her with a smirk. "But please, don't let me stop you if you'd care to brave frostbite."

Kay shook her head. "I only skinny dip in August when the water warms from frigid to brisk. Right now I'm going to go back, take a nice hot shower, and climb into my bed."

Bear opened his mouth as if to say something then shut it again.

"I'll need my rest if I'm going to be sharp at our meeting tomorrow."

"Right." He was quick to snag Shadow's collar, so the dog wouldn't follow her back to the cottage. "We'll see you tomorrow." He held her gaze for a second longer before continuing. His voice softened. "Sweet dreams, Kay."

Chapter Five

Bear watched Kay move with a gentle step up the beach. Her hair was done in a loose, messy braid that swayed in time with her hips. Shadow pulled against his collar. "No, boy. We're not invited up there." Not yet, anyway.

Skinny dipping, hot shower, climbing into bed. His mind played out the whole scene in brilliant Technicolor. The dog looked up at him as if he'd read his mind. "What? Naked is a color. Come on, I'll race ya home." As soon as Bear said the words, the dog took off for the point like a bullet from a gun. The dog had a limited vocabulary, but bone, food, walk, and home were some of his favorite words.

A shower was in Bear's future too, a cold one. Last night, he figured out what was so familiar about Kay Winston and her work, and it was messing with his mind. It certainly explained his instant attraction to her. Part of him wanted to go back and discuss fate with her. Either before or after the climbing into bed part. Both were bad ideas.

His feet pounded along the sand. Bear was used to the linebacker's approach to life. Push ahead. Clear out any obstacles. Shoulder your way past. Beat down your opponent. In business it was a great strategy, but in a relationship it was a guaranteed disaster—just ask Diane, his ex.

"I can't do this anymore. I'm tired of being emotionally tackled every time I open my mouth! You suck at relationships, Bear. You can't steamroll people. Face it, you're better off single."

Maybe she was right. He tried to control everything. Failure was not something he took lightly. His marriage ending was the biggest failure he'd faced since losing everything to one stupid move on the playing field.

Playing football for USC had been his dream. It had been his father's dream, too, but Bear was used to the constant push from his father. He was a Marine. Retired, but Marines were always Marines, retired or not. It had been his father's plan that Bear follow in his military footsteps, until Bear had shown skills on the gridiron.

He was on the fast track to pro. Scouts were approaching him, talking to his coach. How would he feel about moving to LA? Dallas? Cincinnati? Boston? He was getting good grades in his architectural classes. He had life by the balls.

The women...they fell on him like rain. Diane was a monsoon. She was a design major as well. Tall with legs that reached to her chin. A cheerleader, she'd wrap those strong legs around him and squeeze. In bed, she turned him from a fumbling ox into a well-oiled fuck machine. They screwed their way into being in love and figured that was all it took to make a marriage. He'd proposed to her at Christmas.

Then everything went to hell. They'd been playing their rivals, UCLA, the Bruins. Ironic that the Bruins crushed the Bear. Fourth quarter, USC was up by three. The clock was ticking down. UCLA was trying to position their man to go in for the field goal and tie it up. It was a brutal game. Bear made one tackle after another. He'd sacked the QB twice. He hurt all over, but he wouldn't let off. They were after the championship. He was a rumored favorite for the upcoming draft. This was his game.

The ball snapped, he hurled himself toward the line. Connecting with one man, his body twisted and was in the wrong position when he took the hit from their defenseman. He heard his shoulder go. The excruciating pain brought him to the ground. A three hundred pound Bruin held him there. In a single second, everything was over. His career done. The dream gone.

He had to give Diane credit. She stuck with him. Through the surgeries. Through the physical therapy. Through the pain. Through the fear.

His father stood at his bedside and reminded him that fear was a coward's excuse. A man faced his fears, whatever they were. If life knocked you on your ass, you came up swinging a fist. And so, Bear did.

He and Diane ran off and married. With her by his side, he figured he could make it through anything. He dove into his studies with a renewed passion. He was going to make it in this world one way or another.

Bear rushed them into business together. Coulter Designs quickly made a name for itself. He and Diane were fresh blood. Eager. Aggressive. Talented. They soon went from a two-person team to hiring on four full-time architects. Business was great. Diane was brilliant, but she was never fully satisfied.

Neither at the firm, or in bed, or anywhere else for that matter.

****

"Hey, Yogi!"

Bear chuckled. Walter always came through the back door of the inn sounding like Boo Boo from an old cartoon. "Yeah, Walt, I'm in here." He was in the walk-in pantry at the back of the kitchen stacking supplies.

"Mawnin'."

"Morning. Dottie throw you out already?" Bear flattened an empty cardboard box and added it to the growing stack.

"Na. Just makin' the rounds." Walter helped himself to coffee and a donut from the box on the counter. "Come over ta thank ya."

"For what?"

Walt spoke around a mouth full of cinnamon cruller. "Hiring my girl."

Bear shrugged. "She's one hell of a girl. You weren't kidding when you told me she was talented."

"Don't I know it. Came by the other night, just bustin' with ideahs."

"She's due here later. Can't wait to see them." Bear wiped his hands and refilled his coffee. "So what's her story?"

"Whatcha mean?"

"You know, where is she from? You two related? Family? Crazy aunt? A boyfriend? Husband? Maybe she raises boa constrictors for fun." Bear shrugged one shoulder. "I don't know. Stuff."

"Do I look like some gossipin' fishwife?" Walt narrowed his eyes and gave Bear a side glance. "Seems to me, you're going the long way round Robin Hood's barn to find out if she's single."

Bear snorted. "No." He shook his head. "Don't be

ridiculous." Walt shrugged and was silent until Bear broke. "Well, is she?"

"Seems to be."

"What does that mean?"

"Means Dottie figured she was fixin' to get married, and now she's not."

"What happened?"

"Hard tellin', not knowin'." Walt wiped his mouth with the back of one hand, set down his coffee, and crossed his arms over his chest. "Why ya askin'?"

Bear busied himself with another carton. "Like to know the people who work for me."

"Sure you do." Walter jerked his chin toward the sound of hammers above him. "Brian and Skippy…either of them got a crazy aunt? Raise boas?" At Bear's silence, he chuckled. "Well, don't that beat all. You like her."

"Knock it off. I was just making conversation."

"Glad I'm wearing my boots. Starting to get mighty deep in he-ah."

"Forget I asked."

"Hey, no skin off my nose." Walter held up one hand in surrender.

What possessed him to ask about Kay? Possibly the fact he couldn't get her out of his mind. She was due this afternoon at four. It was still hours away. How many times was he going to check the damn clock? Walter was playing this for all it was worth. He'd never hear the end of it.

Time to throw the stick in another direction. "So, what did you find out about the generator you were yammering about the other day?"

It took Bear hours to lose his overalled friend. He

liked Walter, but some days when he was stretched to his limit, the man found great pleasure in jumping up and down on his last nerve. He was one of those guys who claimed to be an expert on whatever subject you were talking about. Always had an opinion even when you didn't want to hear it. But, damn, he knew his way around a hammer and saw, and he was friends with everyone in town. A real asset when being a newcomer was akin to being invisible.

Bear lost track of the number of times he was looking for someone to run some electrical wires, hang sheetrock, or replumb a bathroom, and it had been Walter who'd suggested the perfect person for the job. That included the lovely, talented, distracting Kay Winston.

Kay arrived at four on the dot, wiping her cheek with the back of her hand. "Shadow and I are becoming an item. If he keeps kissing me in public, he's going to have to propose."

Lucky damn dog. "He likes blondes, what can I say."

Kay's hair was loose again. She wore a soft cambric shirt over a print skirt in a mix of earth tones. A wide, tooled leather belt accentuated her narrow waist. Her sleeves were turned back to her elbows and chunky wooden bracelets circled her wrist. She looked beautifully bohemian.

"It's quiet. No saws today?"

"No such thing as nine to five on Fridays. I'm lucky if I can get anyone to stay past three o'clock."

"Beating the weekend rush."

"Getting anyone to work weekends? Forget about it. At least we won't be interrupted." His cell phone rang, and Bear shook his head. "Spoke too soon. Excuse me." He checked caller ID. *Diane.* He'd already talked to her twice today. Hitting the ignore button, he shut off the phone. "Sorry about that."

"Not a problem." Kay set her bag on the floor and unrolled the rubber band off the prints.

"I can't wait to see what you've come up with."

"I hope you like it. After I left the other day, I had a bit of a brainstorm." She pulled a stack of markup boards from her bag. "What do you think of turning the clock back? Celebrate the history of the inn?"

"I like it so far. Go on."

"Well, I went to the library and did some research." She showed him copies of old photographs. "These are all shots of Bell Harbor at the turn of the last century." She handed him the sheet on top. "Here's one of the inn the year it was completed."

Taking two steps backward, she held up a finger. "This is what I'm thinking. Why not celebrate the era of when the inn was in its heyday. I could paint the scenes of Bell Harbor the way it used to be. All the key areas." Kay moved around the lobby indicating placement of the beach scene, Main Street, the church. "Over on this side, the park with the band stand, etc." She spun and gestured to the area to the right of the door. "Tall ships off the beach, and of course, the dock. Fisherman mending nets. Folks strolling in period dress. Buggies, horses, kids rolling hoops. Behind the check-in desk, a painting of the inn itself, but in its new colors."

She crossed back to the table and laid the four idea boards in order. She pointed to the sketch of the inn. "I even put you and Shadow on the porch bench." Retrieving a color board, she handed it to him. "I'm thinking faded brights. I know that doesn't make sense, but given the floor tiles and your exterior paint, I suggest adding some bright undertones to some of the muted hues. A final sepia wash over the finished piece will imitate the aging patina. It will appear as if the mural were original to the lobby."

Tucking hair behind an ear, she leaned in and pointed to the mock-ups. "If you look here, here, and here, I've done something a bit out of the norm, but I think it could work. It's painting past the frame, so to speak. The lost balloon from the park is painted floating on the ceiling. These flowers in the garden spill over the baseboard. Tie the mural into the rest of the inn with a kite string heading up the stairwell. Things like that. It breaks the boundaries, and the effect brings the mural another dimensional layer." She held out her hands. "Now, if you don't like the idea of paint on the baseboards and the ceiling, I can lose it. These are just suggestions at this point." She pulled two more sheets from her bag. "This is a list of supplies, costs, and finally my estimate."

Bear examined each page and card. He was speechless.

"And..." Kay pulled a strip off each mock-up and attached one to the other creating a box. "This is an idea of how the whole project would look all together."

Kay stepped back and folded her arms over her chest. Her cheeks were bright, and her eyes sparkled with obvious excitement. "I'm sorry, I haven't given you a chance to get a word in. What do you think?"

The urge to drag her into his arms and kiss her was overwhelming. "You did all this in two days?"

"I don't sleep much." She tipped her head looking

impossibly adorable. He was in trouble.

"I…I love it."

Chapter Six

Kay ripped into the envelope. *Well done! M.* A neon orange sticky note from Madeline decorated the check from the Bruce Gallery in Boston. A receipt showed the sale price of the piece, the gallery's catalog number, and commission fee.

"Wow, get a load of all those numbers." Dottie peered over Kay's shoulder.

"That's about six summers worth of sketches." Kay grinned back at Dottie. "This day keeps getting better."

Dottie gave her a squeeze. "So your design meeting at the inn went well?"

"Once I stopped rambling on like an idiot. I was a nervous wreck."

"The drawings you showed me were terrific. You had nothing to be nervous about." Dottie began rearranging a selection of hand-thrown pottery bowls.

"I was confident in the sketches. There's just something about Bear Coulter."

Dottie frowned. "What do you mean?"

"He…I…get flustered around him. The way he looks at me sometimes like he's…I don't know, surprised somehow." Kay fanned herself with the check.

"But he liked your ideas?"

"He loved them. Never blinked at the estimate. Liked the color scheme. I start Monday."

"Walter will be tickled. 'Course there'll be no living with him seeing as it was his idea Yogi talk to you." Dottie stepped back to appraise the look of her display.

"I'll make sure I thank him." Kay moved one of the wide bowls an inch to the right.

"You'll puff that man up so his head won't fit through the doorway." Dottie returned the bowl to where she had it.

Kay laughed and slipped the check into her bag. "I should get this over to the bank, and put my supply order in at the hardware store before they close."

Dottie gave her a warm hug and held her close. "Come for dinner."

"Is Friday still pizza night?"

"'Course."

"I'll be back."

Kay rushed through her errands and even had time to return to the cottage and change.

She was looking forward to a relaxing evening. She'd been so wound up about the design meeting, it would be great to relax, eat pizza, and drink some beer. On the way into town, she'd pick up a six-pack of Walter's favorite and grab a couple cheesy movies.

As promised, she returned home with some gourmet cat food for her little friend. The beast had eaten all the tuna she had in the house and seemed intent on sticking around. It still wouldn't come close, but if Kay left the food and water on the deck, it would slink up and fill its belly. Kay guessed it was a female and decided to call her Hope. The name seemed to fit.

She slipped into her most comfortable jeans with the tear in one knee, a soft, short T-shirt with a tie-dyed tree frog flashing the peace sign on the front, and flip flops. Hair pulled into a quick ponytail, and she was off.

Letting herself into Dottie's kitchen, Kay could hear the television blaring. Walter was a tad deaf but wouldn't admit it. "I'm here. I hope you ordered one with mushrooms." Kay pulled three beers out of the six-pack and slipped the rest into the refrigerator. Dottie would only drink half of one, but Walter would *tidy up* for her, like always. "I rented a couple movies, too," she hollered. "A chick flick for Dottie and me. Julia Roberts makes herself look like a duck in this one. And I found one of those awful sci-fi's you like, Walter. Attack of the killer robot somethings." Beer in one hand, movies in the other, she tucked extra napkins under her chin. "The pizza smells great."

Heading into the living room, she stole one of Walter's favorite sayings. "I'm so hungry, I could eat the arse out of a grizzly—Bear."

The napkins fluttered to the floor as Bear Coulter stood. He seemed even bigger in Dottie's chintz-covered living room. He wore jeans and a loose button-down shirt, which looked impossibly white against his skin. His hair was damp as if he were straight from a shower, but his jaw said he hadn't had time for a shave. The combination was lethal.

"Hey, sweetie, come join us." Dottie patted the couch cushion next to her.

"Here." She set the beers on the coffee table. "Oh damn, one short, be right back." Kay fled to the kitchen.

Crap on a cracker! She let out a slow breath. She hadn't expected to see *him* here. Not when she looked like she'd fallen out of a thrift shop dumpster. Tugging at the hem of her shirt, Kay covered her eyes with her hand and groaned.

"Everything okay?" Bear's voice washed over her frayed nerves.

She groaned again. Kay kept her gaze on the pink and gray linoleum tiles of Dottie's floor. "Everything's great."

"Cute shirt."

She closed her eyes and prayed for a gaping hole to appear between the tiles. "Thanks."

He tipped his head in the direction of the living room. "Walter invited me over."

Kay nodded like a bobble-head doll. "Of course he'd invite you. You're buds." She pulled a beer from the fridge and handed it to him. "I'm gonna go. Um, I just remembered, I left…something, you know, back at the cottage." Her eyes locked on the third button of his shirt. "Something hot…like the oven or a candle. Wicked dangerous. I should take care of it."

"But there's mushroom pizza." Amusement tinged his voice.

"Yeah, I'm not real hungry." Kay prayed her stomach wouldn't rumble. She snuck a peek at his face to see if he was buying it. He wasn't.

Bear raised an eyebrow. "You said you were starving a minute ago. Something about eating a bear's ass."

Kay's face burned. Her ears might just burst into flame. "So…you're an organ donor. That's really great."

Bear laughed and tugged on her shirt sleeve. "Come back in. If your cottage burns down, I'll build you a new one."

A beer and a half later, (she did the tiding up) Kay was finally able to relax a little. The pizza was delicious, and the conversation never lagged. Walter and Bear talked about the inn, football, whether Skippy, the hammer-saluting carpenter, would need stitches one of these days.

"I can't wait to see what my girl does to your lobby." Walter puffed. "Told ya she was some talented."

"Hasn't she showed you her design? It's amazing." Bear smiled. "Next time you're over, I'll show you."

"I saw the initial sketches." Dottie nodded. "Very impressive."

Kay's face heated again. "Please, I'm sitting right here."

"You should be very proud. You're a fine artist." Dottie gathered the spent napkins.

Kay began to gather up the dirty plates. "And you aren't the least bit biased."

Dottie patted her hand and took the plates from her. "Not one bit." She kissed Kay's forehead when she passed.

"I'll have the crew priming and taping off this weekend. It will be all set for Monday."

"Prep is included. I don't mind doing it." Kay pointed at him with her bottle. "I've already put in the order for my paint and primer. The guys over at the hardware store said they'd deliver it all to the inn this weekend."

"You're the boss." Bear raised his beer to her.

With Dottie in the kitchen and Walter's eyes slowly closing, Kay was acutely aware of being alone with the handsome man to her left. He lifted his beer to his mouth and took a last swallow. She watched his throat work. Her own went dry, and she tipped her bottle to her lips only to come up empty. She'd done that twice now. How many times was she going to try to drink from an empty bottle?

She set it aside before she started shredding the label like a fidgety loon. "Actually, you're the boss. And you're paying for prep, so you'll get prep."

"I can't wait." He rested his forearms on his thighs and leaned closer. "I had a thought after our meeting. I contacted a local greenhouse about bringing in some dwarf container trees and ferns. You know, after the mural is finished. Thought a continuation of your design with a few real plants and potted flowers. The lobby will knock people out."

"That's a great idea."

"You've inspired me." He smiled again and held her gaze sending lovely fingers of warm tingles to some interesting places.

Dottie returned from the kitchen, and Bear rose. "I should be going. Shadow is waiting for his run. Dottie, thanks for having me. It was great." He tipped his chin toward Walter who snored softly from his corner of the couch. "Tell Boo Boo I said good night."

"I will, Bear. You're more than welcome. Anytime." Dottie patted his arm.

"I should go, too." Kay stood. She kissed Dottie's smooth cheek. "You have an early day tomorrow and Walter's done in. Don't watch Julia Roberts without me."

"I wouldn't think of it."

Bell Harbor was all but deserted as Bear walked her to her car. Without the tourists, the town rolled up the sidewalks early. A cool breeze off the water scented the air. The ring of a buoy bell at the mouth of the inlet bid them a peaceful good night.

"I'm sorry I messed up movie night. The duck movie sounded pretty good."

Kay shook her head. "You didn't mess up anything."

"Maybe not, but you got pretty thrown at seeing me in there." Bear tipped his head back toward the house.

She shrugged a shoulder. "You surprised me, is all."

"A good surprise?"

"More of a *damn I wish I'd worn something better than a frog T-shirt* surprise." She tugged at the hem of her shirt.

"I told you, I like the frog."

"I don't know, ducks, frogs...bears... It was getting a little too *Animal Planet*," she teased. "Speaking of which, you've a dog to take care of, and I-I've still got a dangerous candle burning."

"Right. Hope you're not walking into a fiery inferno."

"Me, too." She dug keys out of her pocket. "Tough running in flip-flops."

"The pink sparkly toenail polish would definitely slow you down."

When had he checked out her toes? She lifted her foot slightly so the glitter caught the light. "On the contrary, sparkles give you superpowers."

His eyes did the crinkle thing that made her heart race. "I had no idea."

"It's why women can tolerate wearing totally

inappropriate footwear. Flip flops, high heels? Sparkly nail polish is the great equalizer."

He laughed. "You're crazy."

Kay shrugged. "You've been warned."

"And cute as hell."

There was no laughter in the statement. Kay met his gaze. In the amber glow of the streetlamps, the world took a breath. The buoy bell rang. "Now, I've been warned."

"Have a nice weekend, Kay. I'll see you Monday."

"Or maybe Shadow will give me more slobbery sweet talk on the beach tomorrow."

Bear shook his head. "We're staying at the inn for the next couple of days. I've early deliveries coming, and I'll be laying tile all weekend. It's easier if we camp in town."

She couldn't help but be a little disappointed at the prospect of two days without seeing Bear and Shadow on their runs. "Sure. That makes sense."

"Besides, I've had a serious talk with Shadow. The boy needed to be set straight. He may have seen you first, but I called dibs." One corner of his mouth tipped into a smile.

Her breath caught, but she recovered. "D-don't you think it's up to me to decide who gets dibs?"

"No." His gaze held her. If he moved half a step closer, he was in kissing range.

Kay blinked up at him. "No?"

"Nope." His voice lowered. "You can't judge until we've both had the chance to kiss you."

"Oh."

He took that half step and leaned closer, tugging on the hem of her shirt. The backs of his fingers brushed the bare strip of skin above the waistband of her jeans. "And I can promise you, I've never slobbered in my life."

Chapter Seven

"Of course, I'm sure. I told you when you called yesterday and the day before, I never worked on the Regency project. I can't help you with this, Diane." Bear rubbed at the ache between his eyebrows. "No, you're gonna have to handle this one yourself." The saws were grinding away upstairs. There was grout to mix. He needed to get back to work. Kay was due this morning. He didn't have time to pacify his ex-wife.

Bear took the cordless phone into the kitchen to refill his coffee. It was going to be a long day, and it hadn't even started.

"Diane, what do you want me to do? What? You've lost it. I'm on the other side of the country up to my eyeballs in construction. I can't drop everything and bail you out. If it's as bad as you think, you should be talking to lawyers, not me." God, she was like a dog with a bone. "I'm not coming to California. Because I'm not. Check the door, sweetheart, my name is gone. It's your business now. You deal with it." He blew out a breath. "Of course I still care, but—" Bear pushed back into the lobby and found Kay had arrived and was looking over the supplies that had been delivered for her over the weekend.

"Hey, I gotta go." He set down his coffee and met Kay's eye. Smiling, he held up a finger indicating he needed just another minute. "I can't be any more clear about this. No. No, I won't change my mind. I'm sorry that you feel that way. Have a nice"—he looked down at the receiver—"day." Diane hung up on him. Having been married to the woman, he wasn't surprised. Relieved, but not surprised. Their last two conversations had ended the same way. He was used to it.

"Problem?" Kay nodded toward the phone he tossed onto the cluttered reception desk.

"Not anymore." His day just got much better. Kay pulled a receipt slip from one of the boxes by her feet. Grabbing his coffee, he joined her. "That arrived late Saturday afternoon. Did you get everything you ordered?"

She checked off the list. "Some of the paint is back stocked, but I can still get started with prep and prime. Hopefully, it won't take too long to get it to me."

Her long hair was secured in a thick braid trailing down the center of her back. Her mottled jeans bore smudges and smears of paint in every conceivable color. A gray hoodie bore similar markings. She slipped the receipt into her back pocket and pushed her pencil into her braid before bending to organize things. Her hoodie rose, and her jeans dipped leaving a pale curve of soft skin. Bear's brain lost a good amount of blood flow.

He cleared the sudden catch in his throat. "Let me know if you have trouble getting anything. I can probably find it through my guys."

"I think I've got it covered, but thanks." She shot him a quick smile over her shoulder.

"You know, I never gave you a tour of the place. Fourth floor is still a disaster, but if you'd like to see the rest."

"Um, I'd love to. Maybe later?"

"Sure, sure. Later." She went back to unpacking quarts of latex paint. He twisted the cup in his hand. "Coffee?"

"No, thanks, I'm good."

He should really stop studying her butt. "You know where the pot is if you want some. Feel free to help yourself. There's donuts, too. Bottled water in the fridge." He was rambling.

"Thank you." She pulled out a set of plush roller sleeves and tossed them to one side.

"Is it too cool in here? I could bump the heat."

"Bear…" Kay straightened, blew out a breath, and crossed her arms over her chest. "I'm great. I don't need coffee, donuts, it's not too hot, or too cold. It's perfect." She shook her head and laughed. She tucked a stray hair behind an ear. "I'm sure you've got your hands full with other things. I'm all set. If I need anything, I'll come find you. I promise."

"That was a nice way of telling me not to let the door hit me in the ass on the way out."

"Handsome and smart." She crooked one eyebrow at him.

"Okay." He held up his hands. "I get it. I'll get out of your way."

"I'd appreciate it."

"But if you need any—"

"Bear."

He threw up his hands in surrender. "I'm going."

And he went, but he couldn't stay out of the lobby for long. He needed to see her work. It fascinated him. She fascinated him. He kept finding excuses to pop back. A forgotten supply order. His coffee cup. A pencil. Had he left his tape measure down here? Where's the phone?

All the while watching her as she made a slow sweep of the lobby, running her hands over the plaster walls, marking with chalk any imperfections she found in the surface. She filled the holes with Spackle, wiped them smooth, and then taped off the baseboard using wide, blue painter's masking tape.

On one of his return visits, he found her at the top of a stepladder taping along the ceiling line. Fear of her falling caught him like a blow to the chest, followed by the sudden, insane desire to catch her if she did. It would all happen in slow motion. She'd lose her footing, he'd drop everything and rush toward her in that split second easily scooping her into his arms. He'd hold her tight while their beating hearts calmed. She'd be so grateful...she'd...she'd...

What an idiot!

By the time five o'clock rolled around, all he wanted to do was pin her against the wall and kiss her. He'd been thinking about just that thing since he left her at her car the other night. Whoa. Let's be honest here, he'd been thinking about kissing her since the first day on the beach.

He knew what the problem was. Lack of rainfall. Monsoon Diane had dried up more than a year ago, and he was in a serious drought. Or...maybe he wasn't a pig and only thinking with his dick. Either way, he needed to hurry up and kiss her, so he could stop thinking about it and get back to work.

Kay was still rolling on primer long after the other workers had left at five.

"Didn't you hear the whistle," he teased. "Work day's done. How about you and I take the tour, and then we can grab a bite to eat. They make a killer burger down at the diner."

Kay set her roller back in the tray and brushed the stray hair away from her face. She put her hands on her hips and sighed at the floor. "I can't do this anymore."

"Great. I'll clean your roller and you—"

"No." She swirled her finger over the paint tray. "Not this." She moved her hand in front of his face. "This."

He opened his mouth to object, but she didn't give him a chance.

"Do you have any idea how many times you came into this lobby today? An Alzheimer patient is less forgetful. Between you and the other guys, this place is like Grand Central Station. I won't be able to work with the constant interruptions."

"I'm sorry. I'll talk to the crew. From now on, while you're working, the lobby is off limits." He rubbed her arm. "What do you say, cheeseburgers and a pile of the best french fries in the state? We can unwind, have a few laughs."

"I can't date you. I don't date clients."

He scoffed, trying to make it sound convincing. "It's not a date."

"Sounds like a date." She tipped her head and narrowed her eyes.

"No. I shave for a date. It's cheeseburgers and maybe a beer."

Kay shook her head and picked up her roller. "Sorry, I have work to do."

"You have to eat."

"I'll eat when I'm finished." She pushed the roller into the pan filling it with paint.

"I can wait." Bear sat on the corner of the desk.

Setting down the roller, she smiled, and brushed off her hands. "I quit."

"Good, so you'll come out with me."

"No. I quit, quit." Kay grabbed her bag and headed toward the door.

He was on his feet and caught her. "What? No. You can't."

"Bear..." She pulled out of his grasp and folded her arms over her chest. "I'm not playing games. Either you let me work, or we're done here."

"Okay, okay. I get it. What about this? I leave you alone. No more interruptions. I'll take Shadow for his run, swing by and grab some burgers, and bring them back here. You can finish up without me getting in your hair, and I'll still get my burger."

"It's not a date. You promise not to shave?"

He crossed a finger over his heart and held up the Boy Scout three fingers. "No shaving. Promise. Hell, I won't even shower."

She wrinkled her nose. "Wow, way to make a girl feel special."

"What do you say?"

For a minute, she didn't say anything. With her hands on her hips, she looked back at the walls. "I'll need at least another hour and a half."

"You got it."

"And soda, not beer."

"Okay."

She picked up her roller again. "No shaving."

"I'm throwing away my razor."

Bear returned ninety minutes later with a sack of fat burgers, a heaping pile of hot french fries and cold six-pack of Cokes along with a serious five o'clock shadow.

The walls were finished. The sharp smell of primer filled the lobby, and Kay was gathering up the last of the drop cloths.

"Let's sit on the porch. You could use the fresh air," Bear suggested. She followed him out and took deep breaths of the easy breeze coming off the harbor. He opened a soda and handed it to her. She took a long pull, then wiped a stray drop of Coke off her lower lip. That insignificant drip brought back the ache he'd been fighting all day. This was not the time to try to kiss her. He'd just keep fighting the urge. He tore into his cheeseburger. "I'm sorry about today." He mumbled around the food in his mouth and swallowed. "Interrupting you like that. I'm surprised you didn't throw something at me."

"I was tempted." She unwrapped her burger and pulled it apart, plucking off the pickles and adding extra ketchup.

"What can I say." Bear shrugged and passed her the fries. "It's the draw of the working artist. Watching someone's talent manifest is intriguing."

Kay took half a dozen fries and set them next to her burger. "I don't like people watching me. It completely throws me off. I'm too self-conscious." She stared out at the water. "I get into a zone when I work. Hyper focused. I can't do it any other way. Hours fly by. Sometimes days." She wiped her fingers on a paper napkin and looked back at him. "Would you have a problem if I worked at night? My hours can get screwy anyway, and the inn is quiet. I won't be interrupted by the crew or the phone or deliveries."

"Or me."

She nodded and gave him a smirk. "Or you. Just another benefit." She patted his arm. "I'm teasing. I just think I'd get much more done."

The last of the lobster boats was pulling into the harbor as the sun set, but the picturesque scene was lost on him. If he agreed to her suggestion, he'd hardly see her. "I don't know how I feel about you being alone here at night."

"Why? What's going to happen?"

"I want to be sure you're safe."

"Bear, look around." She swept a hand toward the water. "This is Bell Harbor, not LA. What could go wrong? Lobster riots?" Her hair shone golden in the fading light. "I'll lock myself in. I'd be fine. If I can't concentrate, this mural is going to take twice as long as it should, and be half as good. That's not what you're paying for and not what I signed on to do. I realize it isn't the perfect plan, but if we can't come to some agreement on this, maybe you need to hire on another artist." She turned those beautiful dark eyes on him.

"Not an option."

"So I can work at night?"

"Under one condition. You can't be alone."

She was quick to shake her head. "You staying here isn't an option. No razor or not."

"We're not talking about me, but what about Shadow? He's crazy about you, and he's a great watchdog. I just installed a new kennel for him out back with a big doghouse. He could be in here with you while you work. I'll set up his bed in the kitchen.

Guaranteed he'll sleep ninety percent of the time. All you'd have to do is kennel him before you leave. Make sure he has water. I feed him in the mornings. Take him for his run. Same as evenings. I'll just drop him back here."

"Sounds like we're drawing up a custody agreement for your dog. Won't he miss you?"

Bear shrugged a shoulder. "He'll be with me all day."

"It seems like an awful lot of running back and forth for you."

"It's only for a few weeks. I'm running back and forth most of the time now."

Kay nibbled the end of a fry and was quiet as she contemplated. "It might work."

"It will work. You agree to a furry night watchman, and I'll get you a set of keys in the morning." He lifted his Coke and held it up to her.

Kay picked up her drink and tapped the bottom rim of her can to his. "I think I could agree to that."

"Fine. Night shift it is."

She took a sip and smiled at him in the fading light. "You should have brought beer."

Chapter Eight

Kay rode home after another long night. The mural was progressing. She was pleased, Bear was thrilled, and Shadow seemed none the worse for wear after he discovered she kept dog treats in her purse. If she could keep up this pace, she might finish the job ahead of schedule.

She was exhausted, but it was a good tired. You know, the brain-numbing fatigue when you finally crawl into bed but are content and satisfied with all you'd accomplished that day—or night.

Pulling into the parking space for the cottage, she met Dottie coming up the stairs.

"Hey! What a nice surprise."

The two hugged. "Hey, yourself, stranger. I was out this way and hoped to catch you. I left a note on your door."

Kay gathered up her bag and pulled her phone off the car charger. "I got your message. I've just been straight out the last few days."

"I heard." She rubbed Kay's back. "Walter brings me progress reports every morning. Wants me to come see what you've done, but I want to wait and see it all finished."

"Hopefully, you won't have too long to wait. I've got everything broad sketched and cut in. I'm working one wall at a time, and it's really coming together. I like it a lot."

"I know Bear loves it."

Kay nodded. "So he says."

"You must be beat, but I wanted to talk to you. Got time for a quick cup of tea?"

"For you? Absolutely." Kay led her down the stone steps and into the tiny blue and white gingham-trimmed kitchen. "Put the kettle on. I need to feed the cat." She filled both the kettle and a bowl with fresh water.

"Cat? What cat?"

Kay scooped some kibble into another bowl and took them out to the back deck. "She showed up last week. Filthy and starving. I named her Hope. She seems to be sticking around."

"As long as you feed her."

"Won't let me near her, but at least she's coming up onto the deck now. We've made great progress." Kay pulled tea bags, honey, and mugs from the cupboard. She joined Dottie at the kitchen table. "So what did you want to talk about?"

"I spoke to your mother the other day."

Kay gave a silent groan and dropped into the chair. "And how is my mother?"

"She says she hasn't heard from you since Christmas."

"Has it been that long? Yes, I guess it has." Kay got *the stare*. The kettle's whistle saved her. Kay leapt up to take it off the heat.

"She didn't know you're staying here."

Kay filled their cups. "Did you tell her?"

"It's not my business to tell."

"Good. Thank you."

"It's also not my business to lie."

Dottie would never betray her, but Kay hated putting her in the middle. She was still her mother's best friend. "You didn't lie."

"Not telling *is* lying."

"Trust me, it's easier this way. I'll deal with her. Soon. Not now, okay?"

Dottie reached across the table and took her hand. "Honey, when are you going to lose that chip on your shoulder?"

Kay stood again and crossed to the sink. Soaping the sponge there, she began wiping down the small countertop. "It isn't so much of a chip where my mother is concerned. It's more like a drag chute." She scrubbed at an invisible spot.

"I have no idea what you're talking about."

She tossed the sponge back into the sink and wiped her hands. "A drag chute is the parachute that releases out of the back of a racecar to stop it in its tracks. It's what she does. I'll be moving along at a great speed, and it's like my mother sucks the road right out from under my tires. She grinds me to a halt. And it takes way too much to get me back to the starting line, let alone back up to speed."

"You need to talk to her."

Kay shook her head. "I can't afford to be derailed. Not now."

"She just wants to know you're okay. And sweetie, you're doing better than okay, you're doing great. Don't you want to share this with her?"

"No." She gave a small laugh. "Absolutely not."

"So what are you going to do—pretend she doesn't exist?"

Kay folded her arms over her chest. "Hey, denial

and running are my best things."

"Some things you can't run away from, Kay. They're going to catch up with you no matter what."

Kay sat and took the woman's hands. "Things are never going to be good where my mother is concerned. It wasn't my idea. She made her choice twenty years ago. I'm just grateful I have you." She kissed the backs of her hands.

Dottie gave her a pitying look. "But I'm not your mom."

"Thank goodness." Kay smiled.

"You know, you only get one."

"Some you get, some you pick. That's why I picked you."

"I just don't want you to get to the day where you regret things. There's still time to mend the fences. Before it's too late."

Kay frowned. "Too late for what?"

"Nothing." Dottie lifted a hand. "I'll go back to minding my own business. I love you both, and it breaks my heart to see you both so unhappy."

"I'm *not* unhappy."

Her words hung in the air as Dottie sipped at her tea. "What happened with Todd?"

Kay was on her feet again. She dumped the rest of her tea into the sink. "Wow, Mom and Todd in one conversation. I may be too tired for this."

"Does your breakup have anything to do with the fact that you're keeping Bear Coulter at arm's length?"

Kay shot her a look over her shoulder. "What?"

Dottie shrugged and spoke into her cup. "The man is sweet on you."

"I am too tired for this." She rinsed her cup and put

it into the drainer to dry.

"You'd have to be blind not to see it."

Turning, Kay braced her hands on the edge of the counter. "Bear is a client."

"So?"

"So, I don't date my clients."

"He's a good man," Dottie insisted.

"I agree."

"Handsome, successful, good-hearted." She counted each quality off on her fingers.

"I agree with all those things."

"Then what's the problem?"

"Besides him being my client, he lives in Maine. I live in New Hampshire."

Dottie scanned the room. "Looks like we're in Maine, now."

Kay narrowed her eyes. "Cute. I'm only here for the summer. What happens come August when I have to go back? I won't even buy a houseplant because who'd take care of it come fall?"

"Bear isn't a houseplant, honey."

"No, he isn't, but I don't want a summer fling. Bear's not a fling guy. He's a forever guy. He deserves someone who is settled and stable. Who's going to be around for the long haul."

"Then may I ask why are you feeding a stray cat?"

Kay huffed out a sharp breath. "Good question."

After Dottie left, Kay showered and slipped into bed. Her body was exhausted, but her mind refused to quit. She tossed and turned and, in frustration, growled at the ceiling before covering her face with her pillow. The day was too warm. Her bedroom felt stuffy and stale. Throwing the pillow didn't help. Air. She needed air to clear her head and cool off.

Slipping on a T-shirt and shorts, Kay headed out to her spot on the point. Passing Bear's house, she replayed her conversation with Dottie. All her reasons concerning Bear were valid. The last thing she wanted or needed was a summer romance. After Todd, her heart couldn't take it, and she wasn't the type to keep her heart out of the mix. Bear Coulter might be sweet on her, but every time she got within two feet of the man, she became some brainless twit. She'd lost track of all the times she'd humiliated herself. Best to keep her head down and do her work. That's all. Come August, she could leave with a solid bank account, maybe a nice reference, and an unbroken heart.

Making her way through the tumble of granite boulders making up the point, she found her place. Her rock. The ancient stone had forever marked this spot. It dipped in on one end, carved out by a million storms and the endless beating of the water. It was the perfect place to sit and watch the waves. Walter called it Fred Flintstone's beach chair. High and dry, the warm stone cradled her tired back.

Kay rolled the tension out of her neck and lost herself to the beauty of the calm sea. The rhythmic waves soothed her. She closed her eyes and relished the feel of the sun on her skin. Out here, the smell of the water was sharp and clean. The air cooled as it came across the sea. It cleared her mind, refreshed her soul, and clarified her resolve.

Dottie meant well, but Kay wasn't going to let a set of big shoulders and a tight guy butt cloud her judgment. Bear Coulter was off limits.

"Kay?"

Kay startled and twisted around. "Bear? What are you doing here?"

"I thought I saw someone walk past the house. You've been working all night. I thought you'd be sleeping."

She looked beyond him. "Where's Shadow? I thought you'd be at the inn."

"Yeah, I left him there. He was busy teaching Skippy how to fetch. I'm expecting a big furniture delivery today. Forgot the damn paperwork."

"Wow, you really are forgetful." She stood up and brushed the back of her shorts. The sun shone in his hair. The gray of his shirt played havoc with the color of his eyes. The way it hugged his body played havoc with her common sense.

"Not usually as scatterbrained as I've led on. Only when I'm trying to spy on beautiful mural painters." He smiled the smile. The one that turned her insides into melted caramel.

"You're here to spy on me?"

"No, this one's legit. Finding you out here basking in the sun was just a bonus."

"And me without my sunscreen. Excuse me." She sidled past him and headed back toward the beach.

He kept pace. "The mural is really coming along. Every morning, I'm excited to walk into the lobby and see what you've done the night before."

"The work is going well. I'll probably be out of your hair sooner than I planned."

"I'm not sure that's good news."

Kay shrugged a shoulder and kept walking. "The project has to be finished sometime."

Bear caught her elbow with a gentle hand. "But

then I wouldn't get to see you."

She pulled out of his grasp, but stopped. Shaking her head, she crossed her arms over her chest as she turned back to him. "You know the old saying, *ships passing in the night*. You barely see me now."

"I see more than you think I see."

She frowned at him and continued walking. "Sounds kind of stalker-ish."

"It does, doesn't it?" He caught up to her in two strides. "What I mean is, you put so much of yourself into your painting. It practically screams your name."

"Well then, when I leave, you won't miss me."

"Could be I'll miss you more." That stopped her. The teasing was past. He was serious.

Bear closed the space between them. The hand at her elbow slipped up her arm to rest at the curve of her neck. His gaze seemed to be taking in every aspect of her face as if he were trying to memorize its features.

"You can't," Kay whispered.

His eyes met and held hers for a long moment before returning his attention to her mouth. "I can't what? Miss you? Or kiss you?"

His fingers trailed up the side of her neck and slipped behind her head while his thumb swept along the line of her jaw. A rush spread through her as the world tipped beneath her feet. She reached a hand out to steady herself, grasping his other arm.

"Neither."

The man was solid muscle beneath her touch. He angled his head and brought his mouth to within a hair's breadth of hers. Her heart was doing its best to pound its way out of her chest. His breath fanned her cheek while she held hers.

"Seems I can't help myself."

His lips captured hers, easily shattering the feeble defense of her words. He claimed her mouth. This was not a teasing timid kiss. Nor was it punishing. It was Bear. Strong, powerful, confident. In other words, breathtaking.

The arm she held slipped behind her waist drawing her even closer as the kiss deepened. Opening her mouth, she welcomed him in. Losing herself to the feeling of being surrounded by the strength of him. Before she knew it, Kay had a hand tangled in the softness of his hair and was pressed tight against the wall of his chest. She returned the fervor of his lips and tongue until the cold wave of sanity made her push away.

Wide eyed, they both stood panting. Her lips felt swollen, and she covered them with shaky fingertips. Her body hummed. After the heat of his body, the cool air raised goosebumps on her arms and tightened her nipples.

"Kay…"

"No." Kay turned and ran back to the cottage.

Chapter Nine

Sweat rolled into Bear's eyes. Three more bed frames to move and assemble and he'd be done. He'd split a knuckle that refused to stop bleeding and continued to sting like a bugger every time he bent his finger, but thank goodness he had some manual labor to keep him moving.

Returning to the inn, he'd chopped half a cord of firewood before the furniture delivery arrived. It beat the hell out of some of the other things he'd considered while trying to make sense out of what happened on the point—banging his head on a rock, punching a wall.

He'd kissed her. All the fantasizing and days of wanting and wondering paled to the mind-blowing reality of that one kiss.

Her tiny gasp of surprise when he slipped his tongue between her lips had almost stopped him, but then she softened beneath his hands. She kissed him back. Held on to his hair, leaned her body along his, and kissed him senseless. The sweet taste of her mouth only made him want more. Another few seconds and he would have picked her up and carried her into the house.

He could have held her forever, but the kiss ended as abruptly as it had begun. He'd been stunned when she bolted. Part of him wanted to chase after her. The other part wanted to throw himself off the point.

Dammit!

Since when did a simple kiss throw him? No, Kay was anything but simple. This had nothing to do with monsoons or drought—there was more heat to her than rain. It was true, it'd been a long time since he'd wanted to kiss someone, and he sure as hell had wanted to kiss Kay. He had the singed lips to prove it.

He couldn't stop thinking about her. She was everywhere and nowhere. Her essence surrounded him at the inn, at home on the point. He tripped over Shadow the other morning on their run all because he was trying to catch a glimpse of her as they passed her cottage.

And now he'd kissed her. He knew how she tasted. How she felt in his arms. In those few maddening seconds, he'd only intensified the desire to know her better. He wanted her even more. All he had to do is get her to speak to him again.

When he returned to the inn later that evening, he was relieved to see her funny little car parked out front. Either she was working—or she was here to *quit, quit.*

Shadow was happy with his new rawhide bone bribe when Bear left him outside in the back kennel. The dog wasn't a fan of his new digs, so dig he did. Bear had already filled in three holes, but if Shadow got his favorite toy or a new bone, he tolerated the short time he was left alone. "Let's see if we're both relegated to the dog house." Shadow whined once in sympathy, and then carried his prize off for some serious gnawing.

As soon as Bear saw Kay's drop cloths spread along the sidewall, he released the breath he hadn't realized he'd been holding. She was working. *Thank you!*

He leaned against the doorframe leading into the lobby, staying quiet as he watched. The earbuds in her ears meant she hadn't heard him come in. What song was she humming?

She was adding a line of pine trees into the background. Tipping her brush, she tapped the paint to the wall. She double loaded the square-tipped brush with two separate colors, which magically mixed beneath her touch. It was as if the trees simply appeared off the end of her brush. One after another, after another.

Kay caught sight of him and gasped. She pulled the buds from her ears. "Jeez, Bear, you scared the hell out of me!"

"Sorry." He pushed away from the doorframe and held up his hands in surrender.

She turned her back on him. Her shoulders set as she added more paint to her palette. Loading her brush, she stood poised to continue, but didn't.

A full ten seconds crawled by. The tension in the room was neon green. He had to say something to make everything right with her, but what?

"Kay, about what happened earlier, I—"

"You scared the hell out of me," she repeated, speaking to the wall.

Bear moved toward her and stopped. "That was the last thing I wanted to do. I'm a big clumsy idiot. I had no right to grab you. I lost my head. I get close to you and…it's no excuse, but I don't want to scare you."

He watched her shoulders rise and fall as she took a deep breath. "It's not *you* I'm afraid of." Her voice sounded small.

"I don't understand."

She set aside her paints and turned around. "I kissed you back."

"Yes, you did." A warm rush ran through him at the memory of her body tight against his, her tongue gliding into his mouth while she tugged at the back of his hair. "I started it though."

"You did. And may I just say for the record, it was epic in that whole *Wow, what a first kiss* kind of thing." She ran a quick finger over her lower lip.

"Epic?"

Kay pressed her lips together and nodded. "Not one hint of slobbering. On a scale of one to ten, it was a rock-solid twelve." Her quick smile disappeared. "That's what scares me. I just got through a really ugly breakup. My feet are barely back on firm ground." She looked away. "Let's not even mention I'm under contract with you, or that I've known you all of five minutes."

"It was one kiss." He shrugged a shoulder. "One mind-blowing, epic, please-God-let-her-kiss-me-again kiss."

Kay gave a quick laugh and sighed. "I've got no business kissing you. We shouldn't be kissing at all."

He took a step closer, fighting the urge to gather her in his arms, hold her, and convince her of all the reasons why she should give them a chance. "Listen, what if you weren't working for me?"

"Are you firing me?" She looked worried.

"Hell, no." She frowned at him and he rushed to explain. "What if we met at the grocery store picking out...peaches?" He shrugged. "We strike up a conversation, you know, about peaches. I invite you for coffee. We hit it off, and I ask you to dinner at the place down by the water because I heard they have amazing peach cobbler. We have a great time. I take you home, walk you to your door, and we kiss good night—just like we kissed out there on the point. Would you still be afraid?"

"Only if I was allergic to peaches."

He laughed. "Exactly my point. Would the possibility of *us* still scare you?

She shook her head. "That's a whole lot of what ifs."

"Kay…" Her name slipped from his mouth in a whisper. "The only *what if* scaring the hell out of *me*, is what if the best thing to ever happen to me never gets the chance to happen? I want to spend more time with you, get to know you, take you out, walk you to your door."

Kay closed her eyes.

He continued, "I'm going to leave. Shadow is in his pen. He's got a new bone, so he won't try to break out, but you can bring him in to keep you company if you'd like. I'll be back in the morning, and I'd really like to take you to breakfast. The Muffin Tin Café has great food."

She looked at him for a long moment before answering. "Do they have peaches?"

"If they don't, we can stop and get some."

****

The Muffin Tin had been crowded. Kay insisted they take Shadow along, to chaperone, which was fine with Mindy the owner so long as they sat at one of the umbrella tables outside. The morning was clear and warm. As if the dog hadn't already been in love with

Kay, after she generously shared her bacon with him, they were definite BFFs.

They talked about the inn, the mural, how Dottie and Walter had become her surrogate aunt and uncle, and the quality of Mindy's peach pancakes.

After, Bear walked Kay back to her car. "See, that wasn't so bad."

"It was delicious. I'm completely stuffed. I should just make it home before the carb coma hits." She ruffled Shadow's ears and kissed the top of his head before laying a hand on Bear's arm. "Thank you for feeding me, again."

Bear covered her hand with his. "Next time you can feed me."

"Next time?"

"Yeah, how about taking a day off?"

"I can't." She tried to pull her hand away, but he tightened his grip.

"Sure you can. You said yourself you're ahead of schedule. I'll clear it with the boss."

Kay raised an eyebrow as she considered. "If I say yes, what did you have in mind?"

"A quiet day on the cove. You, me, sunshine, the mutt."

"My favorite place."

"Convenient, too." He ran a thumb over her knuckles.

"A bit cliché, don't you think?" She kept her gaze on their joined hands.

"Cliché?"

"Having a thing for the girl next door."

"Who says I have a thing?"

She looked up and smiled. "Don't try to deny it.

Even Shadow knows you have a thing."

"I'm not denying it." Bear held her gaze. Her eyes told him everything he needed to know. That kiss had thrown her as much as it had him, but she was still unsure. She didn't trust him. "Come on. Tomorrow. The weather is supposed to be perfect. Spend the day with me." He lifted her hand and kissed the backs of her fingers. "I'll come by at ten."

After a long, agonizing minute, the corner of her mouth tipped. "Make it eleven. I'll meet you on the beach."

"I'll wear a red rose pinned to my swimsuit so you can find me in the crowd?" he teased.

"No roses." Something flittered across her eyes, but it was gone so quickly, Bear had little time to try to figure it out. "I'm sure I'll find you." She pulled her hand from his, gave him a small smile, and was in her car and away from the curb before he could say good-bye.

She took off in such a hurry, he was surprised she didn't leave rubber on the street.

He was standing on the sidewalk in front of the inn watching her car disappear up the road when Walter came down the path.

"There you are, Yogi." He followed his line of sight. "Was that Kay?"

"Yep. The girl can sure leave in a hurry."

"What'd ya say to chase her off?"

Bear shrugged and shook his head. "Beats the hell out of me."

"She's a professional skedaddler." Walter clapped a hand on his shoulder. "Not to worry none, she's never run from a responsibility. She'll get your job done."

"I'm not worried about the mural."

"Then what's got ya in a twist?"

Bear looked him square in the eye. "What happens when the job's done?"

Walter gave him a hard look. "So that's the way things are, are they?"

Bear'd broken the first cardinal rule of men. Never let on you've got feelings. You're just opening yourself up to grief and busted balls. He tried to brush it off and headed back toward the inn. "What are you going on about now?"

"I'm old, but I ain't blind. You're fallin' for her. Don't be trying to deny it either. Not blind. Not stupid."

"If you're so damn smart, then answer my question."

Walter fell in step with him. "Son, I'm gonna level with ya. I know nothin' about women. Hell, I've been with Dottie more than thirty years, and I still don't have that damn fool woman figured out. But Kay's my girl. She's not had a smooth road of it. Never has. Not since day one. I can count on this finger"—he held up his pinkie—"the men who've not let her down. Still don't know what happened with her and her fella back in Stoddard. She's not talkin'. The look on her face when she showed up here a few weeks back told me all I needed to know."

Walter stopped walking. "I like ya, Yogi, I do, but if you're thinking about havin' yer fun and sendin' her on her way, I'm telling ya, you'll have me to deal with. I may be old, but I figure I could still knock your dick in the dirt. Or die trying."

Bear laughed and looked back at Walter. He outweighed him by a good sixty pounds less thirty years, but the man's loyalty to his family trumped all. "I'm not taking you on. You think I'm nuts?"

Chapter Ten

Kay waited until the sun dried the morning's dew off the beach stones before setting her blanket and things out for her date with Bear. *A date with Bear.* The idea of it triggered a host of emotions. After all her protests—to Dottie, to Bear, to herself—the kiss on the point changed everything. Was it too soon to be feeling what she was feeling? Was she fooling herself into believing he was somehow different from the rest?

That damn kiss. It made her skittish. Like Hope, the cat. The wee beast had to be tempted to the bowl each morning. The first few days, she would creep up the stairs, grab a hunk of food, and dash back to safety. Her eyes wide with fear, taking in the movement of every leaf. Ears poised and listening for any threat until hunger overruled her fear.

Was that what Kay was doing? Grabbing a morsel of happiness and rushing back behind her protective walls to savor it? Going out to breakfast, agreeing to this date. Was her desire for Bear superseding the rest?

Hope had relaxed enough to come up on the deck for her food and eat as long as Kay stayed a fair distance away. Perhaps it was time for Kay to relax as well, but keeping Bear at a safe distance didn't seem like an option anymore. The man was catnip.

Shadow raced past her, surprising her as he circled and danced around her legs. His excitement at seeing her always made her laugh. Bear grabbed at his collar. "Easy, boy. We talked about this."

"Good morning, both of you." She scratched Shadow behind the ears. "What did you two talk about?"

"Guy stuff." Bear lowered his sunglasses. "You look great."

Her bathing suit was modest by any standard, black, one-piece, and she'd tied a bright, stained-glass print scarf around her waist as a cover up. But there was something kicking up the *I'm almost naked* level as if she were standing there in her underwear.

"Thanks, so do you." Bear wore a worn USC T-shirt over his shorts. He had great *guy* legs. Tanned. Muscular.

He let Shadow go off to chase seagulls down the beach, and replaced his sunglasses. "Perfect day."

"It's beautiful." Kay scanned the sky.

"I brought some wine." He held a bag aloft before adding it to the small collection of beach bags and the cooler Kay had spread out on a colorful blanket.

She nodded. A flood of nerves had her fumbling for words. "I ran into town this morning and grabbed a couple sandwiches…and some beer."

"Great." He gave an enthusiastic clap.

She frowned. "Great…" They stood looking at the waves. Silence opened like a chasm between them. *Say something else. Anything.* Her mind couldn't come up with a single thing. So much for clever banter. This was going to be a very long day.

"Why the hell is this so awkward?" He laughed, looking at her in shocked amazement.

Kay threw up her hands. "I have no idea."

"We discussed the weather, food, and our mutual appreciation of each other's attire." He ticked them off on his fingers. "That took all of ten seconds."

She shook her head and shrugged. "This is why I don't date."

"We didn't have any trouble with conversation at breakfast yesterday."

"It wasn't a date."

"Sure it was. I shaved. I walked you to your door. Car door, but a door's a door. Would have kissed you good night, but it was nine o'clock in the morning, and you practically ran over my foot getting away."

Kay grimaced. "Sorry."

"Was it something I said?"

"No..." *Yes.* But how do you explain you're a neurotic lunatic without sounding like one? She studied the rocks by her toes. "No."

Bear leaned closer and spoke in a soft voice. "Maybe if I kiss you good night now—you know, get it out of the way." He gave a small shrug. "Then we can relax and enjoy our day."

Catnip. A shiver ran through her that had nothing to do with the cool breeze coming off the water. "Sounds very... practical."

"Practical?" He lowered his sunglasses and peered over the rim. "I've been called many things, but never practical, not when it comes to my kissing."

She grabbed a handful of his T-shirt and tugged him toward her. "Please just kiss me before I say anything else stupid."

He laughed and dropped his sunglasses on the blanket before wrapping his arms around her. "Under one condition."

Kay closed her eyes and groaned. "What?" He brushed the tip of his nose against hers. His mouth hovered. When he didn't kiss her, she opened her eyes. His serious gaze held her captive.

"Promise you won't vanish this time."

She blinked. "I-I can't guarantee that."

He watched her mouth before searching her eyes. "Guess I'll have to take my chances." His arms tightened their hold as he tipped his head and whispered against her lips. "Good night."

His lips were warm as they met hers, but there was nothing soft in the way his mouth played against hers. No hesitation. No gentle whisper of lips across lips. Bear's kisses were potent and heady. He took her mouth, stole her breath, and made her hunger for more.

Shadow bumped against them, and Bear released her before she'd had her fill. Somehow the panic of the kiss on the point was gone. Not that she was powerless against a few killer kisses. Just the opposite. Kay wanted this. She wanted him. She didn't want to think their relationship to death. She just wanted to feel this feeling. The thrill of excitement that runs through you when you know someone's coming to pick you up, or when you hear their voice on the other end of the phone. That delicious inner gasp when you see them. The warm rush of desire when their gaze locks with yours for an extra second. She craved it all. With Bear. It didn't feel as if she were denying all the hurt Todd had caused by her jumping into another man's arms. This felt right. And good.

Bear kept his hands on her hips and studied her face. She gave him a small smile. "I'm still here."

"Yes, you are. Must be my lucky day."

"Mine too." Kay released the grip she had on the front of his T-shirt and smoothed the wrinkles out of the S of USC. She wanted him to take it off. Was it too early in their date to ask to see his tattoo?

Bear lifted her hand and kissed her fingers. "Let's go for a walk."

"Good idea."

Shadow took the lead as they moved closer to the water where the walking was easier. They headed away from the point to explore the far side of the cove.

Kay kicked off her sandals and walked through the very edge of the waves. The sand beneath her feet was coarse and cool. "So why do they call you Bear?"

"The truth?"

Raising her eyebrows, she shot him a glance. "Is it embarrassing?"

"No, not really. But when you're my size and you're a linebacker, people assume I'm called Bear because I was a ferocious defenseman."

"I remember Walter and you talking football the other night. Did you play professionally?"

He turned and indicated the letters on his shirt. "College ball. Wrecked my shoulder my junior year at USC."

"I'm sorry." She hated the idea of him hurt. Kay wasn't much of a sports fan, but she knew enough to know how brutal some of those tackles could be, even with helmets and pads.

Bear shrugged. "It happens."

"That's not why they call you Bear?"

"Nope. Truth is my younger brother had a stutter as a little kid. Couldn't say Barrett."

Kay shot him a smile. "Adorable."

"Don't spread it around." Shadow splashed into the water ahead of them. "What about you? Kay short for Katherine maybe?"

"No. Just Kay. Walter calls me Special Kay. I'm not sure if I'm supposed to be breakfast cereal or what."

"Brothers? Sisters?"

Kay gave a quick shake of her head. "Nope. There's just me. Parents, of course. Well, one parent, one step. Charles."

He looked over at her. "You have a step-Charles?"

She studied the sand as they continued to walk. "We don't talk much."

"How about your mother?"

"We definitely don't talk much." A wave came in close and chilled her feet before ebbing back into the sea.

Bear and Kay reached the end of the cove that curved out to sea and paused for a minute before they turned back. Clouds skidded across the pure blue of the sky. The sun was gloriously warm on her shoulders. It was great learning more about Bear, but she didn't want to dampen the day with a discussion about her parents, so she turned the conversation back to him. "What about you? Any steps?"

"Nope, two regulation, pre-assigned parents."

"And a kid brother."

"Justin." Bear snagged a rock as they walked. "Not pre-assigned."

Kay watched as he turned the stone over and over in his hand. "You don't get along?"

He smoothed his thumb over the bleached pebble. "We're just different. Night and day different. Dad's a Marine. Justin joined the Corps straight out of high school. ROTC. I was on the football track into college, then military."

"But you got hurt."

He nodded. "Sidelined me from a lot." They walked a few paces in silence. If he didn't want to talk about it, she understood. She wouldn't press him, but then he continued. "My dad...he's one of those guys who sleeps at attention. We had crew cuts before we could walk. Justin's exactly like him. I'd never admit it, but getting injured was a blessing in disguise. The military wouldn't have been a good fit for me." He tossed the stone he'd been carrying out into the water and took hold of her hand. "If you think about it, had things not gone the way they did, I wouldn't be here, or own the inn." He gave her fingers a gentle squeeze. "I wouldn't have met an amazing mural painter."

"And you wouldn't have bought the ugly house on the point."

Bear stopped, holding tight to her hand, halting her. "What's wrong with my house?"

She shook her head sadly. "It's ugly."

His jaw dropped. "It's modern," he insisted.

"Modern ugly."

He pointed. "It's based on a design from Frank Lloyd Wright." His tone was incredulous.

"Sorry, still ugly." She pronounced it You-gly. She tugged on his hand, and they kept walking.

Bear huffed beside her. "Wow. I had no idea you had such hatred for my house. And yet you still let me kiss you?"

Kay stopped and flashed him a smug smile. "What can I say, I like your dog."

Chapter Eleven

"I'm sure it's lovely on the inside." She stroked his arm.

"Don't try to make up. You insulted my house." Bear relaxed on the blanket Kay had spread out.

She sat next to him. The print scarf she'd tied around her waist slipped back to reveal the lovely length of her beautiful legs.

"I'm sorry." Kay dropped her chin.

"No, you're not."

She flashed him a coy look. "You're right, I'm not." She pointed. "Your house stole my best spot. I spent hours out there growing up. Buried treasure there when I was seven," she informed him. "Eighty-seven cents, a *very* expensive ring with an actual ruby. I won it at the carnival." Kay counted them off on her fingers. "A perfect piece of pale-green beach glass, and my best periwinkle crayon." She tucked her hands beneath her bent knees and rested her chin on their tops. "Walter gave me the little metal tin to put everything in. I drew the map and everything. Then poof, I came back one summer, and there it was… *that*." She jerked her chin in the direction of his place. "At least my thinking chair is still out there."

"The dipped out rock?"

"Yes, and I don't care if I'm technically trespassing. I was here first."

Bear loved the defiant set to her chin. "You hereby have my permission to sit out there anytime you want. Hell, give me your map, and I'll dig up your crayon."

Kay smiled at him. "You'd dig up your kitchen floor for a crayon?"

"And an actual ruby ring."

She shrugged. "The ruby *might* have been a fake. It turned my finger green."

"But it's still your treasure."

"I was seven." Her eyes looked impossibly blue.

"Bet you were cute as hell."

Kay shook her head and went back to watching the waves. "Knobby knees and Chiclet teeth."

"But look how nice you turned out." Bear fought the urge to touch her.

Pulling a bowl and a bottle of water out of the bag beside her, Kay stopped to give Shadow a drink. He slobbered his way through and flopped in the sun for a nap.

"You spoil him."

"He looked thirsty. And keep it a secret, I brought a F-r-i-s-b-e-e for him." She spelled the word as she whispered it, and glanced back at the dog to see if he somehow, A, heard her and, B, could spell. She was freakin' adorable.

"Warning," Bear whispered back. "Once he gets a hold of a F-r-i-s-b-e-e, he runs off and buries it. You can kiss it goodbye."

"Again with the goodbye kisses." One pale eyebrow crooked. "Do you think of nothing else?"

"It's good-*night* kisses we've been working at. And no, I can't seem to think about anything else." Bear laid back and slipped his hands beneath his head. From this position, he could drink in the sight of her bare back, and still keep his hands to himself. The clouds overhead had started to build, but the day was still bright. "I'm heading down to Portland on Thursday to pick up a few things. How about coming with me?"

She shook her head. "If I keep taking days off, I'll never get your mural done."

"It's one day."

"That's what you said about today."

"I need your artistic eye. I'm scouting some of the shops in Old Port for decorator items. I know jack about decorator items. I could use some help."

She looked over her shoulder. "Can I think about it?"

Bear sat up. His arm brushed hers. "Sure, as long as you say yes."

Kay turned away to rummage through the cooler. "What, and spoil you, too?" She opened and handed him a beer.

"Not possible. I always bring my Frisbees back." Bear took a long pull off the cold brew. Warm day, private beach, beautiful woman. This was just this side of perfect.

Over the last couple of days, he'd spent more time with her, but she was still a mystery. She was unlike most of the women he'd dated. They never stopped talking about themselves. Kay was just the opposite. Every time he tried to bring the conversation back to her, she would turn it around to him, or the inn, or work. He wanted to know more about her.

"Walter told me you don't usually spend all summer up here."

"Not usually." She opened a bottle of water for

herself.

"So why this summer?"

Kay flashed him a grin. "I'm painting the lobby of an inn nearby."

"Cute. No, really?"

Kay lifted one sun kissed shoulder. "Bell Harbor's my *go to* place. My hideaway."

"What are you hiding from?"

"Nothing." She played with her bottle cap. "Bell Harbor is more like where I run. You know, when I have to get away." She lifted that shoulder again and looked at him. "Don't you have a place you escape to? Somewhere where you can kick back and relax? What's your favorite hideaway? I'm guessing you like the mountains. Are you into all that skiing and hiking stuff?"

She was doing it again. Trying to turn the conversation back to him. "I've told you enough about me. Let's talk about you."

"Not my best subject." Kay was on her feet and halfway to the water before he caught up to her.

"Okay, I'll rephrase the question. Are you running from something? Or someone?"

Kay stopped at the water's edge and crossed her arms over her chest. She was quiet for a long moment as if she were debating whether she could trust him.

He bumped her with his elbow. "You're avoiding the question."

She flashed him a smile. "I'm good at that."

"You're a professional."

Kay turned and met his gaze. "My fiancé changed his mind."

"About getting married?"

Her mouth twitched, and she looked away. "About that whole monogamous, fidelity thing."

"Ouch. I'm sorry."

"Better now, than after the *I do's*, right?" She watched the waves.

He studied her profile. "It still sucks."

She nodded slowly.

"What's he, stupid?"

Kay smirked. "I might not be the best one to answer that."

"I am." He snorted. "The man's an idiot."

"Thanks for that." She smiled at him. "So, I got out. I can be fast when I'm properly motivated. Only took me three hours to erase two years, and another three hours to get here."

"Have you heard from him?"

"No."

Her lack of hesitation tugged at him. "Do you want to?"

"No." Kay crossed her arms and hugged herself. "I'm not one to stick around for the post mortem. It's over. There isn't anything more he could say that I'd want to hear."

"Good point."

She tucked a loose hair behind and ear. "I'll need to find another place to live before the fall semester begins, but for now, Bell Harbor is everything it has always been for me. It's safe and soothing as if the water here has magical powers."

"This water is numbing."

She gave a quick laugh. "Maybe numbing is exactly what I need."

He leaned closer and lowered his voice. "Or maybe

you need someone to appreciate how amazing you are."

Kay looked up at him. "I've gotten pretty good at not needing someone."

He retucked that stray bit of hair behind her ear. In the sunlight, her eyes had these little golden specks. "Everybody needs someone."

Her gaze held his for a long moment. "Why do I get the feeling you're applying for the job?"

"Who better?" He grinned. "I already know how amazing you are."

Kay shook her head and looked away. "You know nothing about me."

"I'm trying." When she turned back toward their blanket, he followed. "I know you're beautiful. Talented." Bear reached out and caught her arm. She turned but kept her gaze somewhere in the middle of his chest. "I know how your eyes light up when you talk about your work. You love Walter and Dottie Polk even though you know they're nuts. You've got a great laugh." He wished she would meet his eye. "You drink beer from a bottle and hate pickles on your burger." He stroked the warm softness of her skin. "I know I want to drive three hours to Stoddard, New Hampshire, and push my fist through the face of a guy whose name I've never even heard."

She finally lifted her eyes to his. "I don't know what you want me to say."

"Say you'll go to Portland with me. Tell me you don't think all men are complete jackasses, and even though you hate my house, you'll let me kiss you again."

Kay pressed her lips together before giving him a grudging smile. "You know, for a guy, you sure can talk pretty when you put your mind to it."

"I can be properly motivated, too." The urge to kiss her surged through him.

Kay studied the letters on his shirt before tracing the S with her fingertips. "Can I think about it?"

"Which part?" His voice rasped.

She stilled her fingers. "All of it."

Bear lifted her hand and kissed the back of those fingers. "Sure. Just remember." He turned her hand and laid another kiss in its palm. "You love my dog."

Kay tugged her hand away and scoffed, "I said, I *liked* your dog."

"Your mouth said *liked*, but your eyes…"

She laughed. "My eyes are always running their mouth."

God, she was adorable!

Chapter Twelve

Their day on the beach had started off strained and forced, and there were some moments when Bear saw too much in her "big mouth" eyes. But when he walked her to her door, all she could think about was another good night kiss. Kay kept her focus on the bright USC of his shirt so her eyes couldn't scream out how she was beginning to ache thinking about what a good morning kiss from Bear might be like. You know, after a night in his arms. In her bed.

"Do you want to come in? For a cup of coffee? It's getting chilly, I could start a fire."

"Better not. Shadow's covered with sand and smells like low tide." Bear had been right about one thing. Shadow had caught that Frisbee in midair, raced off with it, and it was never seen again. Okay, he'd had been right about two things. She did love his dog.

Bear pushed the hair away from her cheek and tipped her chin so she had no choice but to look into his eyes. "Plus, if I come in, I won't want to leave."

Then, stay. The words screamed in her brain. Kay pressed her lips together to keep from saying them. She made the mistake of focusing her gaze on his mouth. "I guess it's good night then."

The smallest of smiles curved his lips. Had she not been watching she might have missed it. The tremor it caused to race through her body threw her breathing into second gear. God, he smelled so good. Like summer. All sunshine and sand. Coconutty sunscreen over warm skin.

"*Another* good night kiss?"

"Yes, please."

He stroked the sensitive spot under her chin with a lazy finger. "Yes, please," he mimicked. "Are you always so polite?" His eyes crinkled in amusement.

"Hell, no." Kay traced his bottom lip before testing the gentle dent in his chin. "But other than climbing you like a tree, I figured it was the best way to get you to kiss m—"

His mouth crushed hers with a blazing kiss that ended all the teasing. She opened her mouth to accept the sweep of his tongue. A moan slipped from her throat. Good God, this man could kiss. She nipped at his lower lip with her teeth before returning the heat with a searing kiss of her own.

Steely arms tightened around her, fusing her damp body to his. She trembled with want. If he could kiss like this, what would he be like in bed with those big hands caressing her skin, stroking her? Kissing her all over? *Oh, God!*

Bear moved his kisses to the side of her neck, tasting her there, nipping her earlobe, making major parts of her anatomy turn liquid. His kisses reached across her shoulder to the strap of her bathing suit before he stopped. His warm breath came hard against her skin. His body, a tense coil, wrapped around her until he drew in a deep breath and eased away.

"Timber," he breathed. "I…better go."

Kay nodded. Her ability to speak, gone. She reached back with one steadying hand to grasp the doorframe.

Bear whistled for Shadow who emerged from the woods even dirtier than when he went in. Bear grabbed his collar before the dog could spread his love of mud and give her his own good night kiss.

The light was fading, turning their perfect day into evening. Bear stood for a moment as if he were reluctant to put an end to what might easily turn into a night of beginnings. He seemed to give himself a mental shake before speaking to the dog. "Come on, boy, home." Shadow bolted from Bear's grasp and took off in the direction of the point. Bear held her gaze a moment longer. "Think about Thursday. I want you to come."

She pressed her lips together again and nodded. *I think I just did...*

Kay arrived early to the inn the next afternoon. After missing a day of work, she was eager to catch up. Who was she kidding? She was eager to see Bear. Last night's heated tongue tango on the porch had inspired a night of semi-erotic dreams that left her sweaty and frustrated as hell.

She was no virgin, and she and Todd had a fair sex life, but she'd never been so turned on by the mere thought of a man. Bear's kisses sent her libido into orbit. Zero to sixty in one point eight seconds. She'd been hesitant to start something with him for a host of valid, sound, logical reasons, but for the life of her, when his lips met hers, she couldn't remember a one.

When she entered the lobby, Bear was on his phone.

"Bell. Harbor. Inn. *Bell Harbor*...Yes, Maine. You're joking, right? They were due last week. I've got fourteen beds here with no mattresses." He ran a frustrated hand through his hair before turning and spotting her. A look crossed his face, which she didn't quite understand until his gaze slowly scanned her body down to her ankles and back again. Was she naked? She felt naked. Warmth flooded her face as his eyes held hers. "Beds without mattresses do me no good at all." There was a decided huskiness to his voice.

His eyebrows rose sharply. "Inflatables? Did you just say *inflatables*? Listen, what's your name? Tom? Okay, Tom, here's what you're going to do. You're going to personally hike your ass down to the warehouse and put my order on a truck. Have it to my inn by the end of the week, even if you have to drive it here yourself. Got it? Thank you... That would be great. For you, Tom, I'll try." Bear clicked off the phone and threw it onto the desk. He blew out a sharp breath.

Curiosity got the better of her. "You'll try what?"

"To have a nice day." He rubbed the space between his eyes. "Did you know there is a Bell Harbor Inn in Bell Harbor, Michigan?"

Kay laughed and pulled a roll of brushes from their spot. "I do now."

"Seems they have my mattresses and box springs, and instead of refusing the delivery, someone signed for them before they realized no one had ordered fourteen new mattresses and box springs." He held up a sheet of paper. "But that didn't stop the company from charging my account."

Kay selected a handful of brushes she'd be using today and laid them out according to size. "And in the meantime, they want you to use blow-up ones?"

"Yep." He gave his head a slow shake. "Classic." He rummaged through some more papers on top of his cluttered desk. "Buy an inn, they said, it will be fun," he muttered.

"I'm sorry."

"Not your fault." He looked up at her and smiled. "You're the best thing to walk through that door all day." He checked the clock. "And you're early."

"Need to make up for playing hooky." Kay moved her wheeled paint cart/palette into place. It contained all manner of tubes and pots of paint, more brushes, and anything else she would want at her fingertips. She grabbed a clean rag and slipped it into the back pocket of her jeans.

"A day off isn't hooky. Could be I'm a bad influence."

She uncapped a tube of classic dark red and added a large dollop to her board. "Could be." Using a palette knife, she mixed the red with a touch of brown, a whisper of gray. Kay loaded her one-inch brush with paint. Today, she'd finish up painting the brick skirt of the bandstand before adding in each musician.

Kay shot him a quick smile as she moved in closer to the wall. "I had a wonderful time yesterday."

He was watching her intently. She looked away but could still feel his gaze on her skin. Kay stood poised waiting for the tremor in her hand to stop before she put paint to wall.

"So did I."

There was something in his tone that made her look back at him. He leaned against the corner of his desk in a casual pose. One foot hooked over the other. Arms crossed over his wide chest. Kay could just make out the very bottom of his tattoo beneath the sleeve of his crisp white T-shirt.

Another thing that kept her awake last night. Not the shirt hugging him like a second skin, but his damn tattoo. He'd never removed his shirt on the beach yesterday. She'd been dying to ask. Instead, she'd spent those quiet hours between one and three in the morning wondering about his ink, his skin, his body.

"Made for an interesting night, however," he added.

Wait, what? Was he a mind reader? "Oh?" It had been an interesting night, all right. Moving away from the wall, she swapped her brush to the other hand and reached for a rag to stuff in her pocket only to realize she already had one.

Bear straightened and stepped away from the desk toward her. "Didn't sleep a wink."

She swallowed trying to ease the sudden dryness of her mouth. "You, too?"

His head tipped. "You had trouble sleeping as well? Fascinating." He took a step closer, and Kay's heart rate clicked up a notch or two. "We really need to work on this. Mutual insomnia. Damn. Can't be good for either of us." He shook his head and considered her. "There are some things we could try. Might help."

Her breathing hitched. "I'm almost afraid to ask."

"Nothing drastic." He moved closer. He oozed sexuality—like a freaking fire hydrant. She was drenched. "Warm milk works well," he suggested. "Maybe a touch of brandy?" There was that little glint of mischief in his eyes she'd come to adore. "Or…there are some who swear by a bit of physical activity."

"Before bed?" she asked.

"*In* bed."

If he was trying to fluster her, he'd succeeded. The slight tip of his lips confirmed it. Well, two could play at this game. She fluttered her eyelashes at him. "But you have no mattresses."

He nodded solemnly. "Could be an issue." He was close enough now she needed to lift her eyes to look into the hazel of his. "I'll have to give this some more thought." His voice was smooth as marshmallow Fluff.

"Isn't giving this some thought *why* you're having trouble sleeping?" She raised an eyebrow and tsked. "Sounds like a vicious circle to me." She traced an O in the middle of his chest with her fingertip.

He caught her wrist. "You don't play fair, Kay Winston."

Her breath left her in a rush. "Neither do you."

"What? I'm the Prince of Fair." Bear feigned an innocent look. He couldn't pull it off.

"Not when you kiss like you do." Had the temperature in the room risen? Her cheeks were hot.

He raised her hand and placed a slow, gentle kiss on the inside of her wrist. "You're complaining?" The tip of his tongue skimmed her skin there.

Heat shot clear to her thighs. "No—they...I... Never mind." Her face flamed. "M-my paint is drying."

"Forget the paint." He moved still closer, lifting her hand to drape it over his shoulder while he slipped an arm about her waist. "Tell me. What do my kisses do?"

"I stop breathing," she admitted in a whisper.

"I see."

Had she noticed the way his hair was just long enough to curl around her fingertips before?

"Another vicious circle," he murmured. "You stop breathing, I have to give you mouth to mouth—vicious circle."

"I'm starting to hate those." She sighed.

"Me, too." His gaze fell to her mouth as he bent to kiss her. "Me, too." The words skipped over her lips.

"Hey, Yogi!"

Kay pushed away from Bear as if she'd been burned. The muscle in Bear's jaw ticked as he growled a colorful obscenity about the legitimacy of Walter's birth. Kay was back studying her paints before the man in question pushed through the swinging door between the lobby and the kitchen.

"There ye be. Got the name of that stonemason fella I was—What in the hell! Were ya shot?"

"Aw, shit."

Kay spun around horrified. A large spot of classic dark red paint with a hint of brown and a whisper of gray decorated Bear's shirt. She'd been so engrossed in the prospect of his lips against hers, she'd completely forgotten about the brush in her hand. Bear looked like a gunshot victim. Walter was looking back and forth between the two of them with a frown on his face as if he was trying to figure out just how her paint had jumped those eight feet to land on Bear's chest.

Kay dropped her brush into the wash cup. "Give me your shirt before it dries."

Bear obliged, and in one smooth move, grasped the back collar of his tee and pulled it off. Kay had seen him without his shirt before, but it had been from a distance…at dusk…while he ran the beach. The sight of Bear's naked chest and abs this close…it was so unladylike to drool. Dark hair accented the play of muscles at the center of his chest and led her gaze to follow its sinful trail past his toned stomach to a clear line running straight down into the waistband of his jeans. The clean smell of his skin filled her senses.

His tattoo was nothing like she imagined. A round Celtic design hugged the curve of his shoulder. The work was crisp and intricate with acorns gracing an inter-woven ring around the dark silhouette of a tree. A clean scar sliced through the symbol and distorted the lettering which arched along the top of the branches. *O'nert* was all she could make out at quick glance, but the artistry was beautiful in deep greens and black with touches of yellow in the lettering to give it the appearance of gold. She wondered what the words meant.

Handing her his stained shirt, Bear grabbed a zippered sweatshirt from the back of the desk chair and slipped it on over all those well-defined muscles. *Damn.*

"Special Kay, you all right?"

She'd forgotten Walter was even in the room. "Sure, sure." Heat rushed to her face, and other much less visible places. "Nothing a little mouth to mouth couldn't cure," she said under her breath as she headed past Bear in the direction of the nearest bathroom. His strangled cough behind her made her smile.

In the restroom, Kay ran water through the cotton, washing away most of the paint. Dark red ran into the sink staining the porcelain. The smell of him still clung to the fabric. She pulled the intoxicating scent deep into her lungs before obliterating it with the pink industrial hand soap she pumped from the dispenser affixed to the wall. With a bit of scrubbing, she was able to get rid of the remaining stain of paint.

Rinsing and wringing out the sodden shirt, Kay caught her reflection in the mirror over the sink. Her eyes were bright, cheeks flushed, her slight panicked expression had nothing to do with worries about a ruined shirt.

She searched her eyes looking for the answer to the question her heart and her body had already answered—she was in trouble. Serious trouble. She was falling for him.

Chapter Thirteen

By the time five p.m. rolled around, Bear Coulter didn't know if he was riding a horse or bowling. He'd gone from wanting to play naked finger paints with Kay to her disappearing for the rest of the afternoon.

Walter hadn't helped matters. When he heard the tale of the missing mattresses, he knew a guy who knew a guy who could get him mattresses for *short bucks*. Did it matter if they were slightly used?

Skippy fumbled a nail gun and accidently shot a finish nail into Brian's ass. Brian accidently broke Skippy's nose. Diane called twice, and Shadow had rolled in something muddy, or dead…it sure smelled dead, but Bear hoped like hell it was mud.

It had been one disaster after another. He'd sent Walter home, Skippy and Brian to the ER, hosed off Shadow, and ignored Diane when caller ID alerted him to call number three. He was home now, back from his run, two beers into a six pack, and ready to throw something frozen into the microwave for dinner. Changing his mind, he reached for a third beer instead. A gentle knock on his deck door brought an instant cure for his day from hell.

Kay.

She lifted a hand in a wave when she saw him through the glass. In her other hand she held his shirt from earlier. Opening the slider, he slipped out and shut the door behind him.

"Hey."

"Hey. Sorry to bother you. I'm headed back to the inn, but I wanted to return your shirt." She handed it to him. It was clean and folded. Did she iron it?

"Thanks. It was just an old shirt, you didn't need to go to all that trouble."

"I have to watch where I rest my brush from now on."

"It didn't hurt a bit. Want to come in? Shadow's grounded, but I'm sure he'd love to see you. I was thinking about thawing some dinner." He lifted his bottle. "The beer's cold. You're welcome to stay."

"No thanks, I'm working. Guess my night watchman is off duty tonight. What did he do to get himself grounded?"

"I have no idea. He's not talking, but whatever it was, it stank like the devil and wore him the hell out."

"Sounds like he could use the night off." She nodded and folded her arms over her chest.

It got quiet. The only sound was the waves hitting the rocks on the point. Bear followed her gaze in that direction. He lifted his beer and took a swallow before continuing. "Where'd you disappear to today?"

That earned him a shrug. "I had a shirt to clean."

"Couldn't have anything to do with this obvious thing we've got going on between us."

"Thing?" She chewed at her lower lip.

He couldn't tear his eyes away from that lip. "I'm not sure what else to call it."

Kay tucked her chin. "How about we don't call it anything."

"I don't know if we can ignore it any more. I know

111

I can't."

"I'm not saying we ignore it. I'm saying...I wish I could explain it better, but I'm a painter, not a poet." She looked at him with wide eyes, as if she was just caught stealing candy. "I like you," she confessed. "A lot..."

Bear's stomach took a dip. Wasn't this how all those *let's just be friends, it's not you it's me* conversations started. He braced himself. "But?"

"No buts." She shrugged. "I think you might like me a little bit too."

Relief washed over him. If she hadn't looked so serious, he'd have laughed. "Just a little." He held up his hand with his thumb and forefinger and inch apart.

"Then maybe we should take your *little bit* and my *a lot* and...see what happens. Leave the labels off, just let it be what it is."

"Keep it easy," he suggested.

Kay agreed. "Exactly. Easy."

Bear leaned back against the doorjamb and considered her. "Easy isn't a word I'd use to describe you in any way. And *easy* sure as hell isn't what I'm feeling."

"I can't promise you any more than that." She studied his feet.

"So what does this mean?"

Kay straightened and squared her shoulders. "It means I'll go with you to Portland on Thursday."

"And after?" He knew he shouldn't press. Maybe it was the beer talking, but he needed to know. He had no intention of playing games. Not with her. It had taken a lot for Kay to come out here, but he wanted there to be no more question as to what he wanted.

She took a breath and gave him a quick smile. "How about we get there when we get there."

"Okay. Thursday. Walter's taking Shadow for the day and lending me his truck. I'll swing by and pick you up on my way over there."

"Sounds good." She looked relieved and started to walk away. "I'll see you then."

"Wait." He straightened from the doorframe. "I need to be clear here. We're great at this verbal sparring business. I don't care what we call what's happening between us. Truth is, I want you. Plain and simple. We can go as easy as you'd like, but I can't deny how I feel about you."

"That's not what I'm asking you to do." She was back to looking out past the point. "I don't want to examine us to death. I don't want to stress over everything I say and do. Dissect every moment. Replay every conversation in my head searching for hidden meanings. I don't want that." She looked back at him. "I want to spend time with you. Be with you, and not worry about either of us making it more than it needs to be."

"Understood." He wished she didn't look so panicked. The last thing he wanted to do was frighten her off, but he was past the flirting. She was scared. He got that. It was time to prove to her he wasn't like the others. He wasn't out to hurt her, take whatever he could get and walk away. He wished he had the words to convince her. "We'll take it nice and easy. No strings."

"Perfect." She smiled. "That's all I want."

"You got it." It was the first time he'd outright lied to her. No strings? He was so tied up in her now, he could knit a sweater. There was no way he could do the friends-with-benefits thing. Not with her. But he had to give her credit. Whatever her reasons, she was being honest. He was walking into this minefield with his eyes wide open. If his heart was blown to smithereens, it was no one's fault but his own.

"Great. Then I'll see you Thursday."

"We'll be crawling through some dusty antique shops; dress casual. But pack a change of clothes. I'm taking you to my favorite restaurant for dinner after."

Thursday finally came following a week of relative calm. If you call wading through building inspections, half a dozen calls from Diane, and needing a new septic tank calm. But every night Kay arrived to work. With her came quiet. The phones stopped ringing, the saws and hammers went silent. It was as if her paintbrush was a magic wand. Bear would leave for home much more collected than he otherwise would have.

And in the morning, he would enter the lobby, and marvel at what her magic wand had done in the night. Before the chaos of the day, he would take his coffee and stroll through the latest addition to the mural. Her attention to the tiniest detail was amazing.

He discovered her humor there. Subtle and hidden like secret Easter eggs. Everything was period, and perfect, but if you looked very close, that's where you'd discover treasures. Tiny things you wouldn't notice at first glance. You had to look. The tuba player on the bandstand wore two different colored socks. The fire department was rescuing a cat out of a tree until you looked close enough to see it was a poodle. The child fishing off the dock caught a boot with a fish tail sticking out of the top. Was there a pirate flag on one of the tall ships? Losing himself in Kay's painting made every morning feel like his own private scavenger hunt.

He was in love with her.

No hidden surprise there. What surprised Bear was the lack of panic usually accompanied that fact. He was acting like a twenty-year-old. Hopeless and horny. His body in a constant state of want. Thinking about spending the entire day with her only perpetuating the wooden discomfort in his shorts.

He refused to be that guy. The desperate one who sends flowers every day or leaves notes on her car window. But his mind kept coming up with little romantic things he wanted to do for her. What the hell! He was Bear Coulter. Women came after *him*. When had the tide turned? He knew when. He could tell you the exact day.

It had killed him, but he'd forced himself to keep his distance these last few days. Monday night's exchange on his deck had convinced him to slow the hell down. Had he invited her into the house, shown her into the bedroom…that would have been the end of it. We're talking smoking tire tracks. She would have run so fast, he'd never have found her. He was in love, and technically a liar…but he was no idiot.

Picking up Walter's rust bucket of a Ford was fun. The way hitting yourself in the head with a hammer is fun when you stop. Shadow had been crazy with excitement at seeing Kay and Walter. Dottie insisted on packing them a few snacks for the road.

"Who ya feedin', woman? Coxey's army?" After commenting on the ton of food Dottie was pushing at them, Walter took twenty minutes explaining how the emergency brake pedal in the truck was broken, and if you had your fingers on the wrong side of the pull handle, you'd most likely break a knuckle when it released. And thank goodness the weather was due to be clear, because the windshield wiper motor was temperamental. The wipers would wipe, but they wouldn't come back the other way. He'd meant to fix it, but in the meantime, there was a string. "Takes a far bit of coordination ta drive a beat-ah, but you'll get the hang of it."

Bear swapped a sack of sandwiches and God knows what else with a bag of Shadow's food, favorite bones, and instructions on what to do if they put him in his nemesis, the kennel. Yesterday he'd dug a hole half way to China and shimmied beneath the fence when Bear had caught him. Dog was too smart for his own good.

It was all worth it, however, when it was finally just him and Kay. Driving down the shore route took them through one picturesque village after another. They discovered wonderful out of the way places for antiques and found some great things. The best finds were an old brass telescope, some sailing charts Kay thought would look amazing framed, and a period washstand complete with its original pitcher and bowl.

Kay had a great eye. After each stop, she would hop back into the cab of the old truck, fasten her seat belt, and cross her legs. She'd worn a sassy pair of cut off denim shorts and simple cotton top. And off the tips of those sparkle-pink toes, a flat, strappy sandal would dangle, threatening to drop. Bear spent all day fascinated by her sandal...and the long beautiful leg attached.

"Where to next?" The seat belt clicked, the legs

crossed, the sandal hung precariously—his jeans tightened.

"Umm…there are a few more places in Old Port down along the water. Then maybe we could take a run out to Cape Elizabeth."

"Sure. What's out there, more antiques?"

"No. The light."

A few hours later, they pulled into the small state park. Following the road past the remains of the fort which used to be there, Bear pulled the truck into the parking lot. To their left, out on a small jut, stood Portland Head Light.

"Oh, Bear," Kay breathed, "this is beautiful."

"I discovered it a few months ago. It's becoming one of my favorite places."

"Favorite places, favorite restaurant later? Am I getting the Coulter VIP tour of Portland?" Kay slipped her arm through his.

"I've only been down here a handful of times. There are some great spots, but I'm still exploring." He took her hand as they walked down the small hill toward the light. "I like sharing it with you."

Kay smiled. "It's been years since I visited the city, and I'm embarrassed to say, I've never been to Cape Elizabeth." She pulled in a deep breath of sea air. "This is gorgeous."

They walked the path past the hedges of sea roses, alongside the former lighthouse keeper's residence, which was now a museum. They passed an elderly couple heading the other way. Being late on a Thursday afternoon, they pretty much had the place to themselves. Long shadows stretched toward the sea. Kay leaned against the brilliant white of the light's tower and closed her eyes. A contented Mona Lisa smile graced her lips.

"Have I worn you out?"

She opened her beautiful eyes and smiled at him. "No. I was listening. The gulls, the buoy bells, the wind, the light clicks as it rotates."

"I hadn't noticed any of those things. I was too busy noticing you and wondering how the hell I'd been with you more than six straight hours and I haven't kissed you yet."

"I was going to ask you about that." She tipped her head and gave him a coy look. "I mean, what's a girl gotta do?" She held out her hand to him. He closed his fingers over hers, and she gave his hand a slight tug.

Bear narrowed the space between them. "I can fix this."

He fit his mouth over hers erasing the hours of building desire after days of denial. She was eager to open her lips to the insistent searching of his tongue.

Kay purred her approval beneath him as her hands found the belt loops of his jeans and pulled his hips toward her. Heat rushed to his cock as he pinned her to the lighthouse tower and she straddled his knee. The roughness of the stucco surface of the tower pricked the palms of his hands as the kiss reached white hot level.

Squeals and laughter of children heading in their direction from the visitor's trail ended the kiss abruptly. Bear pushed away from her and the tower and moved quickly to the fence line keeping visitors away from the rocky edge. Standing close to the short chain-link fence, he hoped like hell to hide the evidence of his arousal. His body thrummed with need. He could still feel her lips against his and taste the sweetness of her mouth on his tongue.

Half a dozen kids bounced off the chain link and raced behind him, followed closely by two women pushing strollers. After they passed, Kay came to stand beside him. She slipped her hand through the crook of his arm again and pressed herself against his side.

"Damn kids," he muttered.

Kay tightened her hold, blew out a breath, and gave a small laugh. "Wasn't their fault."

"I know. It was mine."

"How was it yours?" She kissed his arm and rested her chin on his shoulder.

"When am I going to learn to kiss you somewhere where we won't be interrupted?"

"That could be dangerous." Her warm breath on the side of his neck wasn't helping matters.

"I'm counting on it," he growled. Turning his head, he stole another kiss.

"Folks? 'Fraid I have ta kick you out. Pahk closes he'ah at dusk." The park ranger tipped his hat and moved along, giving the same message to the two women juggling all those children.

Bear grumbled after the ranger, but his gaze never left hers. "Could we continue this conversation at dinner?"

His hoarse whisper seemed to amuse her. She tightened her hold on his arm and held his gaze for an extra second.

"I'd like that."

Chapter Fourteen

Kay ran a brush through her hair and smoothed the skirt of her dress. The low, square neck of the classic little black dress complemented the one piece of *real* jewelry she owned—a short strand of small cream-colored pearls her parents had given her on her sixteenth birthday.

Immediately upon opening the long thin velvet box, her mother had snatched them from her and shown her the proper way to determine whether pearls were real or fake. "If you run them over your teeth and they feel smooth, they're the cheap ones. They need to feel rough if they're real." She ran Kay's gift across her teeth and smiled. "Here, try." Kay had declined and put them back in the box, vowing they would never come anywhere near her teeth. Ever.

On second thought, Kay took them off and tucked them back into her bag. Tonight had all the signs of being a special night, and Kay wanted nothing to spoil it.

She and Bear had left the picturesque lighthouse and stopped at a small coffee shop in Portland to change their clothes. Her body still held the warmth from their exchange at the light. Her lips still pink. He'd held her hand all the way back to the truck, and reached for it again as they began the drive back into the city. Now they were off to a nice dinner at his favorite restaurant, which was famous for their crème brûlée. All she could think of was how fast could they get back to Bell Harbor. She wanted to be with him. Alone.

Kay tossed her sandals into the backpack she'd brought along, and pulled out a pair of black satin pumps with a thin heel. She had forgotten stockings and for one scandalous moment considered slipping out of her silk panties and going completely bare beneath the dress.

She laughed at her reflection. Bear would burst into flames if he knew. She'd felt the firm ridge of his erection pressed into her belly when they kissed against the lighthouse. He wanted her as much as she wanted him. If she walked out there and casually mentioned she wasn't wearing panties, they'd never get further than the parking lot. She really didn't want to have their first time be in the front seat of Walter's junky pickup.

Smoothing a light gloss over her lips, she fluffed her hair. It had been a long time since she dressed up, and even longer since she'd been so excited to be with a man that she contemplated losing her underwear. She wasn't sure she could calmly sit through a nice dinner and then the two-hour drive back to Bell Harbor.

When she walked out of the ladies' room and caught the expression on Bear's face as he took in the sight of her in her dress and heels, she knew she needed to suggest another alternative.

He took her hand and lifted it over her head leading her into a spin. "I'm…speechless. You look amazing."

He wore a black jacket over a white oxford shirt and jeans. The effect was dressy casual and he fit it perfectly. "You're pretty amazing yourself."

Bear leaned toward her and growled, "I'll never make it through dinner."

Kay laughed. "I just had a similar conversation with my reflection in the mirror." She moved closer. An older couple drinking their coffee and sharing a muffin watched them. "So why don't we make a slight change of plan."

Bear sighed. "God, you smell wonderful. I'm listening...talk fast." His voice had a low sexy rasp she felt in her thighs.

Kay held his gaze. "Take me home."

"What about dinner?" He was close enough to kiss her.

"Dottie packed us enough food for three days." Kay ran a gentle thumb over the slight clef in his chin. "We can eat on the way."

"But candlelight, wine list...crème brûlée." Bear watched her mouth.

Kay bit her bottom lip. The man could make love to her with just his eyes. "I have candles and wine at my place. No crème brûlée, but I have stale cookies."

A smooth smile graced his mouth. "I love stale cookies."

"Then what are we waiting for?"

Just before they reached the Maine turnpike, Kay licked chip dust off the tips of her fingers before leaning over and kissing Bear's neck. "Damn," she whispered against his skin. "I forgot something back at the coffee shop."

Bear checked his side view mirror. "I can turn around."

She sat back in her seat and crossed her legs. "No, don't bother." She flipped her hand and then smoothed the hem of her skirt across her thigh. "I can always buy another pair of panties."

A mile later, blue lights filled the cab of the truck, and Bear was passing his license and Walter's registration out the window to the waiting officer.

"Yes, sir, I did know I was speeding."

"Is this your vehicle?" The Statey shined his light onto the documents in his hands.

"Um...no...I borrowed it from a friend, Walter Polk. I had some antiques to pick up in Portland. I can lift off the tarp—"

"Do you know how fast you were going, sir?"

Bear snuck a look at her. Kay pressed her lips together to keep from laughing. "Not fast enough," he murmured. To the officer he tried to joke. "I didn't expect this heap would ever go over seventy-five."

The officer wasn't amused. "I clocked you at eighty-six." He shined his official flashlight on her. Kay leaned toward the driver's side and smiled. "Good evening, officer."

"Can I see some ID, ma'am?"

Kay pulled out her license and leaned over Bear to pass it to the officer. "I'm Kay Winston. Walter Polk is my uncle. I can call him for you. He can vouch for everything."

He examined her identification and handed it back. "Won't be necessary. Stay in the vehicle. I'll be right back."

"Don't you dare laugh," Bear muttered as soon as the officer was out of earshot.

"I wouldn't dream of it." Kay stowed her license, settled back into her seat, and crossed her legs.

Bear watched her every move with a look of pure

lust on his face. "This is all your fault."

Kay raised a hand in surrender. "I take full responsibility. If I hadn't accidently left my panties—"

"You like playing with fire, don't you?" he growled.

Blue lights strobed, and the blinding spotlight made it look like they were on stage. Kay gave him a coy smile. "Only with you."

He shifted slightly in his seat, shook his head, and smiled back. "If I get a ticket, I'm docking your pay."

Kay took her finger and ran it slowly along the square edge of her low neckline. Bear's eyes followed its path. "You won't get a ticket. Did you see where his flashlight was pointed?"

****

The door hit the wall as they pushed blindly into the kitchen. Bear pinned her against the wall, and gave her a kiss that melted her high heels. "Nice place. Cozy," he murmured against her neck.

Kay could only gasp, trying to catch her breath. "Y-you want the tour?"

"No." His kisses moved along her collarbone.

"But I have mattresses. Two," she offered as he slipped her dress off her shoulder and kissed her there.

Bear lifted his head. "Show off."

"One is much too small." She rushed. His hand teasing the hem of her dress was making it hard for her to think.

"Is the other *just right*, Goldilocks?" His eyes held hers.

She could only blink. "That's up to you, Papa Bear."

Bear slipped her hair behind her ear before kissing

it and rasping, "I'm nobody's papa."

Kay's knees liquefied. "Good to know. Wasn't his…bed…too hard?"

"Mmhmmmm." He agreed against her neck. "Too hard."

"Some things are better hard."

"Some things are much better soft." He palmed her breast. "Are you going to show me this perfect mattress, or am I going to be forced to test the strength of your kitchen table?"

"I thought you promised Officer Dan you would take it slow."

"Oh, I plan to. Just as soon as I get you out of this dress." His hand moved to the zipper on the back.

"W-we should shut the door first."

"If we have to." He let go of her and stepped back, stripping out of his jacket. He tossed it over the back of one of the chairs.

Kay slipped past him, and closed the door. She turned on a small lamp all the while feeling his eyes on her. Feeling his desire wrap around her. The air in the room pulsed with it.

"I promised you wine." She ran a hand over the wild mess of her hair.

"And stale cookies." He worked on unbuttoning his shirt, and pulled its tails from his jeans.

"I lied about the cookies. It was just a ploy to get you back to my place. I have Triscuits."

He moved closer and slipped his arms around her waist, drawing her close. "So you planned to seduce me all along?"

Everywhere he touched her tingled with a delicious shimmer. "Just since the lighthouse." She flashed him a smile.

"The wine and crackers can wait." He found the tab of her zipper and lowered it slowly.

Kay stroked the slight patch of dark hair in the center of his chest. "Are you sure you're not too tired? It was a long drive."

"The next time you decide to seduce me, could you make it closer to home?"

She gasped as the zipper of her dress hit bottom and his warm hand slipped around her bare back. "You insisted on making all those stops."

He rested his lips against her temple. "Two stops. Cops and condoms. Crucial on both counts."

"You're very responsible." She released the metal button of his jeans.

"USC." His breathing sounded labored.

"USC?" She couldn't think. His fingers played across her back.

In one deft move, he found the back clasp of her bra and unhooked it. "Trojans." He growled a second before his mouth claimed hers. Kay clung to the fabric of his shirt and melted into the kiss. Bear pulled her tight against the hard ridge of his erection still trapped inside his jeans. He broke the kiss resting his forehead against hers. "You said something about a mattress, Goldilocks."

Taking his hand, Kay led him to the narrow stairs leading to her bedroom. On the first step she stopped, turned, and wrapped her arms around his neck. The shift in height was perfect. Their mouths met on an equal plane.

Bear wrapped his arms around her waist and lifted her off her feet. He didn't stop until the top.

Chapter Fifteen

"Left or right?" he breathed.

"My right, or your right?" Kay gasped between kisses. She pointed, barely able tell up from down.

Three steps into the room, Bear lowered her, easing her down his body like water over a rock. "I lied." He rested his forehead against hers. She could feel his heart hammering against his chest.

Kay's breath caught. "Oh?"

A thread of chilled concern flitted down her spine until he cupped her cheek with his hand and raised her chin up to kiss her. "To hell with Officer Dan. I can't promise slow. Not the first time, anyway." He nipped at her lower lip with his teeth. "God, I want you."

"Oh…"

"I can't see your face. Is that a good *oh*, or a bad *oh*?"

Kay stepped away and lit the two fat candles she kept on the corner of her dresser. The scent of warm vanilla rose to greet her. She lit another on the nightstand next to the bed. Soft light flickered. Standing there in the soft glow, she finished what Bear had started down in the kitchen. A shrug of one shoulder and a slip over her hips, and her little black dress dropped to her shoes. Kicking it aside, she stood in nothing but her heels.

"Oh." Bear sounded like he'd been punched. His

eyes made a slow scan from top to bottom and back again.

The only sound was the ocean stroking the shore and the blood rushing in her ears. "For someone who was in such a hurry, you're not moving."

"I'm trying to remember how to breathe."

She was having no trouble breathing. With her heart trying to beat its way out of her chest, her lungs were working double time. "You have done this before, right?" She tried to joke.

He flashed a quick smile. "Not with you." His gaze held her. "You're gorgeous." Bear closed the distance between them. Kay ran her hands up the solid muscles of his chest and slid his shirt off his shoulders before he pulled her into his arms and lowered her onto the bed.

Kay leaned back on her elbows as Bear lifted her leg. He plucked the satin pump from her foot and tossed it aside. He nipped the top of her knee as he removed her other shoe. The sensation shot straight to her sex and made her gasp.

Bear gave her a wicked grin and was quick to remove the rest of his clothes and sheath himself with his Trojan pride condom. He lowered himself between her legs pushing her back into the mattress.

Kay looked up into his hooded eyes. "I see you've remembered how to breathe."

Balancing on one arm, he trailed a finger down her throat to circle the tip of one breast. "Are you always so damn sassy?"

"Always." She ran a hand up his supporting arm relishing the feel and contour of muscle. The man was satin over granite.

"Good. I like sass," he rasped before crushing his

mouth to her, ending any need for a witty comeback.

Kay arched into the warmth of his hand holding her breast as his tongue slipped between her parted lips. She raised one knee, running her thigh up the line of his hip while he swept his hand over the dip of her waist to play at the curve of her ass. He lifted her to him. Pressed the heat of her tight to the hard length of his erection.

Bear tore his lips from hers, moving his kisses to her jaw, sucking the lobe of her ear into his mouth, and ran the tip of his tongue slowly along the rim before nipping his way down the side of her neck.

Kay was aflame. The blaze that started on the ride home burned white hot. When his hand moved between her thighs, she whimpered and ducked her head so she could kiss him again.

"You're so wet." His fingers swirled over her swollen flesh as he growled against her mouth. "I can't wait, Kay."

She clutched at his back, at his hip, dropping her knee to one side. Opening for him. Urging him on to end her sweet torment. "Please. Now," she moaned.

In a single thrust, he buried himself deep within her. Kay cried out as her body stretched to receive him. Lights burst behind her eyelids. He engulfed her. Surrounded her. Filled her. Hard, fast thrusts rocked her. She kept pace with him to start with, but soon his rhythm raced ahead of hers. The pressure of her climax built too quickly. Wrapping her legs around Bear's waist, she hung on. His body pounded into hers. Sweat made their skin slick.

"Ah!" Her body tensed with the initial wave of her orgasm. "Bear!" All of a sudden, it was as if he'd run her to the top of a mountain and tossed her off a cliff. The muscles within her clenched and squeezed. She pressed up hard against the continuing power of him. A soaking heat filled her as she struggled to catch her breath.

Bear drove faster until with a final plunge he ground out her name. His tensed body welded into hers. His hand gripped roughly at her hip, as he pumped into her as deep as he was able. "Kay, my God—"

His panting mouth found hers. Gasping, he kissed her mouth, her cheeks, her forehead, her closed eyes. He'd dropped down onto one elbow. His body a delicious weight on her. In her. His other hand continued its caress of her from waist to hip.

"You *have* done this before," Kay gasped.

"I didn't mean...I should have... You were just so sexy standing there. The way your hair... The shoes... Dammit, did I hurt you?" He cupped her face, brushing her cheek with his thumb. "I'm sorry."

"Stop. You didn't hurt me. You were—"

"Out of my mind." He gazed down at her. "I wanted our first time to be amazing, not some mindless f—"

Kay silenced him with a kiss. "It was amazing." She murmured against his lips, pushing her fingers into his hair. "You were...amazing."

He nipped at her lower lip. "I can do better."

****

Kay slipped from her bed and extinguished the last flickering of the candles. Bear was asleep. Somehow they ended up in a tangle of sheets, sideways in the bed. She covered him with the quilt that had fallen off the end and wrapped her robe around her.

Bear's *better* had been two hours of the most incredible sex she'd ever had. Was there a *Guinness Book of World Records* for the number of orgasms experienced in one night? She may just be a record holder and not know it. The way he touched her, stroked her. After the power of the first time, the gentleness of him made her weep. He found places on her body—pulse points—where a kiss, or a touch, the sweep of his tongue made her quiver and gasp with breathless rushes of pure pleasure.

She tiptoed downstairs on legs which still trembled. All she had to do was remember his mouth at her breast, a nip on her inner thigh, the tip of his tongue on the back of her knee...God, she should bronze that tongue of his. And the rest of him. The smell of his skin. The play of muscle over bone. He was beautiful. Potent. Addictive.

She stepped out onto the deck; the cool air of the night chilled her. She pulled the thin robe tighter, hugging herself. The moon's light filtered through the pine trees casting lacy patterns on the decking. The soft hush of the waves whispered up to her from the beach.

Perfect. Everything was perfect. How was that even possible? When had anything in her life been so painfully blissful? It didn't happen. Not to her. Never to her.

Something Walter was fond of saying kept running through her head. "Every dog has their day." Was this her day? Could she trust it? Could she trust Bear? God, she wanted to.

He'd done nothing wrong, and yet she couldn't help but pile all the sins from boyfriends past onto his shoulders. She hated herself for doing it, but there it was, and one night of amazing love-making couldn't rid her of those scars.

Dammit, she was doing what she swore to herself she would not do. Did she always have to dissect everything to death? What happened to keeping it easy?

She knew the answer…Bear happened.

And in one perfect day he had swept her off her feet. She wasn't the strong, sassy, *easy* woman she made herself out to be. The kind of woman who could fall into bed and not have it mean something.

It meant something. And it was the enormity of the something that had her standing there shivering in her robe instead of wrapped around the incredibly hot man in her bed. Not just any man. Bear.

She noticed the empty dishes by the stairs. She'd left food and water out for Hope. Maybe the cat was finally brave enough to come up and eat. Savor it instead of snatching a mouthful. Kay refilled the dishes.

Realization dawned. That was it. That was the piece of her heart she'd lost along the way. Hope. Maybe she'd destined herself to one heartbreak after another because she hadn't hoped for anything better? She expected most of the people in her life to fail her, and they did. But Bear…what was happening between them…it filled her with possibility. She'd lowered her guard and let him in. She trusted him. She was in love with him. He'd filled the hole in her heart and given her hope.

"There you are."

Kay startled and spun around. Bear stood leaning against the doorframe. He'd slipped into his jeans. He hadn't buttoned the top button, pushing his sexy quotient up a thousand points. Moonlight dappled his face and bare chest. He was just the most beautiful man.

He held up one of her shoes. "Here I was prepared to start searching the kingdom." His voice was husky from sleep. "You left the dance a little early, Cinderella." He moved toward her.

Butterflies kick boxed in her chest. "I've never understood that fairy tale." Her breath caught. "I mean, the man had been dancing with her all night, fallen madly in love, but couldn't remember what she looked like?"

A smile curved the corner of his mouth. "Maybe he was proving a point. You know, enduring all those smelly feet to find her." Bear ran the toe of her shoe slowly down the lapel of her robe. "So what are you doing out here in the middle of the night?"

"F-feeding the cat."

Bear looked past her, scanning the deck. "You have a cat?"

"Sort of." Kay's hand swept the bushes. "Her name is Hope. She was lost. We kind of found one another."

"Don't let Shadow know. He's the jealous type. You'll break his heart."

"Maybe he'd like her."

Bear shook his head. "Shadow and me—not big cat fans. Shadow thinks they're crunchy chew toys. And me? My father had a mean old son of a bitch cat when we were growing up. MacArthur. See this scar?" He pointed to a long white line along the side of his neck. She'd never even noticed it before. "I was five. It bled like a bitch."

Kay kissed him there. "You don't have to worry about Hope. She'll never get close enough to lay a claw on you or let Shadow chew on her." She traced the small scar again before running her finger along the crest of his shoulder. Over his tattoo. "What about this scar?"

He followed the path of her touch. "Four surgeries to fix a shoulder beyond fixing."

"I'm sorry." She kissed him there, slipping her hand around the swell of muscle defining his arm. Her other hand traced the intricate artwork. "It looks like lightning struck the tree. What did the words say?"

"O'nert Go Nert," Bear murmured into her hair. "It's Celtic. Means from strength to strength." A soft thud to the deck sounded a heartbeat before his other arm wrapped around her. He pulled her tight to him and kissed her. A quick tug untied the belt of her robe before his large warm hand slid beneath to caress the tightened tip of her breast.

"Y-you dropped your shoe, Prince Charming."

"Don't need it," he growled. "I already found you."

She ran her hand over the firm swelling in his jeans. "How will you know if it fits?"

"Oh, it fits…"

Chapter Sixteen

Bear left Kay's early the next morning. He needed to return Walter's truck and pick up Shadow. Before leaving her naked in a tangle of sheets, he made her promise she'd rearrange her work schedule—at least on the weekends.

He wanted her nights all for himself.

They'd hardly slept. He should have been exhausted, but everything that had happened in the last twenty-four hours defied logic. Days of keeping his distance and the whole day leading up to the new land-speed record for getting from Portland to Bell Harbor. One hour, twenty minutes. Including the stops for condoms and cops. It was worth the hundred and ninety dollar speeding ticket. Kay was right, her generous display of cleavage would have gotten them off with a warning had Walter's taillight not been broken as well. Least that's what Officer Dan said…not about the lovely cleavage, just about the light.

Bear was working on the fourth floor. The brass telescope they'd found yesterday looked fantastic as if it had always been here. He couldn't wait to show Kay.

This room was the best in the inn. The bridal suite, or penthouse of sorts. It was the only room on this floor. A beautifully carved, four-poster bed—still with no mattress. Tom the mattress guy was now officially on Bear's shit list. Floor to ceiling windows afforded a panoramic view of the harbor. Sunrises were amazing, and unless you were being stalked by a seagull, keeping the windows without curtains afforded plenty of privacy without compromising any of the view. A wraparound widow's walk allowed access to a narrow deck with new wrought iron railings. On a clear day, you could see for miles.

He picked up the new hardware for the bathtub while he was in Portland and was busy installing the faucet. At first, he questioned the positioning of the tub. It wasn't in the bathroom. The cramped little water closet adjoining the main room was more than adequate. Small, but it had all the necessities: toilet, sink, tiled shower. It was as if the tub had been an afterthought. But the sexy lines of the deep, cast iron slipper tub looked perfect within the main room. He pictured romantic baths by the light of the fireplace. Bubbles and bubbly—a complimentary bottle of champagne for some happy couple.

Correction, not some happy couple. Them. Him and Kay.

He could picture them. She'd make that pleasured sigh she makes as she stepped into the steaming bath and sank beneath the fragrant water. Her hair a messy knot on the top of her head. Stray pieces framing her face, curling in the steam. Drinking champagne with a thick froth of soapy bubbles caressing the curve of her breasts, decorating her shoulders, allowing her nipples to play hide and seek.

With a little inventive navigation, he bet there'd be room enough for two in the tub. If he put his leg there, and she straddled…

Bear groaned and shifted the position of his

erection. How was it possible after hours of sex, he *still* wanted more of her. His body still ached the delicious ache of a passion-filled night, and yet, if Kay were here right now—

"Coffee?"

"Hey." He jerked his hand off his pants like he was thirteen and Kay had caught him with his father's Playboy magazine. "What are you doing up here?"

"Looking for you, of course. Did I scare you? You look…startled. Skippy told me where you were. I brought coffee, and those amazing muffins from Mindy's. The tar water you have in the kitchen makes my hands shake, so I thought we could both use some caffeine and sustenance."

"You surprised me, is all. I could use some sustenance right about now. Thank you."

Kay handed him his coffee and did a slow sweep of the room. "Bear, I love this. It's stunning. Everything. The windows. The view is spectacular. Oh, our telescope. It looks like it has stood there forever."

"I thought the same thing."

She made a slow turn. "Such a great room. What are you thinking about for colors? Oh, the tub…" She ran her hand down the wide rolled edge. "I could live in this tub."

"I was just imagining you in it."

"Oh?" Kay smiled. "What were you imagining?

"Us, actually. You, me, bubbles." He moved closer, setting aside his coffee, taking hers from her as well.

Kay slipped her arms around his neck and pressed her body to his. "It might be a tight squeeze."

He like the way they were fitting right now. The

way she stood on tiptoes to match her curves along his. "We'd manage." He took her mouth hungrily and snuck his hand under the hem of her shirt to skim the smooth warm skin of her back.

"If only this room had a bed," she murmured against his lips.

"I'm hiring a hit man for my buddy Tom first thing Monday morning." Bear buried his nose into the sweet curve of her neck. "Been doing a lot of thinking about you. About last night. This morning…"

Kay tipped her head back, giving him access to the pale length of her neck. "And I thought your first kiss was epic."

Bear breathed in the scent of her. For the life of him, he couldn't describe it. It was like no perfume he'd ever smelled. She held his head, and let out that little whimper that drove him over the edge. "God, I can't get enough of you. On second thought, I'll kill Tom myself."

"There's always the tub," she teased, then gasped as he gave a not too gentle bite to her collarbone.

"Water's shut off," he grumbled.

Kay breathed into his ear. "We're running out of options."

He tucked the tip of one finger into her waistband. "We'll figure something out."

"What about Skippy and Brian?"

"Let them get their own girls." He flicked open the button on her jeans.

She laughed. "No, you crazy man, they could come up here any minute." She tried to pull away.

He pulled her back by the front of her pants. "I don't care."

She laughed again, lifted his hand, and kissed it. "I have work to do."

"You're going to leave me? Now? In this condition?"

"You'll survive." She picked up her coffee and held out a shaking hand. "Maybe it isn't the coffee downstairs that makes my hands tremble. I think maybe it's you." She ran a fingertip over his chest and leaned close. "It took close to an hour for my legs...and other more sensitive parts...to stop quivering after you left this morning."

Bear groaned. "Are you trying to kill me?"

"Trying to save poor Tom." She stroked his arm.

"Who's gonna save me?"

Kay cupped his cheek. "You are going to go back to work and think about baseball." She smiled before laying a tender kiss on his mouth. "And I am going to go put all this pent-up energy into your mural."

"Add one of your hidden treasures, for me."

"Like?"

He shrugged and gave her a wicked smile. "One of those proper Victorian ladies...put a man under her skirts." He brushed her breast with the backs of his fingers. "Or a caressing hand where it shouldn't be? Or a couple *coupling* back in the trees?"

She laughed and raised an eyebrow. "You want me to turn your mural R-rated?"

"Sure, why not?"

Kay considered it. "You're the boss."

Bear scribbled his signature on the paperwork. Fourteen mattresses and box springs. Tom's ass was saved. Bear helped the deliverymen spend the last hour moving each set into its assigned room. It was well past quitting time. The rest of the guys were gone. He was spent.

He found Kay still working. She wore her earphones, so the clamor of the busy inn wouldn't be such a distraction. Too bad he didn't have something to distract him from her. After this morning's little scene upstairs, he'd been *distracted* all day.

Kay stepped back, tipping her head as she appraised the area where she'd been working. Evidently satisfied, she dropped the brush into her wash cup. She extended her arms over her head, working the tension out of her shoulders. The hem of her shirt rose giving him a glimpse of the two gentle dimples gracing her lower back. Kay reached around, fisting those very dimples and arched into a stretch.

Maybe he wasn't as spent as he thought.

She caught sight of him and pulled the earphones from her ears. "Hey."

"Hey."

She cocked her head, listening. "It's quiet." She pulled her cell phone from her back pocket. "What time is it?"

"Time for you to kiss me," he suggested, crossing the room.

A wide smile curved her lips. "Is it that late already?"

Bear hauled her against him and backed them into the space behind the desk. "Come here." He pinned her against the wall.

Kay blinked up at him. "You are my employer. Technically, isn't this sexual harassment?"

"Are you feeling harassed?" He watched her lips as he lifted her leg to hook around his hips. His hand smoothed over the curve of her ass.

One side of her mouth tipped. "Not sexually."

"Come home with me," he pressed.

"I have to work."

"You promised I'd have your nights."

"I was physically compromised when I agreed to that. Would have promised anything. Tomorrow. I swear. Let me turn my schedule around today, and I'll be all yours tomorrow night."

He groaned. "Seven o'clock. No arguments, no work. I'm taking you to dinner. I'll make reservations at the Chart House. Wear that little black dress you had on last night. Dear God, please wear panties—or not—just don't tell me."

"Wouldn't it be worse if you weren't sure and had to leave the wondering to your imagination?"

"Here I thought you were such a sweet woman. You enjoy getting me crazy."

"Just another of my superpowers," she teased. "Fine. I swear, I'll wear something special under my skirt. I have the perfect pair. Black. Lace. It looks like a delicate butterfly."

"Kay…" he warned.

"But wait…do thongs really count as panties? I mean, they don't cover much. More a suggestion than an actual article of clothing."

"You're evil."

"No, I'm not. I only use my powers for good."

Chapter Seventeen

Kay folded the last of her drop cloths and grinned at the tiny addition she'd made to the mural just for Bear. It was high on the wall and so well hidden, he'd probably never find it. The thought of him searching made her smile.

Physically, she'd hit her own wall. Exhaustion claimed her. She had superpowers, but she was no Wonder Woman. Locking up the inn, she stopped to take a deep breath of sea air. The weather was becoming wonderfully warm into the evenings. Tourists had started their descent into the sleepy little harbor. The typical quiet of a Friday night was no more with several of the businesses in town keeping their doors open for late shoppers. Traffic was heavier with folks coming up early to start their weekends, but the mood was light and carefree.

She passed a small group of six, three couples by the look. They were laughing and talking excitedly about their plans. Kay was still smiling when she settled into her car and fit the key into the ignition. She was happy. Feet-not-quite-touching-the-ground giddy. And all because she'd taken a chance and allowed herself to trust Bear.

He was wonderful. Fun, kind, and caring. Not to mention gorgeous, sexy, and insatiable. It was a thrilling rush knowing how she affected him. Knowing he wanted her as much as she wanted him. They could barely keep their hands off one another. She'd never been so bold, but then she'd never been with anyone like him.

Before she could start the car, her cell vibrated. Dottie had left a message earlier asking Kay to stop by for pizza night again. She'd lost track of time and hadn't returned the call.

"I'm so sorry, I forgot to call you back. I hope you went ahead and ate without me."

"It's me, Kay."

Todd. Her first instinct was to throw the phone away from her as if it were covered in hairy spiders. She pulled it away from her ear and stared at the screen while contemplated hanging up. Her heart fumbled for a beat.

"*Kay?*" She heard him calling to her.

She lifted the phone to her ear. "What?"

"Where are you?"

"What difference does it make?" All the emotions she'd so carefully tucked out of sight flooded back. Hurt. Betrayal. Anger.

"I've been looking all over town for you."

Anger was leading the wave. "I can't imagine why."

"We need to talk."

"No, we don't," she snapped.

"Okay, I get it, you're pissed, and I totally deserve it. I'm an fucking asshole.."

"I'm hanging up now." She pulled the phone away from her ear to push the disconnect button.

His voice reached through the phone to stop her. "No! Don't. Wait. Please."

"No, you wait," she barked. "I left Stoddard weeks ago. Not that it makes one damn bit of difference, but why are you calling now?"

"I miss you."

Kay choked out a bitter laugh. "Bullshit."

"I *do*. I still love you, Kay-Kay," he pleaded in the sappy sweet voice she remembered so well.

"Don't call me that." The familiar nickname squeezed the air from her lungs. "And you don't get to say you love me. Not anymore."

"We were getting married."

The punch to her heart made her wince. "I remembered. It was you who forgot."

"We can work through this. Other couples do. I think maybe I was having cold feet. You know, about the wedding. We can go to counseling or something."

"I don't need counseling." Kay watched another tourist couple walk arm in arm up the sidewalk. They stopped in front of the inn. The woman pointed toward the top floor before they kissed. The quick flash of a diamond ring decorated her left hand. Perhaps they were planning to stay at the inn for their honeymoon. They started taking selfies in front of the sign. Kay had to look away.

"I think I might have a sexual addiction, Kay."

"How convenient for you." The pain in her chest twisted her gut.

"It's a real disease. Don't you care?"

"If you're sick, get help. If this is just a sad excuse to somehow justify your screwing around, I feel bad for you, because you'll never be happy and you'll have no one to blame but yourself. Go live your life, Todd. Do whatever you want. Whoever you want. It doesn't concern me anymore."

"I want you back, Kay. I'm sorry. So sorry. Say it's not too late."

Kay rubbed at the space between her eyebrows. "It *is* too late. It's over. I've moved on."

"What does that mean?" His voice took on a sharp edge. "Are you seeing someone else?"

"Yes," she answered with no hesitation. Bear's last kiss had her shifting in her seat. The way he'd held her tight against the plastered wall, pinning her hands above her head, ravaging her mouth as he pressed the hot, hard length of his body against her. "Yes, I'm seeing someone."

"Well, that was fucking quick. So much for true love. What's his name?" Todd's raised voice bellowed through the receiver.

"Don't you dare preach to me," Kay shot back. "You have no right. True love? What do you know of true love? You're the one who cheated. How *is* Gwen?"

"How long, Kay?" He conveniently dodged the question about his ex. "How long before you hooked up with this new guy?"

"You and I were done weeks ago."

"So you're already sleeping with him," he snipped.

"I'm not discussing this." The couple in front of the inn had moved on. Kay could still see them in her rearview mirror. They were holding hands as they walked away.

"Well, that's a yes."

"It's none of your business."

"Jeez, I almost feel bad for the bastard."

Kay frowned. The last thing she wanted to do was play one of Todd's games, but she knew if she didn't ask, it would eat at her for days. "Why would you feel bad for him?"

"'Cause he's your rebound guy. It'll never last. Rebounds never work. I give it two, three weeks, max."

"Shut your mouth." The twisting in her gut dropped. Had they been face to face, she would have slapped him. "You don't know what you're talking about."

"It's classic." Kay could hear the smirk in his voice. "Wait and see if I'm right."

"Goodbye, Todd."

"I'll just bide my time. You'll be back. Wherever you are, you have to come home to Stoddard eventually. No way you'll walk away from your degree when you're so close to graduating. You've only got one more year. By the time fall semester rolls around, whatever this thing you've got going is sure to be over. I can wait. Give me a call when you get to Stoddard."

"I won't be calling you."

"Yes, you will. You'll see."

Kay slammed the phone onto the seat. "Aaaahhhh!" She lowered her forehead onto the steering wheel. "No. I'm not listening to that lying bastard. I refuse to let him get to me." She spoke to her lap. "He's full of shit. Rebound guy? He knows nothing."

She lifted her head and started the car. Checking the mirrors, she pulled out onto Main Street, and she noticed the engaged couple had started to walk back the way they'd come.

In a rush of jealousy, she punched her foot on the accelerator. "Todd knows nothing."

Loading her palette the next morning, she was still

reliving the phone conversation and cursing Todd. She hated that he'd managed to work his poison into her brain. He was so wrong about her and Bear. What they had was the real thing. The entire notion of her becoming involved with him as some feeble attempt to recover from Todd's betrayal was beyond ludicrous.

Forget about it. Think about something else! How many times had she told herself that over the last twelve hours? But his words kept playing over and over in her mind like a song that gets stuck, slowly driving you crazy. "*I almost feel bad for the bastard, he's your rebound guy…*"

Kay added more white to the paint she was working with. It was still too dark, but she couldn't seem to bring up the tone and lighten the color. Each time she tried, it screamed at her from the wall. Frustrated, she wiped it all away with her rag. By now, her palette resembled a mud puddle. She scraped it all into the trash and hit the kitchen for a cup of coffee. Cutting half of the murky mess with milk, she ignored the box of day-old bagels and stale donuts and propped herself against the counter. She winced as she tasted the bitter brew, and added more milk.

It was where Bear and Shadow found her when they arrived. The dog beat his master to her, jumped up to put his front paws on her chest, and gave her a sloppy chin kiss.

"Hey, off," Bear scolded. "She's mine." He pulled the dog to one side and held him away from her while he kissed her hello. "I like this. Seeing you here in the morning. Knowing I'll be seeing you again tonight." He kissed her again. "I'm liking this a lot."

"Good morning." She forced a smile.

He grabbed a cup and poured himself some coffee. "I thought you hated my coffee?" He drank it black.

"I do, but I forgot to stop on my way over." She stared into her cup. "At least if I drink this I can blame my shaky hands for a lousy paint day," she mumbled.

"What do you mean lousy? Everything okay?"

"It's fine." She gave a quick shake of her head. "You ever have days when your work seems...off?"

"Sure." He came to stand in front of her and rubbed her arm. "It's not fair to be brilliant every day." He smiled.

"I'm not even close to brilliant today. What's the exact opposite? I hate this when it happens, but I've been doing this long enough to learn there are some days I need to step away from it before I end up ruining it."

"You won't ruin it." When she wouldn't look up at him, he nudged her chin. "Hey," he whispered. Kay couldn't stop the sudden rush of tears that had been threatening since she hung up the damn phone last night. "Whoa. Don't cry." Bear gave her a small kiss before he took away her coffee and lifted her to sit on the counter. He moved between her knees as he cupped her face. "Sweetheart..." He brushed the stubborn tear away from her cheek. "You're being way too hard on yourself. It's okay. You're just having an off morning."

Kay buried her face into the now familiar smell of Bear's neck and wrapped her arms around his chest. He crushed her closer and held her, stroking her back. Shushing her as if she were a child waking after a bad dream. Shadow whined at her feet and pawed at her sneaker.

"I'm sorry," she mumbled into his shoulder.

"Stop. You've nothing to be sorry about."

Kay pulled back and wiped at her eyes. She gave herself a small shake and tried to pull it together. "Way to be professional. I should add *occasionally cries on boss* to my resumé." She smiled as she brushed at his damp shoulder.

"I'm not your boss right now. I'm the man who cares about you."

"I'm fine." The worry in his eyes threatened to undo her. "Really." She kissed him. "I don't know what's come over me. The moon must be in retrograde or something ridiculous." She reached down and patted Shadow's silky head. "I've even upset your dog."

"He loves you." Something in the way Bear said it made Kay's breath catch. She met his serious gaze. "The dog loves you...and the man who cares. I love you, too."

Chapter Eighteen

And she loved him. The dog, and most definitely the man.

She'd said as much before he'd practically crushed her in his arms. Her eyes had filled with tears again, and for a moment, he'd lost his mind. When had he become one of those men who crumbled at the sight of a woman's tears?

He'd been preparing to tell her how he felt after dinner that night. Whether before, during, or after he'd properly seduced her, he hadn't decided. But when he came in and found her so upset. It tore at his heart. The words had just tumbled out. Not that he regretted saying them. He'd meant every word.

Kay loved him. He'd taken the blame for her rotten morning. It was his fault she'd tried to switch her schedule. No wonder things weren't working as well as before. He was being selfish, but he didn't care. He wanted her. He needed to be with her.

He offered to take her home, but she insisted she was fine. Better than fine. In fact, because the workday had taken such a beautiful turn, she was going shopping. She wanted something special to wear tonight. Panties included, although she wouldn't elaborate on what defined the term *skimpy*. He could only imagine. That was the problem. If he imagined any more, he'd never make it through the day.

Bear was due to pick her up at seven. He was early.

He heard her call down to him from upstairs. "Come on in. Door's open. I'm almost ready."

Bear let himself into the kitchen. "You shouldn't leave your door open. It's not safe. I could be a serial killer," he called.

From overhead he heard, "This is Bell Harbor, not LA."

"They still have serial killers in Maine, you know."

"I'm safe. They'd never work weekends."

"You're right." He chuckled. Bear walked out into the shade of the back deck to wait. He shifted the cellophane-wrapped flowers he'd brought to his other hand and noted the fresh bowl of cat kibble. Scanning the surrounding greenery, he realized he'd yet to lay eyes on Kay's cat. What was the feline's name again, Hope? "Are you sure you have a cat?" he teased, talking to himself. "I think you're making her up. Would that make you Hope-less?"

Bear turned laughing to find Kay standing in the doorway. The laughter died on his lips. She was drop-dead gorgeous. Her hair was loose and fell into soft curls at her shoulders. Gold earrings caught the light. The dress she wore crisscrossed her body to form a wide, low V-neckline and tied into a bow on one side. It hugged her curves like a Ferrari. A cherry-red Ferrari.

"Kay…" Bear made a sound like he'd been punched.

She smiled. Her lipstick matched her dress. "You clean up nice. I like the suit."

He smoothed a hand down his tie while his heart knocked around in his chest. He stepped toward her. "I love the dress."

"The color is a little bold for me, but the salesclerk told me it made my butt look good. So I had to buy it."

Bear held up a hand and spun his finger in a tight circle. Kay gave a sassy turn. The salesclerk was right. "I'm buying you two more," his voice rasped. "Make that an even dozen." He pulled the bouquet of twelve long-stemmed red roses from behind his back.

Kay stared at the flowers. "You bought me roses."

"They even match." He held them out.

"They do." She stood twisting her hands. Her hesitation struck him as odd, but it was short-lived. She gave him a small smile and took them from his hand. "Thank you. You really shouldn't have."

"I wanted tonight to be special."

Kay set the flowers aside without another glance, and smoothed her hands down the lapel of his jacket. She gave him the briefest of kisses and wiped her lipstick from his lips with her thumb. "I want that, too. Can we go?"

He'd made reservations for them at the Chart House. It was an upscale restaurant at the end of the harbor, with amazing seafood and an equally amazing view.

The maître d' welcomed them and led them through the room. Tourist season was in full swing, and the restaurant was crowded. A loud group, all sporting plastic lobster bibs, were looking at the boiled crustaceans on their plates like something out of an episode of The Weirdest Thing I Ever Ate.

Bear had arranged for a private table for two tucked into a corner away from the main dining room with a stunning view of the back bay. According to the woman who secured his reservation, the intimate table was quiet, secluded, and the sunsets were guaranteed breathtaking.

Bear held her chair. The maitre d' handed them thick, leather-bound dinner menus as well as their wine list and left them to enjoy their meal.

Kay appreciated the view. Bear appreciated Kay appreciating the view. She caught him staring and reached across the table to take his hand. "This is lovely. Thank you for bringing me. I haven't been here since I was a little girl. I think they called it the Compass Rose back then. I remember thinking how fancy it was." She opened her menu and leaned forward. "I was only six, however, any place where they used cloth napkins and your food didn't come with a toy was considered fancy." She blinked at him and frowned. "What? Why are you looking at me like that? Is my lipstick smeared?" She shielded her mouth with her fingertips.

He squeezed the hand he held. "No, woman, your lipstick is fine. I'm just trying to get over how beautiful you are tonight."

"There you go, saying the perfect thing again." Color brightened her cheeks.

"I counted at least three other guys as we walked through the restaurant who're considering fighting me in the parking lot for you right now."

"Idiots," she scoffed. "Have they seen your shoulders?"

He lifted her hand and kissed her fingers. The waiter arrived, and Bear ordered a bottle of wine. Kay looked over the menu while he told them about the specials for the evening.

"Lucky pie." Kay smiled as their server left. "The

dessert special is lucky pie. Maine blueberry. I doubt it's as good as Dottie's, but I adore blueberry pie."

"What makes it lucky?"

"Dottie." Kay grinned.

The wine arrived and as Bear went through the motions of tasting and approving, Kay continued with her explanation.

"Dottie's blueberry pie is magic. For my birthday, every year since I can remember, I've asked for her pie instead of cake. She told me she always bakes good luck into the crust, and Walter taught me to eat it backward."

"Why backward?"

"According to Walter, if you eat the point of the pie last, your wish will come true." Kay paused as Bear poured her wine. "I remember one year, all I wanted was a bubble-gum-pink bicycle with a glittered seat and purple sparkly tassels off the handlebars. I found it in a catalog. I cut out the picture and left it everywhere I could think, hoping my parents would get the hint. They didn't." She shrugged. "Walter and Dottie always had a special dinner for me to celebrate, and when she brought out my pie that year, she said she put in extra luck."

Kay sipped at her wine. "I made my wish, blew out the candle, and made sure to eat it from the crust side just like Walter said. Sure enough, as the last bit of pie reached my mouth, a bell began to ring on the back porch. Dottie and I rushed out. There was Walter ringing the little tin bell attached to my new pink bike."

"With sparkly purple tassels?"

"Of course." She shrugged again. "Lucky pie."

"That's a great story.

"Dottie made me lucky pie the night before I came to the inn for my interview," she said coyly.

"Then it was lucky for both of us."

As they waited for their meals to arrive, a woman strolled through the restaurant with a large basket of single-wrapped roses offering them to the men to give to their female companions.

"Rose for the lady?" she asked Bear.

"No, thank you," Kay was quick to say to her. To Bear she said, "You already got me some."

"There's no such thing as too many roses," he argued, peering into the basket.

"No." There was the look again. Flustered, she flashed a quick smile at the woman. "Thank you, anyway." When she left, Kay took a large swallow of wine and asked for a bit more.

Bear wanted to ask what was wrong, but Kay was quick to turn the subject back to something else, and the moment was lost and soon forgotten.

Dinner was delicious. Bear ordered a second bottle of wine. They had a wonderful time. Kay got delightfully tipsy. By the time it came to ordering dessert, they both were too full, but Bear made sure to order an extra large piece of their blueberry pie, to go.

His plan had been to invite her back to his place for a nightcap, but after ordering a second bottle of wine, he decided the evening's plans had capped enough. At least for Kay. He'd only had the one glass. The second he poured just for show, but she'd kept tipping a bit more into her glass. He took her home.

Back at the cottage, she hung onto his arm and suggested he take her straight to bed. Bear put the kettle on for coffee instead. He loosened his tie and unbuttoned the top button of his shirt.

Turning from the stove, he caught her as she stumbled. "You're drunk, Ms. Winston."

Kay giggled. "The perfect obber...opportunity to take advantage of me, Mr. Coulter." She slipped her arms around his neck and pressed against him.

He smiled down at her. "I don't take advantage of drunk women."

"I'm not drunk. Maybe I am a little. But it's not taking advantage if you've been *asked* to take advantage. Nicely, I might add." She ran her fingers through the back of his hair.

"Why don't you sit down, and I'll get you some coffee."

"You know what you are? You're too damn nice." She dropped into a seat at the kitchen table and picked up the bouquet of roses she'd tossed there before they left. She lifted them to her nose, and breathed in their scent. "Too damn nice. Had anyone else brought me these." She waved them at him. "I'd have dropped them straight in the trash. I might have stomped on them first."

Bear frowned. "What do you have against roses?"

"Shhhh." She put her finger over her lips, then motioned him closer. She pulled him down and whispered in his ear. "I h-hate them."

"You do?"

Kay pulled back, traced his ear with her fingertip, and nodded. "I really wanted to like your roses, Bear. They are so beautiful. And *you* gave them to me, but I can't like them. It's not your fault. They're ruined."

"You've lost me, sweetheart."

She held up her thumb. "See this scar?" She held it

way too close to his eye for him to see anything. She sat back examining it herself while she told him about her ex-fiancé, Todd, and the rose petals.

"I was fine," she insisted. "I'd gotten over the whole thing. I was happy, dammit. Really happy. But it's like an alarm goes off somewhere. Oops, Kay's happy. Can't have her happy. Quick, Todd, you better stop that shit. So, of course, he called. Thought if he said Kay-Kay, I'd forget what a bast—"

"Whoa, back up. Todd called? When?"

"Last night. After I left the inn."

Everything started to make sense. Of course she'd be still upset this morning. Giving her the flowers and bringing it up again at dinner, no wonder she kept refilling her glass. Bear pulled her into his lap and held her. "I'm sorry."

Kay rested on his shoulder. "Please don't be nice to me, Bear. You'll make me cry again."

He tucked her under his chin, and kissed her hair. "I have to be nice to you. I love you."

"Todd said he still loves me too, but he's not nice."

"Then he's lying to you."

The kettle began whistling. Bear moved Kay gently to the adjoining chair and shut off the flame. Making her a cup of coffee, he set it before her.

He swept the roses off the table, dropping them to the floor. Smashing them through the cellophane with the heel of his shoe. The bruised scent of them wafted up to him. He made sure to crush each tight head before gathering the mess of mashed petals and broken stems and throwing them into the trash. Kay looked at him with wide eyes shimmering with tears. Her lower jaw had gone slack in surprise.

Bear knelt next to her chair and cupped her cheek. He kissed her. "I promise, I'll never give you roses ever again."

Chapter Nineteen

Bear left Kay's a short time later after agreeing to return. Given he'd hoped they end up at his place, he needed to head back to the point and let Shadow out for a quick, but by now, necessary break.

"I don't want to ruin our wonderful night." She stroked his cheek. "You didn't even get your dessert. Come back after you take care of Shadow."

"I think you should go to bed."

"I do, too, but with you." She smiled. When he hesitated, she insisted. "I'll drink two more cups of coffee while you're gone." She held up a three-fingered Boy Scout gesture. "In fact, bring Shadow with you. I'll make him a bed in the living room. Turn down service with a Milk-Bone on his pillow. He'll love it." She left his arms long enough to pull a key off a hook. "Take my spare key. In case of serial killers, I'll lock the door and wait for you upstairs."

Bear stroked her arms. "What'll be on my pillow?"

"Just me."

Shadow raced past Bear as he entered the house on the point. Guess the boy needed to go. He pulled the tie from his neck and tossed it on the counter just as the phone rang.

Diane. Again. She'd called earlier and twice again while he and Kay had been at dinner. He'd switched his phone over to vibrate, and the blinking four on the answering machine told him she'd tried to reach him at this number, too.

He grabbed the handset and pushed the talk button. "What do you want, now?"

"Finally. Where the hell have you been? I've been calling for hours."

"Is someone dead?" he asked.

"Of course not."

His jaw tightened. "Fire? Earthquake? Aliens invade California? Are you under attack?"

"Don't be such an ass," she snapped.

"Just trying to figure out what's so damn important to make you call me eight times in four hours."

"If you'd picked up the phone when I called the first time, it wouldn't have been eight times. Where were you?"

He planted a hand on his hip and studied the tie on the counter. "I was on a date." A familiar unease washed over him. Why did it always feel weird telling Diane about his relationships? There hadn't been more than a couple since they divorced, and it wasn't as if she cared about who he saw or held onto any hope of reconciliation. Was it always like that with an ex?

"Kind of early to be home, isn't it?" Smugness oozed through the phone. "It can't even be midnight there. Not like the Bear Coulter dates I was used to."

"Date's not over, sweetheart." He grabbed Shadow's leash off the hook by the door. He didn't want him getting away from him on his way back to Kay's.

"Is this the same artist you've been going on about? What's her name again? Things must be getting serious with you two, but if she's there with you, why'd you answer the phone?"

"'Cause you keep calling." Bear tugged on a fistful of his hair. If he still lived with the woman, he'd be bald. "Now I know no one has died, I'm hanging up."

"I have to talk to you."

He sighed and opened his back door. He didn't see Shadow at first. "If I say I'll call you tomorrow, will you stop bugging me?" Bear held the phone away from his mouth to give a quick shrill whistle. "Come!" he shouted.

"Oh, honey, is that your technique now? No wonder your date sucks. You used to be so suave."

"Goodbye, Diane."

"You'll call me tomorrow?"

"Yes." He pressed the disconnect button. "Maybe."

Shadow raced into the house as he'd raced out, slobbered through a fresh bowl of water and gave himself a good shake before sitting. Bear clipped his lead to his collar. "Now, when we get back to Kay's, there'll be no three in the bed, understand?" The mutt wagged his whole body at the mention of her name. The dog tipped his head as if listening. "You stay downstairs like a good dog, right?" Shadow stood and gave a single bark in agreement.

Kay had left the light in the kitchen on, but true to her word, she'd locked the door. Shadow tugged at the leash after Bear had let them in. "We're guests, remember. No chewing, scratching, or peeing on anything unauthorized."

A thick blanket had been laid on the floor by the fireplace for the dog. Shadow found the treats she'd left and inhaled them. "Now, lie down, and stay."

Shadow was a trained lie-downer, but he needed

work on his stay. Bear had only climbed two steps when he was bumped in the back of his knee by a disobedient nose. He returned the dog to his blanket and tried again. With more authority. "Shadow, down." The dog shifted his eyebrows as if considering. "Listen, I've got a beautiful woman waiting for me upstairs. Have a heart. Lie down." Bear pointed to the floor. Shadow lowered himself and dropped his head to his front legs with a huff. "Good man."

Closing the bedroom door behind him, he let out a breath he hadn't realized he'd been holding. Kay was sitting in bed, a sheet tucked provocatively about her breasts. Her shoulders were bare. Was she wearing anything under that sheet? She set aside the book she'd been reading.

"I thought you might have fallen asleep."

"After three cups of coffee?"

The dress she'd worn to dinner was lying over the back of a chair. "I don't suppose you'd like to put that back on so I can know what it's like to take it off?"

"It's simple. No zipper. Just untie the bow and unwrap."

"Like a present?"

"Just like a present." She rose off the bed, dragging the sheet with her. "I saved you a couple of bows you could untie." She held the sheet to her with one hand and slipped the other around his neck. She stood on her toes to kiss him. "I'm so sorry about earlier."

"Don't apologize."

"I don't generally drink so much. I'm an idiot for letting Todd's phone call get to me."

"He's the idiot." He ran his hands down the bare skin of her back. "Could we not talk about him any more tonight?"

"Deal." She unbuttoned his shirt. Using both hands caused the sheet she held to fall to their feet. The bows Kay referred to earlier were strategically placed, low on each hip. They were thin purple lacings that held the tiniest scrap of multi-colored silk in red, purple, and gold. His brain lost a good amount of blood flow.

"Sweet God." He crushed his mouth to hers. When he reached to grab at her hips and pull her to him, his hands found nothing but skin. Running his palms over the naked rounds of her ass, he groaned into her mouth. Bear eased himself toward the bed, taking her with him. He lay back. Kay stood before him and finished undressing him before she straddled his hips.

Not a thing separated him from her heat save a bit of silk and a fragile length of string. His impatient fingers traced the length of string from where it disappeared to follow the crease of her ass, to where he found the first bow. The tiny tail knotted when he tugged on it. His cock pulsed in frustration as his fingers worked at the tangled silk. Bear snarled. His patience spent. With one swift yank, he ripped the panties from her.

Kay gasped into his mouth. He braced himself for her to be upset, but shredding the delicate thong only seemed to heighten her passion. The fervor of her kisses deepened. He drove his hands into her hair, holding the back of her head as her hand raked down his chest. She reached between them, grasped him, and encircled him with her fingers before caressing him from root to tip in slow torturous sweeps. Bear moaned and rocked his hips against her strokes. The ache for his release raged.

Her body trembled beneath his hands as she

continued to fondle him. She kissed his panting mouth. "Did you make a wish?"

His brain was in a sexual fog. "I...don't understand."

Kay reached over to the nightstand and lifted the Styrofoam container from the restaurant. Dipping her finger into the sweet filling of the blueberry pie, she spread it over his lower lip before licking it away. "You need a wish before you have lucky pie."

She fed him a piece of flaky crust with her fingers before breaking off her own bite. "I'm already feeling pretty lucky," he breathed. She painted a sugary swath across the pink of her nipple. A fiery surge rushed to his sex. *Good God.* Purple stained her skin. Kay lifted another bite of pie and held his gaze.

She curved the corner of her mouth and blinked. "Oops." A good-sized portion tumbled from her fingertips to drop warm and sticky into the middle of his chest. "Oh, I'm so clumsy. Let me clean that off." Before she lowered her mouth to him, she *clumsily* fumbled more fruit and crust down over the ridges of his abdomen and across the head of his penis. Her fingers painted the inside of one his thighs.

Bear arched his back and ground out her name as she proceeded to lick blueberries from his chest and stomach. She moved lower. He closed his eyes to the sensation of her mouth and tongue driving him wild. "Kay!"

Clutching her arms, he lifted her and rolled them both over. He peered down into her face. His breath coming so hard it fluttered the hair on her cheek. "No fair," he huffed. "Hand over the pie."

Chapter Twenty

Kay stuffed the ruined sheets into the trash with a smile. They were past saving. Last night had been one of the wildest nights of her life. How she would ever eat another piece of Dottie's lucky pie without blushing to the roots of her hair was beyond her, but it was worth every intensely sultry, sticky memory. By the time they both hit the cramped little shower upstairs, the sheets were a total loss to their passionate pastry frenzy.

The shower had been wonderful as well, cleaning away the blueberry smears on their bodies under the warm rush of water. Bear had washed her hair and soaped her already sensitive skin. His slick fingers insistent on bringing her to yet another orgasm.

After, they'd stripped the bed and wrapped themselves in a clean quilt. They slept in each other's arms until all hell broke loose downstairs.

Shadow met Hope. Or, at least according to their best guess, he tried to make her acquaintance through the glass door of the slider when she'd come up onto the deck to eat.

At the first explosion of rabid barking, Bear was out of bed, pants-ed, and down the stairs before Kay could comprehend what was happening. By the time she'd joined the party, Hope had vanished back into the safety of the underbrush. Her food scattered across the deck. Bear had Shadow firmly by the collar as he continued to bark as if they were under attack.

"I'm sorry," Bear yelled over the din. "He probably scared the crap out of your cat."

"Poor Hope. Poor Shadow." She patted the dog. "It's okay. She scared the crap out of you too, didn't she?" Shadow settled down, and Bear was able to release the death grip he had on his collar.

Bear groaned and pulled her into his arms. He kissed her forehead. "I'd love to go back to bed and work on a friendlier, gentler wake up, but he needs his breakfast and a run. I should go." He didn't move, but held her gaze before lowering his mouth to hers again. "Really, I need to go." His arms wrapped tighter as she opened her mouth to the sweep of his tongue. "Really."

Kay lifted onto her toes, hanging onto the solid span of his shoulders. "Right...bye..." She tipped her head to the left angling the kiss, opening her mouth to the invasion of his tongue. The heat coming off his body sent a delightful shimmer through her.

When his hands lowered to cup her ass, her body purred. Giving a small arch to her back, she pressed her chest against the wall of his, before she rolled her hips forward again. His hands gripped her stronger, hauling her against the hard length of his erection.

Shadow bumped into them with a whine and a sharp bark. Bear huffed against her mouth, "We hate this dog."

"We love this dog," she countered.

Bear glared down at Shadow. "You're lucky she's here to save you."

Kay peeled herself away from Bear's body and closed the robe he had skillfully untied without her knowing it. Robe ties and bra clasps were no match for

Bear. It was as if they dissolved at the touch of his fingers. "We can meet up later at the inn?" She ran her fingers through the crisp hair on his chest. "I have to drop some more cards and sketches at Polka Dots, but I should be there by noon."

Bear cocked a mischievous eyebrow. "Let me know if Dottie is making pie."

Packing up the last of her things, Kay heard Bear come back a short time later. He used his key. She called to him from the living room. "Did you think I snuck back to bed, or were you hoping to drag me there yourself?" She laughed. "You will never guess where I just found a blueberry."

She came around the corner into the kitchen and froze. "Mother?" She slapped a hand to her heart. "What are you doing here?"

"I could ask you the same question. You obviously were expecting someone else." Claire Winston stood stock straight in her signature linen sheath dress with a classic strand of real *rub-them-on-your-teeth* pearls. "I thought we had an understanding. You'd let us know when you planned to use the cottage. Seeing as I haven't had a word from you in more than six months, I had no idea you'd be here."

"I-I'm here on a job," she half-lied. It was easier that way. "I'm painting a mural at the Bell Harbor Inn."

"And I'm here meeting with my Realtor."

Kay's world tilted. *Realtor?* "You can't mean…"

She looked around the kitchen and gave a slow disapproving shake of her head. "I'm thinking of selling the cottage."

"You can't," Kay gasped.

"I think I can." She frowned. "Does Dottie know

you're here?"

Kay wouldn't throw Dottie under the bus. She turned her back on her mother and moved into the living room. She was too good at spotting a lie. "I'm not sure."

Her mother was still too shrewd. She followed Kay. "Of course she knows. You tell her everything. She probably found you the job at the inn." She ran a pale hand over her forehead. "I'm so tired of her running interference for you. Protecting you."

"Someone had to," Kay murmured.

Her mother's eyes flashed. "What is that supposed to mean?"

Kay was still reeling. Even though she had spent the last six years putting as much distance between her and her mother, here they were again. Stuck in the same endless groove. As far apart as they could be, yet still attached. The ultimate game of tug of war with no hope of there ever being a winner. Kay sighed, "It means, Mother, if I hadn't had Dottie and Walter all these years, who knows where I'd be."

"Don't be so melodramatic. Your stepfather and I have done everything we could to give you a good life." Kay opened her mouth to argue, but her mother beat her to it. "It wasn't what *you* wanted. I understand. We're horrible." Her patronizing tone stung.

"I'm not getting into this with you." She gathered her things to leave.

Two strides into the kitchen, Bear balanced a take-out cup holder with two giant coffees and a waxed bag in one hand. In his other, a stack of folded fabric tied with a large blue bow.

"Surprise, I'm back with all essential provisions,

coffee, donuts, new sheets. Two sets, in case we want to get crazy again." He frowned when he saw her face. "I...left Shadow with Skippy. What's wrong? Somebody die?"

"I'm what's wrong." Mother stood in the doorway of the kitchen looking as if someone had just crashed into her BMW. "I'm Kay's mother. Who the hell are you?"

Bear coughed, looked back at Kay, and set the things in his hands onto the table. He wiped his palms on the front of his jeans as he straightened and stepped forward with this hand extended. "Mrs. Winston, forgive me. Kay didn't tell me you might be visiting."

"Kay didn't know," she shot back. "That still doesn't answer my question."

"Barrett Coulter. Most people call me Bear, ma'am."

Kay closed her eyes and winced. If there was one thing her mother hated above all, it was being called "ma'am." She opened her eyes and beheld her mother's face. She knew this face. It was not a good face.

The vein running down the center of her mother's forehead could have cut glass. "Other than bringing my daughter sheets to *get crazy* on, why are you here?"

"I live here," he blurted.

Kay rushed to add. "On the point, Mother. Bear lives in the house on the point."

"I see." Frost formed on the inside of the windows.

"I also own the Bell Harbor Inn downtown."

Kay was hit with bone and brain matter as her mother's head exploded. She spun on her. "He's your *employer*?"

"Yes. And my neighbor. And, not that it's any of

your business, the man I'm dating."

"You mean, sleeping with," her mother snipped.

Kay folded her arms and nodded. "Yep, that too."

"I think I've heard quite enough." Her mother held up one manicured hand and marched past them and out the kitchen door.

"Mrs. Winston—" Bear called.

"Don't bother." Kay caught his arm as he turned to follow her out.

He looked back at Kay. A deer in the headlights look frozen on his handsome face. "What the hell was that?"

She hugged him. "Claire Eustace Fenton Winston. Of the Stockbridge, Massachusetts, Winstons." Kay rubbed his arms. "I'm so sorry you had to experience her, but trust me, the searing headache will subside soon. The eye twitch takes about a week to stop. Good news is you *will* see color again."

"Shit." Bear looked back at the kitchen door. "The woman is scary."

"Yep, that's Mom."

"Were you adopted? Did you see her face when I called her ma'am?"

"I know, sweetheart. You need to just walk it off." She gave him a quick kiss.

"Does she pop in often?" Poor man looked slightly panicked.

"We haven't spoken since December. I haven't seen her in two years. I can't even remember the last time she was up here. I've been the only one to use this cottage for years, but she's putting an end to that. She's probably listing it as we speak."

"She's selling?"

Kay nodded. "Looks like it." She dropped into a chair. "I had some foolish notion they'd hold on to it for a few more years, then I could buy the place."

He sat next to her and frowned. "What if you talk to her, tell her how much you love it here?"

Kay threw her head back and laughed. "I do love you. You think like a normal person."

"I'll talk to her."

"You're very sweet, but no. One close encounter with Claire Eustace is enough for you. I've had twenty-four years of conditioning." She placed a fingertip under her eye. "See, no twitch."

"I'm sorry."

"Don't be." She smiled at the handsome man who was ready to tilt at windmills for her. How was it possible, in the midst of the storm which was her mother, she was more in love with him now than when he'd left her just a few hours ago? "I never did thank you for the coffee, donuts, and sheets. No man has ever given me sheets before."

He pulled her onto his lap. "Ever get lucky with any other man?"

"Not lucky pie, lucky."

"I can't tell you how happy that makes me."

"You deserve to be happy."

"So do you."

She stroked his cheek. He hadn't taken the time to shave. His scruff tickled her palm. "I am."

Whether or not Bear's goal had been to come back and ply her with coffee and donuts before seducing her again, Kay would never know. Her mother took care of any such plan. Work beckoned for them both so they, once more, agreed to meet up at the inn.

After another gentle kiss at the door, Kay sent Bear off. She turned and looked around the blue and white gingham kitchen she adored. She'd made the curtains herself. Turning, she played with the bow on top of the sheets Bear had given her. It was going to be a summer of first and lasts. And the last thing she was prepared to do was let her mother ruin the best thing that had ever come into her life.

But first, she and Dottie had to work a few things out.

Chapter Twenty-One

Bear stood in the lobby of the inn. Kay was eighty percent done with the amazing mural gracing the walls. She had begun work on the final scene behind the desk. The painting was so much more than he had imagined when they'd started. *She* was so much more than he could have dreamed.

Kay was this mural. Beautiful, captivating, but with a wicked sense of humor and a sharp wit. She drew you in, so you wanted to spend hours learning every inch of her. Discovering all the small facets. Finding those things hidden from eyes too blind to see.

He ran a fingertip over the tiny lovers she'd painted high on the mural. His request. She'd placed it at his eye level. So tiny and seamless in the mural, and yet so detailed. Did she have a paintbrush with one bristle? It was them. On their beach, making love amongst the rocks. If you stood more than a few feet away from the wall, you'd never notice it, but now he'd found it, he saw little else. It was the same now he'd found Kay.

She could be tough, skittish, cautious, but Bear understood what created those things in her. Shit, he'd met her mother and learned what an ass her ex had been. Looking past all those things, Kay's true beauty lay tucked away just below the surface. It wasn't the Kay she allowed many to see. The caring, sensitive, incredibly sensual side. And somehow, he'd become the man she let in. Given him the golden ticket few would ever have. At the same time, she'd awoken the sleeping Bear.

Coming east had been a sort of a hibernation for him. He was tired. Dead tired. Tired of the high pressure hounding his every waking moment in LA. Coulter Designs had been a dream—but it was quick to become a nightmare. Diane was incredible at bringing in new clients, until his vision of a uniquely personal, small design firm was no longer recognizable.

He'd started a company where they spent time walking their customers through the process of designing their retirement cabin on the lake. Adding on the addition to welcome a new baby. High priced jobs, but not high stress. Before he knew it, they were taking on clients wanting business complexes and high rises. Industrial designs worth hundreds of millions of dollars.

The money had been great, but the cost had been even greater. What started as a partnership with Diane had quickly become a bitter battleground. It consumed their lives and devoured their marriage. But where Bear had wanted to crawl into a hole and pull the world over his head, Diane had flourished. She ate stress like multivitamins. It drove her.

It drove him too. Drove him to buy an inn in Maine in the middle of February. He gave a bitter laugh. Talk about hibernation. The first week he was here, every time he tried to venture outside, his balls froze off. The point house became his cave.

Surviving the first winter here gave him back his sanity. The inn, his soul. As he finished each room, a small part of him was restored as well. And then came Kay. She had restored his heart in ways she didn't even know, and it was time to tell her.

He'd wanted to last night. That had been the plan. He'd take her to dinner and back to his place and tell her the truth, come clean. Well, we know how that worked. Instead of coming clean, he'd spent the night getting down and dirty with Kay and pie! Talk about erotic finger painting. Shit, he'd never look at pie the same way ever again.

Last night had been like the tiny lovers in the mural. It was Kay's gift. She sprinkled starlight along her path. Little points of brilliant light which changed how he'd forever see the world. It wasn't pie that made him lucky.

Let's hope his luck held. He'd invite her over to his place for dinner. If not tonight, then soon. Take her mind off her mother and the situation with the cottage. Then he'd explain the whole thing. She had to believe in fate, right?

Bear took a cup of coffee out onto the screen porch. Shadow flopped onto a shaded spot and curled up for yet another nap.

The day was warm. Not hot by LA standards, but for Maine, summer had arrived. It was creeping toward midday. The lobster boats were long gone, but the harbor was still busy with all sorts of pleasure craft. Outboards and jet skis. An elegant sailboat glided past the inn.

Punching the numbers into the phone, he called Diane.

"Shocker. You actually called back," she answered on one ring.

"Hello to you, too." He propped his feet onto the railing bisecting the screening. Crossing his ankles, he sipped at his coffee.

"*Hello.* Do we really have to go through all this? Okay, how are you? I'm fine. How are things? Good? Great. Me? Things suck." Bear heard the click of her cigarette lighter. She paused in her little rant to inhale. "There. Happy?"

"Wow, Diane, you're a little ray of sunshine this morning, aren't you?" Diane was famous for her displays of mood. She was a giver. The kicker was she didn't want you to help get her out of her foul mood. She wanted everyone to join in. Pissy parties she called them, and she made no excuse for them. It had taken Bear a long time to learn that lesson. Some people just aren't happy unless their world is in crisis mode. They feed on it like zombies at a fresh brain buffet. Diane was their queen.

"I don't have time to shine for you, Bear. I'm up to my eyeballs in shit."

"As much as I'd love to help you shovel yourself out, there's a reason I moved to the other side of the country. Remember?"

"You still don't get it, do you? Why do you think I've been calling you day and night? You're as deep in this mess as I am." She exhaled. "We're in trouble."

Bear tipped back in his chair. He wouldn't let her panic spill infect him. Distance was his immunity. "Are you still freaking out over the Regency project?"

"I heard from the lawyers yesterday. They've scheduled a deposition."

"So, what's the big deal? Tell them Coulter Designs wasn't responsible for those shoddy materials. The contract agreement with the subcontractor was solid. If they decided to cut corners, it's on them. The project passed inspection, right? As far as CD is concerned, all the I's were dotted and the T's crossed. Like always."

"They don't want to depose me. It's *you* they want."

Bear snorted. "And you told them I didn't work on the project."

"Your signature is on the final work order."

"Impossible." There was a long silence on the other end of the phone. An all too familiar churning began in his gut. "Diane?"

"I messed up," she confessed.

Cold fingers ran down his spine. He pulled his feet down off the rail and sat up straight. "What do you mean, you messed up?"

"It was right after you left," she said in a rush. "The head of the Regency project didn't want to work with me. Thought I was—what did he call me— difficult. Bastard. No, he refused to deal with me, he only wanted to work with you. But you'd left. Abandoned me and the business."

"I hardly abandoned you."

"The point is, you weren't there when I needed you. I was desperate to close the deal. The money was too good. And with the divorce and everything else, I...I suppose I wanted to show everyone I was just as capable as you. One Coulter was just as good as two."

"What did you do?" The muscle in his jaw threatened to crush his back teeth.

Again, the silent pause froze the phone lines. "I might have signed your name to the final paperwork."

Bear leaped to his feet. He practically shot through the ceiling. "What?"

"Remember how you used to joke I signed your name better than you did?"

"You didn't?" he railed.

"I did," she moaned. At his string of colorful curses, she insisted, "I can fix it...but I need your help."

"I don't believe this! Are you insane? The Regency project was *your* baby. It's all I've heard about for months. You practically rubbed my nose in it every chance you got. How it was the biggest deal the agency ever had. How they'd been following your career and begged to work with you. And now? Shit, Diane, you are some piece of work. I can't believe you pulled something like this. How are you planning to fix this? What are the lawyers saying? Never mind, I'll ask them myself. I'll give Adam Dunbar a call as soon as I figure out a way to reach through this phone and wring your neck."

"We're not represented by Dunbar & Pratt anymore."

Bear took the phone from his ear and looked at it as if it were defective. Unbelievable. The hits just kept coming. He put the phone back to his ear. "Why the hell not?"

"Adam Dunbar is an ass."

Bear gave an exasperated huff toward the ceiling. "He's only an ass because he never noticed yours. The man's gay. Get over it."

"No," she snapped. "It's not only that. It's called housecleaning. After you left—"

It took all his control not to punch a fist through one of the screens, but he'd only have to fix it later. He forced a breath through clenched teeth. "Who represents Coulter Designs now?"

"Alfred, Becker, and Stevens."

He bit out a curse. Alfred, Becker, & Stevens was the firm that handled Diane's side of the divorce. They were just this side of slimy. He didn't trust any of them after watching the way they fawned over his wife. "Which one are you sleeping with?"

"Hey!"

He rubbed at the two-by-four that had become his neck. "You don't get to be the one who's pissed off, Diane."

After a silent pause, "I need you to come out here," she pleaded in a small voice.

"No way." He gave a bitter laugh.

"Regency can't know you've relocated to the east coast."

"How is it they still believe they're dealing with me directly? That's not possible."

"Most of our communication with them is through email, text, so—"

"Unbelievable!" His shout caused Shadow to jolt up and bark.

Diane rushed to add, "You just need to make an appearance. I know you can smooth this over. You're good at it. That's why everyone wants to work with you and not me. You're the easy-going, *everyone's-your-friend* guy."

"Lucky for you, I am, or I'd be hanging you out to dry faster than you can max out a credit card. I'm done talking to you. I need to find out the depth of this hole you've thrown me into. I'm calling Adam Dunbar."

Unfortunately, during the ten-minute, hundred-dollar phone call, Adam didn't have much to say. Not being associated with Coulter Designs any longer, he had none of the necessary information, and all Bear could tell him was what little he'd dragged out of Diane. He chose to keep the fact Diane had forged his signature out of things for the time being. He wasn't going to take the fall for this, but he didn't want to destroy her. Even as furious as he was, he'd worked too hard to build Coulter Designs. If there were a way to save it, he'd do it.

Adam's suggestion was to drop the blame solely at the feet of the subcontractor. "Don't worry yet. Let me look into it and see what I can find out. If there are any other complaints against this sub, we could cite their history of incompetence. I haven't heard of anything outright against them, but you never know what's been hushed up. I'll do some digging and get back to you. Give me a couple of days. In the meantime, I'll see what I can do about the deposition. If we suggest a video feed, they'll know you're no longer in the city. Maybe we can convince them you're visiting a sick aunt or off celebrating Grampa Fred's one hundredth birthday or something." Bear thanked him and hung up.

Standing back in the lobby of the inn, he drew on the calming sense he got from Kay's mural. If this thing with Regency escalated, they'd end up suing him for everything he had. Coulter Designs, the point house, the inn.

There was no way he was losing this inn. Not now. Dunbar was good. He'd eased some of the panic, and Bear trusted him. If it meant he'd have to go back to California to put the matter to rest, he would, but not until he secured things with Kay.

He supposed he should tell her what was going on, but where did he begin the conversation? It's not like he'd done much more than mention Diane before this. Better to let it play out without making more of it than need be. Right now, Kay was his priority. Their love for one another was so new. Like a foal, it was still finding its footing. He'd be a fool to mess it up.

Bear traced a fingertip over the tiny lovers hidden in the painting. In his own mind, he painted the perfect scene. Candlelight dinner, soft music. A gentle sea breeze drifting through the open windows. Waves licking at the rocks. He'd sweep Kay into his arms and carry her into the bedroom. Between kisses, whispering how he'd come to love her. Be forthright with everything going on with Diane. Explain serendipity.

It needed to happen. Soon.

Chapter Twenty-Two

Kay pushed through the door at Polka Dots. Dottie was helping a small group of women. The shop was busy with tourists buying some little thing to fit into their suitcase to remember their time spent in Bell Harbor.

"Oh, here's the artist now," Dottie beamed. The women turned and flooded her with compliments regarding her greeting cards. Behind them, she met Dottie's gaze. Kay's frown soon dissolved the grin on her face.

Kay pasted on a smile of her own and thanked the women, answering their questions. She shot Dottie an impatient look.

"I see you've brought some more items." Dottie pressed nervous lips together. She gave Kay a worried frown. "Ladies, if you'll excuse us. Keep looking around, we have a ton of great things. I'll be back in a jiff."

Kay led her into the office. Dottie followed and shut the door behind them. Kay spun on her. "Why didn't you tell me she was coming?"

Dottie's forehead puckered. "Claire?"

"Of course, Claire. You knew, and you didn't tell me."

"I didn't know for sure until last night," Dottie held up her hands in surrender. "She mentioned something about coming up, but you know your mother. She doesn't do well with schedules."

"You could have at least given me the heads up."

Dottie sighed and gave her a sad look. "And what would you have done?"

The edge to Kay's anger softened. "I don't know. Been more prepared. Dug a moat. Hired sharks."

Dottie shook her head. "You have to stop this. The two of you. I'm tired of being in the middle."

Kay held Dottie's gaze. This was a familiar argument. It was the same one they'd had for years. "Then take my side," Kay begged.

"I love you both," Dottie insisted.

Kay countered in a small voice. "Love me more."

"Kay…"

"No. She doesn't deserve you. I deserve you." Anger pushed past the hurt. "And she doesn't get to show up here after how many years and…and…screw things up again. I can't take this any more. I'm done. If I've learned anything in these last few years of being on my own, it's that I don't need her in my life anymore. Besides you, the only good thing between us was the cottage, and now she's selling it. Did she tell you?"

A long, pregnant pause followed before Dottie answered. "She might have mentioned it."

The words hit Kay like a slap. "So you lied to me?"

Dottie was quick to defend herself. "I didn't lie. I just didn't tell you."

"Not telling *is* lying. Aren't you the one who is famous for saying that? Were you ever going to tell me?"

Dottie reached out and took Kay's hand. "Sweetheart, I understand you're upset, but there is so much more to this. So much you don't understand. If you don't swallow your pride, sit down, and talk with her—"

"I've already swallowed enough, thank you."

"Kay…"

She pulled out of Dottie's grasp and rubbed chilled fingertips over the ache between her eyebrows. "Don't, Dottie. You can't wrap this all up in a pretty bow. You, better than anyone, know what's she's like. I won't do it anymore. I don't care what her reasons are. I've spent a lifetime trying to understand, and I'm done."

"Dot? You back here? You've got folks lined up at the register." Claire pushed into the office with a sack of groceries in her arms. "Oh, there you are. I stopped to pick up a few things for dinner and found two bottles of the horrible wine you dr—" When she saw Kay, she came up short. "Kay." She sighed, shaking her head. "Twice in one morning. I'm not sure I'm up for another go-round with you."

Dottie fussed and took the bag out of Claire's arms. Putting it on the desk, she shot Kay a worried glance. "I have to get back out front." Her gaze darted between the two of them. "Maybe you two should make up a pot of tea and have a nice long, *calm* talk."

Kay met her mother's eye. "You're staying here?"

Her mother crossed her arms over her chest. "Dottie insisted."

"Well…" Kay's brain slammed shut. Grabbing her bag, she dropped her chin and pushed between the two women. Dottie reached out to catch her sleeve. Kay shrugged her off, never breaking stride. "Don't."

Laughter from the customers in the shop deflected her into the storeroom as if she'd been a pinball. She pushed out the back door and nearly knocked Walter over on his way in.

"Special Kay."

"I-I'm sorry, Walter. I'm in kinda a hurry." Angry tear stung the backs of her eyes.

"Hold on." He grabbed the same arm Dottie had seconds before. He dipped his head to look into her face when she refused to look at him. "Are you okay?"

Kay blinked at him. "Whose side, Walter? Whose side are you on?"

He cupped her cheek. "Not sure I know what you're talkin' 'bout."

She sniffed and pointed. "My mother."

"Oh, that." Walter stood tall and rubbed at her arm. He gave her a sheepish shrug. "Ya know I gotta be on Dottie's side, honey."

Her heart weighed heavy in her chest. Part of her went numb. "Right. I get it."

Walter cupped her shoulder and gave it a squeeze. "She's only trying to get you two to make some sort of peace treaty."

Kay shook her head and patted Walter's chest as she moved by him. "She's about twenty years too late. Goodbye, Walter."

She didn't turn around. Making her way along the tourist packed sidewalks, Kay headed for the docks. She was due at the inn for work, but needed to pull herself together. All she wanted was to run to Bear and dissolve into his arms and let him kiss all the hurt away. But she didn't want to be that girl. Hell, she'd never been that girl. She'd learned to stand on her own two feet long ago. As far as Bear was concerned, she'd already brought enough drama.

It would never work with her mother. Losing the cottage was hard enough, but the thought of losing Dottie and Walter in all this mess truly made her chest hurt. She guessed she couldn't blame them. Dottie and Claire's friendship went back decades. And Walter, well, he might be gruff around the edges, but he loved Dottie more than anything. He was as loyal as a Saint Bernard.

Kay strolled past the weekend fishermen lining the dock. The sun was warm as she stood at the very end and looked out onto nothing but sea. The mural would be done by the end of the week. Then what? She couldn't stay at the cottage. The smart thing would be to go back to Stoddard and find a new place to live before the fall semester began, but...Bear. How could she walk away from him? It would crush her.

Seagulls swooped and cried. In the back of her mind, Kay knew come August they'd have to part, but somehow between blueberry-infused sex and falling in love with him, she'd let herself drift into the blind world of denial. Distance wouldn't be a challenge. It would be a romantic opportunity to spend weekends together and share long lusty phone calls and suggestive e-mails. Absence would make the heart grow fonder. Reunions would be measured on the Richter scale.

There had to be a solution. She just had to get past the giant roadblock otherwise known as Claire and figure it out. Kay looked into the sky to watch the clouds skim by. "Some kind of sign would be nice."

No sooner had the words left her mouth, Kay's cell phone buzzed in her pocket. It was a New Hampshire number, but she didn't recognize it right away. She almost didn't answer it for fear it was Todd. If that was her sign, she'd throw herself off the dock.

Holding her breath, she pushed the button to connect. "Kay Winston."

"Hi Kay, it's Maddie Sullivan."

"Oh, hi." Relief flooded her. "Caller ID didn't tell me it was you."

"I'm calling from the house. I've got some good news."

"I could certainly use some."

"Everything okay?"

Kay turned back and headed for the inn. "It will be. What's the news? Did I sell another painting? Make Daniel Bruce another tidy profit?"

"Not quite, but this may be just as good. I've been doing a little digging where you're concerned, and I hit pay dirt."

"Oh?"

"How'd you like to finish up your last year at Stoddard an entire semester early?"

Had she heard properly? She put her finger in her opposite ear to block out the street noise. "Is that even possible?"

"After our last discussion, I did some looking. I know how disappointed you were to miss the internship you were hoping for this summer. But even without it, your credits, now you're in Luc Girard's hot glass class—Jeez, say that three times fast. Anyway, it would be enough to let you graduate early."

Maddie must be confused. "I can't graduate without completing my internship."

"Exactly."

"Now I'm confused." Kay stopped on the walkway to the inn.

"I spoke to the Internship Committee, and happened to mention your name. The success of the Bruce Gallery show has several people talking about you."

"What has that got to do with the committee?"

"I've talked to a couple of the members and told them how you were working in Maine this summer. Well, they thought if your employer would agree to sign off on the project once it's completed—you know, verify your time, scope of the project, satisfaction, et cetera—then they would consider your internship obligation satisfied."

"Really?" Hope bubbled up in Kay's chest. If she finished early, she and Bear wouldn't have to spend so much time apart.

"I already dropped the paperwork in the mail. To the address I mailed your check. Care of Polka Dots, right? You should have them in a few days.

It meant she'd have to face Dottie again, but maybe that was good news, too. Everything could work out for the best. "That's great."

"Yep, I thought you'd be happy." Maddie chuckled. "'Course the committee wants me to make sure we don't have a repeat of what happened *last* year. Having a student get involved romantically with their internship provider has never happened before. I told them, you wouldn't be foolish enough to have an affair with the inn's owners. Ridiculous, right? I reassured them you're engaged, but they're such worriers."

Kay's hope took a nosedive. Looking toward the inn, she caught sight of Bear. He was installing the new porch lights flanking the front door. He was halfway up a stepladder, with his back to her. Kay stopped to stare.

His shirt molded to the muscles across the span of his back. She'd soaped those muscles in the shower this morning. The snug fit of his jeans hugged the rest. What they were doing was so much more than an affair. She loved him.

Bear climbed down from his task and dropped a pair of pliers into the toolbox at his feet. Seeing Kay, he smiled and started toward her.

Maddie continued talking into Kay's ear. "We sure as hell don't need *that* kind of scandal again. I mean all's well that ends well. Emily Baskins and Maximo Vega came out of their mess fairly unscathed. Did you hear they got married on Valentine's Day? Daniel Bruce says both their work is back to selling strong on the west coast. Sometimes a bit of hot gossip works to help sales. But I don't have to tell you, the school came under a serious firestorm from the alumna for their forbidden tryst. I sure as hell don't need that headache again." Maddie laughed. "Whatever you do, for Pete's sake, don't sleep with the man."

Chapter Twenty-Three

Bear's arm circled Kay's waist. She gave a nervous laugh into her phone. "Not a chance, Maddie." He moved to kiss her, but she dodged him by switching the phone to her other ear and placed a halting hand upon his chest. "You don't have to worry about that." Not to be deterred, Bear brushed his lips along the side of her neck.

"Gotta run," Kay insisted, her voice a full octave higher. "Bye." She pressed the disconnect button just as Bear nipped at her collarbone.

"I didn't mean to interrupt your call," he murmured into her hair, tracing the outside of her ear with the tip on his tongue. "I was just thinking about you."

A wave of scorching desire clashed with the sudden icy chill of panic as if Maddie could somehow see them.

"I was thinking about you, too." Kay tried to take a step back, but he held her firmly by the belt loops of her jeans. When he tipped his head and lowered his mouth to hers, she was quick to lay two fingers over his lips. "Maybe we should go inside." She shot a quick glance over her shoulder.

"Right, your mother could be lurking." Bear kissed her fingers and released her. "I'm just starting to see color again."

Kay gave a tight laugh and followed him as he

gathered his tools and collapsed the short stepladder. "That's only the half of it." She held the door open for him. The coolness of the lobby after the heat from outside raised goosebumps on her arms and tightened the sensitive tips of her nipples.

"Did you hear from her again?" He propped the ladder against the welcome desk and stowed the toolbox behind.

"We crossed paths."

"I'm sorry. I should have gone with you."

"Thank you, but I think there's been enough collateral damage for one day." Kay rubbed a hand over her eyebrows. "There's something else I need to ask you about, though." She shifted her head from one side to the other trying to ease the tightness in her neck.

"Turn around." Bear held her by the shoulders and nudged one side.

She stood firm and held up a hand. "I'm fine, it's just—"

"No arguing, turn around," he insisted.

Doing as he asked, Kay sighed as Bear's large, warm hands gently kneaded the tension from her shoulders. "Oh my God, that feels good."

"What did you need to ask me?" His voice was low and caramel-ly behind her.

"It can wait," she purred.

Neither spoke for a long moment. The heat of him penetrated the thin cotton of her tank, warming her back. Bear kissed the top of her head as he continued the bone-melting massage. "Can we go back to thirty seconds before Shadow set off the cat alarm at your place this morning and start the whole day over?" His thumbs moved in firm circles. "It went seriously downhill from there."

"I don't know. This is pretty nice." Kay sighed and leaned against the strength of his chest.

His mouth returned to the side of her neck. "You're right. We can keep this part." His hands moved down her body and spanned her ribs. "I get close to you and all I can think about is being with you. Kissing you. Makes me forget everything else."

"Everything?" Kay moved one of his hands higher to cup her breast, arching into his palm.

He bit her earlobe. "Right now, I'm having trouble remembering my name."

Kay turned in his arms and met his kiss with her own. She gasped his name into his mouth when those magic massaging fingers pushing their way under her top. "Bear…"

"I do remember some mention of mattresses," he murmured again her lips as his gentle touches made her knees weak. "Fourteen to be exact."

She smiled against his mouth. "So many. Do we need to test every one?"

"Not all at once."

Standing on tiptoes, she wrapped her arms around his neck. "And you promise to make the rest of the world disappear?"

"Totally gone." He tightened his hold and lifted her off her feet. "Just me and you. Nothing past these doors."

"Please tell me they're locked."

"Tighter than Fort Knox."

"And Shadow?"

"Asleep on the screen porch." He kissed her again. "We're all alone. Think desert island." One hand moved lower to cup the round of her behind.

"Escaping to a desert island... Isn't that called avoidance? Denial?"

"Only if you say no." He raised an eyebrow as if to challenge her.

Kay laughed. "To you? Doesn't seem possible."

"Now that, I'll remember." He pecked her lightly on the lips and set her down. "I want to show you something. Upstairs."

"Etchings?"

"Close." Bear gave her the boyish, mischievous grin sending shockwaves straight to her thighs. "Follow me." He kissed her fingers and then held them tight in his hand as he pulled her toward the stairs.

"We finished setting it yesterday. I couldn't wait to show you." At the top floor, Bear pulled his keys from his front pocket and unlocked the door to the "penthouse."

When Kay last saw this room, she'd fallen in love with the lines and the view and how lovely the room could be. She couldn't have imagined just how beautiful it would turn out.

Walls of a soft buttery cream flowed into the crisp white of the trim around the doors and the windows capturing the sights of the harbor and far out to sea. The ceiling paint was the palest shade of blue.

The bedding pulled in the warm, rich wall color with a thick spread and shams and accented with the coolness of the soft blue with an arrangement of pillows. A brass framework crowned the bed's four carved posts. Sheer panels of white flowed at each corner to pool onto the floor. The construction mats she remembered from the other day had hidden the beautiful oak floors, which now shone beneath the gentle tones of several oriental scatter rugs.

Their telescope gleamed at the window, and the tub now sported lush towels hung over one side and a brass wired tray across its span to hold soap, a rough sea sponge, and a jar of bath salts. It even had a place to set a book and a glass of wine.

"You like?"

"Bear…" Kay looked at him over one shoulder as she took in each detail. "I love it…"

"What do you think of the prints?" He gestured to opposite wall.

She hadn't even noticed the artwork. In gold-leafed frames of various shapes and sizes, sepia photographs of historic Bell Harbor's dock and waterfront graced the walls.

"Your mural inspired me. The new, celebrating the old."

"They're perfect." She held her arms wide. "The whole room is…perfect." Kay couldn't come up with a better word. "It's soft without being too feminine, warm, yet light and airy. Totally romantic."

"I'm glad you think so." Bear pulled her into his arms and angled his head to kiss her.

"You're very good at this."

"Kissing?"

She smiled against his lips. "That, too, but I was talking about decorating."

"I'm a man of many talents." He moved her slowly backward.

"So I've been told." Kay lifted her chin as he laid a line of warm kisses along the curve of her throat. "Oh, I love the chandelier."

"Mmhmm."

Her legs hit the edge of the mattress, and she stumbled back across the bed. Bear wasted no time and covered her with his body, pressing her into the creamy bedding.

"We can't." Kay protested with as much conviction as a starving man pushed toward a smorgasbord.

"Of course we can."

She blinked up at him. "We'll mess up this perfect bed."

"I'm good at that too, remember? There's a reason they call them throw pillows." His arm swept the bed before lifting off her tank top.

Kay needn't have worried. The rich comforter and thick blanket hit the floor seconds before the rest of her clothing and all but his pants.

The afternoon sun warmed the room. Had it not been for the clean breeze tickling over her skin, it might have been too hot, but then hot took on a very different meaning when she was in bed with Bear Coulter.

In one swift motion, she went from under him to on top, straddling his hips, while he held tight to hers. His erection strained against the denim of his jeans.

"I like the view from up here," Kay teased.

"So do I." Bear's large hands skimmed over her waist, cupping the sides of her breasts.

Kay traced the high sweep of his cheekbone as she studied him. Beyond the smolder in his hazel gaze, he looked drawn. Serious. As if the day's stress was written about his face. Around his eyes. "Did something else happen after you left the cove this morning?"

His eyes held hers, and he forced a small smile. "Nothing I can't handle. Nothing I want to talk about.

Not now." His thumbs toyed with the pebbled tips of her nipples. "Desert island, remember."

Each circle of his finger sent ever-increasing waves of pleasure through her. Escaping with him into an afternoon of sexual abandon was intoxicating. "Quite a tree house you've built on your island."

"Beats getting sand in your shorts." He threaded a hand into her hair and pulled her mouth to his.

Kay opened her lips to the insistent plunge of his tongue and rocked her hips slowly over the hard length of him. Reaching between them, she released the metal button from its buttonhole. "Helps if you're not wearing any."

Before adding his jeans to the scattering on the floor, Bear fished a condom out of the pocket and tore the foiled package open with his teeth. Sheathing his erection, he was quick to pull her back astride him. "There...happy?"

"Oh, yes, very happy."

"Good. Let's shoot for ecstatic."

Kay left a sleeping, post-ecstatic Bear briefly to put Shadow out on his run. She'd heard him pawing at the door shortly after Bear had gathered her tight to him and murmured that he loved her and he'd run away with her anytime she wanted.

Donning her tank and panties and following the dog to the kitchen door, she held tight to Shadow's collar. Like a member of a SWAT team, she checked the backyard for anyone who might catch her as she dashed half naked to secure him outside before zipping back inside again.

She padded back through the lobby toward the stairs with two bottles of water she'd snagged from the huge stainless steel refrigerator. Kay paused to give the painting her ever-critical appraisal. The work was good. She was pleased. Another day or two and she'd be finished.

The conversation with Madeline Sullivan crept back in to worry the edges of her mind. There was no question if she asked Bear, he would sign off on her internship, but given Maddie's final warning, it meant they would have to hide their relationship. At least for the remaining time she was at Stoddard.

She didn't want to hide. She wanted to stand on rooftops and yell to the world she had fallen in love with the most wonderful man on the planet.

But if there were so much as a hint of anything going on between them, it would not only threaten her degree, but also the school. He'd never be able to visit her there. She'd have to use Dottie as an excuse to keep coming back here. It would be lies on top of lies, and Kay hated even the thought of that. She seemed surrounded by dishonesty and half-truths lately. Between Todd, and now Dottie.

Something was going on between Dottie and her mother. She could feel it, but being blind-sided by Claire and losing her beloved cottage had only solidified her decision not to try and figure it out. If they wanted to keep things from her. Fine. She didn't want to know. She didn't care anymore—damn it, now she was even lying to herself.

Focused on the tiny lovers tucked into the rocks, Kay worried her lower lip. She hated secrets almost as much as she hated the thought of waiting six months longer to be with Bear. If she were honest and refused to use the mural as her internship, she would still need to complete the requirement. She couldn't decide which would be worse.

Todd. Todd would be worse. He'd guessed there was someone else the other night on the phone. *I almost feel bad for the guy.* If she went back to Stoddard and hid her relationship with Bear, Todd would boast he'd been right about it not lasting more than a few weeks. He'd never stop telling her "I told you so."

The town was too small. The school, even smaller. She'd have to cross paths with him daily. If he suspected things were still going on, he wouldn't hesitate to let the Internship Committee and the Graduate Board know. It would be a semester of walking on a tightrope across a shark tank.

She couldn't do it. No matter how tempting. Kay wouldn't cut corners to get her degree early if it meant she'd have to lie about her and Bear.

Kay slipped back into bed and snuggled against the broad warmth of Bear's back. She traced the silvered line that cut through his tattoo. Strength from strength. That's what he said it had meant. She'd count on the strength of what was building between them to get her through the next year. Losing the cottage. Dottie. A lonely year at school and a long-distance relationship. Thank goodness she and Bear were solid.

Chapter Twenty-Four

Warm breasts pressed into his back as Kay wrapped an arm around his waist. Her breath tickled his shoulder a moment before she laid a kiss upon his tattoo.

Rolling onto his back, Bear gathered her close.

"I didn't mean to wake you."

"Glad you did." He sighed. She felt good tucked into his side. "I could get used to this." He tightened his hold. "Where did you disappear to?"

"I left the island temporarily. Shadow needed to go out."

"Didn't even hear him."

"You were recharging." She smiled against his chest and teased the hair there.

"What did you want to ask me?" He rested his lips on the top of her head breathing in the sweet scent of her hair. "There's a very good chance I'll say yes to pretty much anything right at the moment."

"No need."

He shifted so he could look at her face. "I thought you wanted—"

Kay shrugged a shoulder and gave a quick shake of her head. "I've decided to handle it another way." She trailed her fingers down the plane of his stomach. "But make no mistake…you would have said yes."

"You decided?"

"Mmmhmm." She snuggled against him again.

A flare of irritation raced through him. Maybe it was lack of sleep, maybe it was all the business with Diane, maybe it was his curse for being attracted to strong women, but there it was. He pulled back and sat up. "Did this decision have anything to do with me? Us?"

"Well, yes, in a way, but—"

"And you didn't think you should let me in on it before you made up your mind?" He got out of bed and found his jeans.

"Bear…"

Turning to look at her, some of the anger evaporated. He wasn't mad at her. He was furious with himself. With Diane.

He raked a hand through his hair and blew out a breath.

Kay was on her feet. "I didn't mean to exclude you. It wasn't like that." She told him about the conversation with the director from Stoddard and her internship. "As much as I want to be with you—and I do. I want this. You and me. I don't know how or when or where. I just don't want a lie to get in our way."

He was an ass. What right did he have getting upset with her? He was the one hiding things. "I'm such a jerk."

"No." She closed the space between them and wrapped her arms about his waist, resting her cheek on his chest. "I was going to tell you, I promise."

"I believe you." As he wrapped his arms around her and held her, he prayed when he said those exact words, she'd believe him as well. He'd better make it soon. "What are you going to do about the cottage?"

"I don't know if there is anything I can do." She moved away from him and sat on the edge of the bed. "It might not sell for months, but I don't feel right staying there now. My work here is almost done. I suppose the smart thing to do is to pack up and head back to Stoddard. Use the rest of the summer to find a place to live, find a job."

"Stay with me."

Kay shook her head. "I have to go back sometime."

"Not right away. You can stay here." He swept the room with a hand.

"I can't afford to stay here."

"Sure you can. I know the owner. He'd give you a sweet deal."

"You're trying to start an inn. You can't be giving rooms away."

"Then stay with me out on the point."

She gave him a quick frown. "I don't know."

"You hate it, I know, but it's not ugly on the inside. You'll see. I've a crazy week with the guys here to lay the stone out back and finish the final landscaping. How about Friday night? My place. I'll wine and dine you. Build a fire in the fireplace. Shadow will wear a tie."

Bear sat beside her and took her hand. "I've wanted to show you things out there. The view alone will seduce you. And we can talk everything through. Figure things out. Together."

Kay looked at him with concern. "You're still upset about the internship."

"No. I'm not upset." He cupped her cheek. "I get it. You're absolutely right. We can't build something around a lie."

****

Bear sipped his coffee while he leaned against one of the poles holding up the new pergola. It crowned the inn's back patio, which consisted of huge slabs of cut New Hampshire granite. The stonemasons were building him an outdoor grill area off to one side as well. It looked great. He could picture small private parties on the back lawn, family gatherings, intimate summer weddings. It was finally coming together.

The last few days had been a frenzy of activity. Months of stressing that the work would never get done, and then suddenly there seemed to be a mad race to the finish line. The stone guys were concerned about the rain moving in for the weekend, and they wanted everything set and covered before then.

The phone had already started ringing with bookings. If he kept up this pace, there was no reason why he couldn't be up and rolling by Labor Day. Next few weeks, he'd start advertising for a cook, housekeepers, servers. Who knows, if he found a great chef quick enough, he might even be able to open the dining room for dinners before then.

As for things with Kay, he was ready to settle everything tomorrow night. It was all planned. Food was set. Hell, the wine was already chilling. He'd been rehearsing just what he wanted to say.

The last couple of days had been easy between the two of them. They were both busy with work, but still managed to steal a kiss or share a cup of coffee when their paths crossed. She was looking forward to dinner.

The subject of the cottage hadn't come up again. Claire Winston hadn't bothered to talk to Kay. Seemed the standoff continued.

Walter had stopped by as usual, but he told Bear

he'd decided to play *Switzerland* where Dottie, Kay, and her mother were concerned. Said Claire had been a damn fool all these years, but he knew better than to come between his wife and her best friend, no matter what his opinion happened to be.

And by some miracle of miracles, Bear hadn't heard from Diane in close to forty-eight hours. Had to be a record. He'd had another brief phone conversation with Adam Dunbar. Adam was working an angle on a continuance. Diane's lawyers were giving him the run around, but for right now, anyway, the deposition was on hold.

Bear grabbed a refill and headed toward the lobby to pull up the designs for the final landscaping. The sod should arrive next week. He glanced up at the sound of the front door closing.

"Bear, good morning." Dottie Polk gave him a small strained smile. Kay's mother eyed him over Dottie's shoulder.

"Dottie. Mrs. Winston. What brings you two out so early?"

"We…" Both women stopped to look around. "Oh, Bear," gushed Dottie. She placed a hand to her heart. "Walter said the mural was beautiful, but I had no idea. It's breathtaking."

Claire Winston took a step closer to the wall leading toward the dining room. "My Kay did *this*?"

"No. *My* Kay did this," Bear countered. Her incredulous tone made the muscle in his jaw tense. He didn't care if his eye twitched for a solid year, he wasn't going to take any crap from this woman. If she said one disparaging remark about Kay, she'd find herself back on the sidewalk. Stockbridge Winstons be damned.

"I can't quite believe it." She turned to Dottie. "Who knew she was so talented?"

Bear crossed his arms over his chest, tucking his fists. "The bigger question is, why don't you know?"

"Bear," Dottie warned.

"I beg your pardon." Claire turned on him. "I don't think I care for your tone, Mr. Coulter."

"And I'm not sure I care for you in my inn, Mrs. Winston."

"I don't know what you think you know about my relationship with my daughter, but I'll thank you to mind your own business."

"Kay's happiness *is* my business."

"Hold on, hold on." Dottie moved between them and put her hands up. "We didn't come here to start a pissin' contest." She turned to Bear and showed him an envelope. "Kay got a letter from Stoddard. The last time it was a nice fat check. I thought we should bring it right over. Is she here?"

"No. She's not due until after noon. As far as I know, she's at the cottage. Packing." His voice chilled the last word.

Claire Winston's chin notched a bit higher.

"You could always leave it with me. I'll make sure she gets it," Bear suggested.

"No." Dottie shook her head and gave Claire a pointed look. "We should head over there. It could be real important." Turning to Bear, she laid a calming hand on his arm. "The inn is gorgeous, Bear. Really. The mural. Everything." An apologetic smile filtered across her face. "We shouldn't have interrupted your morning. I'm sorry."

"Don't worry about it." He glanced in Claire's direction. She was once again studying Kay's work. He lowered his voice at Dottie. "Go easy, okay?"

Dottie gave his arm a squeeze. "I love her, too, remember."

"She may need reminding."

Pressing her lips together, Dottie blinked back the sudden shine in her eyes. She nodded and turned to leave.

Bear shook his head at the door closing behind Dottie and Claire. He was in full protect mode, and part of him wanted to rush to the cove to what…warn Kay? Shield her? Soothe away the hurt after her mother got through swinging her haughty sword of disapproval?

How could she not see what the rest of the world saw? Kay was incredible. Talented. Beautiful. Kind and loving. For a moment he almost felt sorry for Claire Winston. She'd missed it. She didn't know her own daughter. Didn't have a clue as to what Kay's life was like, or where her passions lie. All she saw was that Kay wasn't a carbon copy of her.

"Thank God," he mumbled as he once more picked up the designs for the back gardens.

When the door opened for the second time, Bear gritted his teeth before looking up. "Back so soon? Come to apologize?"

"Hardly."

Bear's head snapped up. "What the fu—*Diane*."

She stood with her hands planted firmly on her hips. "If you care anything about this inn or about me, you'll go pack a bag. We have a plane to catch."

Lisa A. Olech

Chapter Twenty-Five

Kay stretched the clear tape across the length of the cardboard carton. It was premature to be packing, but she was an expert on quick getaways. It was one of the benefits of not owning many things. With so much up in the air where the cottage was concerned, it didn't hurt to box a few things now.

She thought back to her conversation with Bear. It was tempting to think of staying with him for the rest of the summer, but living out at the point house would mean seeing the cottage every day. It would be hard watching strangers moving in and changing things.

And what about Hope? She wasn't about to abandon her. The cat had finally come to trust Kay enough not to bolt back into the underbrush each time Kay stepped onto the porch. Now in the mornings, when Kay placed her food down, she'd sit and wait for the cat to come up onto the deck to eat. Not too close, but each day the distance between her and the skittish cat was becoming less and less. Trust was a funny thing, even with animals. Forever to build, mere seconds to destroy.

Kay found a pet carrier at the secondhand shop a few days ago. Maybe if she set it out and started putting Hope's food inside, the cat would trust her to crate her when it came time to leave. But to where, and when? Kay hated not knowing.

The only thing she did know, she was falling in love with Bear Coulter more and more every day. And not for the big reasons like he was beautiful to look at and a-may-zing in bed. No, it was the little things that really touched her heart. It was the way he rubbed her shoulders when she was stiff and sore after painting for hours. Or the way he went out to get her coffee in the afternoons, so she wouldn't have to drink the sludge passing for coffee in the kitchen. He valued her opinion. Made her feel cherished. Came undone when she cried. It was a heady combination, and she couldn't remember ever having feelings this strong.

It was hard to explain, but she'd spent so much energy making her own way. Ferocious in not having to depend on anyone. Not financially. Not emotionally. Even when she was with Todd, there was an underlying feeling she could manage by herself if things went wrong. Perhaps she had a sixth sense she and Todd wouldn't last.

Adding the carton to the small pile next to the couch, Kay stood and stretched her back. Don't ask her how she knew, but somehow, wherever she landed or when, having Bear in her life gave her the sense all would be well. Maybe she didn't have to do it all by herself.

A tap sounded at the back door. When Kay pushed back the curtain, there was Dottie. She held up a letter and gave Kay a sheepish smile. Ah, the internship paperwork from Stoddard. Maddie was fast.

Kay swung open the door.

"May I come in?"

"Since when do you have to ask?"

"Given our last conversation, I wasn't sure if I was

welcome."

"Of course, you're welcome."

Dottie moved past Kay before handing her the envelope. "This came for you, and I thought it might be important."

"Yes, and no." Kay studied the Stoddard School of Art logo above the return address. "It's just some paperwork I don't really need any more."

"Oh…" Dottie shoved her hands in her pockets and shifted her stance. "Well, we stopped by the inn first. Bear said—"

"We?"

"Your mother and I. She…she decided it might be better if I came out here on my own."

Kay fought to urge to ask why. She wasn't used to walking through a verbal minefield with Dottie. Her mother was a full on frontal assault, but with Dottie, it had never been this tense. She played with the corner of the letter. "I hate that we fought."

"I hate it, too." Dottie reached out and stroked Kay's arm. "We saw the mural. It blew me away, sweetheart. Walter's been telling me, but even my imaginings were nowhere near accurate. It's spectacular."

"Thanks." She'd said "we," hadn't she? Despite every stop sign her mind threw at her. Regardless of a deep-seated knowing of what the answer was, Kay couldn't help herself. "So what did Claire think of it?" As soon as the words found air, she regretted them. Regretted her seven-year-old's need for some sliver of praise. She'd once more set herself up. The quick frown on Dottie's face told her everything. "Never mind. It doesn't matter."

"It does. Your mother is—"

Kay held up a hand to stop her. "Don't."

Dottie dropped into one of the kitchen chairs. "I'll be damned if I can understand what goes on in Claire's head sometimes. With you especially. I don't get it, but there's something you need to know."

"I'm done, Dottie." Kay leaned on the back of a chair to steady herself. "She can sell the cottage, she can forget she even has a daughter. There's nothing you can tell me that will change anything. I'm sorry."

"She's sick."

Kay pushed away from the chair, folded the letter from Stoddard, and shoved it into the back pocket of her jeans. "I don't want to hear this."

"And I don't want to be the one to tell you. She swore me to secrecy, but jeezum rice, you're her daughter."

"How sick?"

Dottie didn't answer, but once again, Kay could read her face. The tumble of emotions choked her. How was she supposed to feel? Anger sparred with guilt. Worry pushed through apathy. After the initial wave, all that truly remained was sadness.

"I'm sorry."

"That's all you have to say?" Dottie looked shocked.

"What did you want me to say?" Kay threw up a hand. "She swore you to secrecy because she didn't want me to know. What does that tell you?"

"She's protecting you."

"That would be a first," Kay scoffed. "Nothing has changed. And now, I guess, it never will."

"You know," Dottie snapped. "If you don't lose the

damn chip on your shoulder and work it out, you'll regret it. It's hard, but that's life, Kay. Believe it or not, Claire does love you."

"Three words, Dottie. Three simple words."

"They're not so simple for some." Dottie sighed and reached for Kay's arm. "You need to be the bigger person."

"I'm not the bad guy here, Dottie. I'm not the one who turned her back on this relationship. How much more do you want me to do?"

"Aren't you even upset?"

"Of course, I'm upset. Once again, my mother has decided to keep me out of her life. She didn't want me to know this. It's why you kept it from me. For her. It's always been about her. And yes, I'm sad. I'm sad she's sick, and I'm sad she doesn't feel it's important enough for her to tell me. It's what *she* wants. What I'm most sad about is what never was. I'm her daughter, her only child, and yet we're more like strangers. We could have had an amazing relationship, but she picked Charles over me. She made her choice a long time ago."

"You have to try," Dottie pleaded.

"I don't know if I can." Kay crossed her arms over her chest to squeeze the sudden hurt there. "And I'm not sure I want to."

"Then you aren't the Kay I know."

****

Kay pulled the Mini tight to the curb down the block from the inn. Parking was tough with all the tourists in town. The scene with Dottie circled around and around her mind. She wasn't heartless, but Claire's demand she not be told only confirmed what Kay had already mourned. Yes, she was losing her mother, but hadn't she already lost her?

Before Dottie left the cottage, she told Kay about the scene between Bear and her mother. She wished she could have witnessed that herself. Bear getting all…Bear. When was the last time someone defended her? If she hadn't already loved him…

She came into through kitchen, hoping to find him working out back. There was so much she wanted to tell him, but first she simply craved the feel of his arms around her. No Bear by the new patio, no Shadow greeting either. The dog was an Olympic napper. Give him a sunbeam, and he was a goner. But Bear's car was here, so he had to be around somewhere.

Kay pushed into the foyer. A tall red-haired woman in a beautiful sage-colored suit was behind the desk speaking on the phone. "Yes, flight two eight one nine. Can you tell me if it's on schedule?" Kay caught her eye. Cool green eyes appraised her. She smiled. "Thank you."

Hanging up the phone, the woman smoothed the lines of her jacket before checking the time on her gold watch. "Can I help you?"

"I was just going to ask you the same thing." Kay frowned, but shrugged it off. "I'm Kay Winston. I work here."

The woman lit a cigarette and blew the smoke toward the ceiling. "Oh, yes, you're the artist."

Kay looked down at her paint-smudged clothes. "Good guess."

"Bear has told me so much about you. I love what you've done here." Her manicured hand swept the lobby. "It's…nice."

"I'm sorry, but who are you?"

"Mrs. Diane Coulter, Bear's wife."

"Ex-wife." Kay was quick to correct her.

Diane gave her a cool smile. "Technically, yes." She shrugged a shoulder. "But not for long. I'm happy the inn is almost done, so he can come back to California for good this time. Dual-coast relationships take so much work. But who knew the sex would be better *after* the divorce?" She lowered her voice as if she were sharing a secret and gave a coy smile. "Bear doesn't do alone well, though. Likes having someone warming his bed, and the separation hasn't been good for either of us. If we didn't have our phone dates several times a day, I'm not sure we'd have made it this far." She glanced back at her watch. "Did you need to talk to him? He just ran over to leave Shadow with a friend of his. Walter? Wait, isn't he your uncle, sort of? Bear's told me such stories about all of you. It's nice to finally put faces to the names. I do hope he's hurrying. I understand Walter can be quite the talker. If we don't get going, we're going to miss our plane."

Kay's stomach gave a vicious twist. She took a great gulp of air to keep from being sick. They spoke several times a day? Had Bear even mentioned his wife after that first day when Kay interviewed for the mural job? Her mind raced to remember. This woman certainly knew who she was. Who Walter was.

Bear was planning on going back to California? That couldn't be true, could it? He'd have told her.

"Diane," Bear called from the back. "Did you check on our flight?"

Black crept around the edges of Kay's vision as she rushed to leave. She shoved her way through the front entryway.

"Kay? Wait!" Bear called.

She didn't realize she was running until she hit the sidewalk. For a moment, she couldn't remember where she'd parked.

It was half a block before Bear caught up to her.

"Kay, wait." He grabbed her arm and pulled her to a stop. "Hey, I just left you a message." He held up his cell phone.

She jerked her chin toward her car. "I was…running to grab something out of my car," she panted. "Forgot my lucky paint rag."

"Okay." He frowned before dipping his head to peer into her face. "I have to go out of town, but—"

"I heard." Her body shook with the effort it took to hold herself together. She pointed toward the inn. "Your…um, Diane filled me in."

"She's in a real mess. She needs me in LA. A business contract gone bad. She showed up out of the blue." He swept a hand toward the inn. "I should have said something before, but it wasn't a big deal, then it became a huge disaster. I was hoping it would all work itself out somehow."

Kay looked everywhere but at his face. "I understand."

"You do?" He rubbed at her arm.

"Sure. These things happen." She nodded like a bobble-head doll. "You do what you have to."

"Can we move our dinner back a few nights?"

"No problem."

Bear's cell vibrated. He looked at the screen and hit ignore. "Damn it, Diane, I'm coming," he grumbled. Kay's mind flashed back to all the times she'd seen him do the same thing over the last few weeks. The icy truth encased what remained of her heart. Had he been lying all this time?

"She calls a lot?"

"You have no idea. I think her record is twelve times in one day." He ran his hands through his hair. "You know the old saying, *like a dog with a bone*, that's her. She can be relentless."

Behind Bear, Kay caught sight of Diane standing on the porch of the inn. Relentless was right. Kay jerked her chin in toward her. "You shouldn't keep her waiting."

"You sure you're okay?"

"Of course, why wouldn't I be?" Suddenly, he didn't deserve the truth.

"I'll call you as soon as I get to LA. Walter is taking care of Shadow, so you don't have to worry about him. Just remind him the spare key for the point house is in the stupid rock that doesn't look like a rock by the side door."

"Will do."

"Are you sure you're okay?"

"You need to stop asking me that." She forced a smile.

His cell buzzed again. "I gotta go. I'll call you."

"I'll be waiting." She met his gaze and held it as the words soured on her tongue. He wouldn't know she was lying if she didn't look away. "Oh, before you leave, could you do me a favor?" Kay fished the letter from Stoddard from her rear pocket. She folded it over so he couldn't read the letterhead. "The final supply order. I need a quick signature."

Chapter Twenty-Six

"You're awful quiet."

Bear pushed the phone back into his pocket. "Kay's not picking up."

"She probably took the day off. The boss is out of town. Cat's away and all."

"Kay's not like that."

"Oh, honey, everyone's like that." Diane pulled her bag out of the overhead compartment. "Come on. I need a drink and a cigarette. We have a two-hour layover here in Chicago. I plan to use my time wisely." She cranked an eyebrow at him. "In the bar."

Bear grabbed his carry-on bag and followed her out of the plane. "Wasn't the free champagne in first class enough for you?"

"I think they water it down."

"I doubt it."

Diane made a straight shot for the smoker's lounge. Bear stood outside. The enclosed glass cubicle set aside for smokers reminded him of the monkey cage at the zoo. You couldn't look at them all surrounded in their blue smoked haze without feeling a bit sorry for them.

He tried calling the inn again. No answer. Where was she? She wouldn't have taken the day off. Something wasn't right. He'd sensed it when he said goodbye. He sensed it all the way to Portland and on the flight here to Chicago.

It wasn't what she said when he caught up with her at her car. Kay had been nothing but understanding. He expected her to be more upset, but she was great.

He pictured her with her headphones on, lost in her work. While she was in her zone, maybe she couldn't hear the phone. Everything was fine. He was worrying for nothing. If he could just shake this uneasy feeling.

Diane emerged in a toxic cloud. There was an edge to her now that Bear didn't quite recognize. Still beautiful by LA standards, but there was a hardness. She was almost brittle in the way she walked, spoke, the way she treated their driver and the flight attendants. Had she always been like this? Had he just never noticed? He was certain of one thing, however. She no longer resembled the young, eager design student from USC.

She slipped an arm through his and tugged him along. "I could use a martini."

Sidled up to the bar, Bear opted for coffee, which may have been a mistake. He'd forgotten how bad airport coffee could be. Even the inn's sludge was better. He took a sip, grimaced at the bitter, acrid taste, and pushed it aside. "What time is the meeting in the morning?"

"I don't know, nineish." Diane rubbed her thumb over a chip in her manicure.

"Ish? You don't know? Six hours ago you made it sound desperate."

She swirled the olives in her drink. "I never said desperate."

"No, you tossed around the words like *emergency, urgent, Federal lawsuit, bankruptcy.* Any of those sound familiar? Why else would I be sitting in an airport bar in Chicago?"

"It is urgent."

"And I only have to show my face, and then Regency calls off their vultures?"

Diane nodded and ate her olive. "That's what Fred Becker said."

Bear frowned. "You're a hell of a lot calmer about this than you were this morning. Why?"

"Because you agreed to come back with me. Saving the day like the superhero you are." She smiled at him over one shoulder.

"Adam Dunbar can't make the meeting. He's in court all morning, but he's agreed to talk to me prior. You have the court order demanding my presence? I'll want to see it. Adam needs to hear the exact wording, so I'll know how to respond."

Diane flipped a hand. "Sure, sure. It's at the office."

"Wait a minute. You left it at the office?"

"That's where we're heading now, isn't it?"

"But you didn't know for certain when you decided to fly clear across the country to get me."

Diane flashed him a smug smile. "I know you better than you think I do, Bear. I never had any doubt that you wouldn't come back with me. I mean, once I explained everything in person. Come on." She placed a hand on his knee. "When have you ever been able to say no to me?"

There was something in the way she said the words. It made the tiny hairs on the back of Bear's neck prickle. He couldn't put his finger on what it was, but Diane was right. They both knew one another too well. It was foolish to underestimate her.

"What's the name of the judge?"

Diane blinked at him twice before giving her head a quick shake. "What?"

"The judge," he reiterated. "What's his name?"

"How should I know?" She took a large swallow of her drink and signaled the bartender to bring her another. "I don't remember those insignificant details. That's what I have lawyers for."

"Fine." Bear pulled out his phone. "Give me Fred Becker's number."

"What for?"

"He can tell me the judge's name, and tell me what time we're meeting in the morning, so I can make my flight arrangements back to Maine."

She sighed. "Relax. You need to see this through. I may have guessed at the time thing. It might take more than just one meeting. You'd have to stay in LA a bit longer. Would that be so awful?" She stroked his thigh.

Bear removed her hand. "That's not what I agreed to, Diane."

"Why the hell do you have to rush back anyway? It's not like the inn is even open yet." She stroked his cheek. "You look tired. Maybe this could be a blessing in disguise. Get you away for a few days. I've missed you. We could spend some time together. Visit some of our old haunts. Do you know I haven't eaten at Jacob's since you left? Remember how delicious their paella was the night we were there celebrating your birthday? I'm off carbs, but, yum, I could make an exception."

"This isn't a vacation, Diane. Dragging me across the country to face legal charges is hardly *getting away*. Do you think the inn will open itself? I'm on a deadline. I have contractors lined up, inspections. I promised you one day."

Diane notched her chin and huffed. "And spending time with me would kill you, I suppose? I thought once I got you away from that little backwater town you'd see how ridiculous you've been. You don't belong there. Maine? Give me a break. I mean it's beautiful, but you don't move there. You should be with me. In Los Angeles. Coulter Designs needs you back. I need you, too."

"Is that what all this is about?" He narrowed his eyes. "If you're playing me, Diane, so help me…" He lowered his voice and hissed. "Tell me there really is a lawsuit. Tell me you haven't made this whole thing up in some cockamamie scheme to get me back to California."

"Would you be sitting here otherwise?"

"That doesn't answer my question. I want the truth. Now."

"I have told you the truth. I've done nothing else for weeks. I can't make it without you. If you don't come back, I'm bankrupt. I'll lose it all. I need you in California. You're Coulter Designs. No one cares that I risked everything, sacrificed *everything* for this company. Built it from a second-hand computer and a slide rule. I thought once I had the name and the company, that would be it. I'd finally get some of the credit, but no. They don't want me. Never did. They want you, the great Barrett Coulter. Do you know how many times a day I heard, *Where's Bear? Can we talk to Bear?*" Diane leaned into him and hissed back. "And then I call you and hear how wonderful things are for you in that stupid inn and you're falling for little miss paintbrush? How do you think it made me feel?"

Bear's hands curled into fists. "I can't believe what I'm hearing."

"We were good once, Bear. I was there for you when everything fell into the crapper. You were supposed to play for the Dallas Cowboys. I was supposed to be a team wife with all those beautiful perks. But it all ended, and who was the one who had to help you after the surgeries? Me, that's who. Getting you cleaned and dressed. Taking you back and forth to doctors and PT. And then you decide we're done?"

"You're the one who filed for divorce, Diane."

"Right, because you didn't have the balls to do it yourself. We didn't have a marriage anymore. And I was okay with that because of the business. If we couldn't be marriage partners, at least we were business partners. But then you decided you'd had enough of that as well. What the hell did you expect?"

Bear was speechless. The sound of his heartbeat pulsed in his ears. Diane had pulled some crazy shit before, but this was beyond anything he could even wrap his brain around. His back teeth were in danger of shattering.

Diane turned back and spoke into her drink. "The Regency deal fell apart six months ago. I paid Fred Becker to dance around Adam Dunbar and feed him the continuation story. I was trying to buy time. There haven't been any commissions since." She shot him a glance. "It *was* desperate. *I* was desperate. I'm sorry I tricked you, but if we're to find our way back, back to where Coulter Designs used to be, back to one another, we need to be in the same damn time zone." She drained her drink as the second one arrived.

"You're insane." He was on his feet and grabbing

his bag before he wrapped his hands around something else, like her throat.

"Admit you're not happy there, Bear. Just be honest with me. You bought the inn to hurt me. Maine was just as far as you could run and still be in the same country. I didn't want to lose you." Diane followed him. "When I met Kay, I got more than a little jealous. I'm not proud of it, but there it is. I may have fibbed a little about you moving back to California, but I'd do it ag—"

Bear spun on her. "You did what?"

She held her hands up in surrender. "I said, you were considering, just *considering* coming back." Her lips thinned. "I may have insinuated that we…you and I…you know."

Red rage clouded his vision. "Do you have any idea what you've done?" Bear headed back toward the terminal.

"Where are you going?" Diane called after him.

"Where do you think?" Bear dodged the other travelers while dialing the inn on his cell.

"Slow down, will you. I can't keep up with you in heels!"

Still no answer. He tried Kay's number. It went straight to voice mail. He stopped to look at the departure board. Portland Jetport would be the closest airport to Bell Harbor, but they didn't handle very many flights in and out and it looked like the only flight listed had been canceled. Maybe there was a later flight not yet listed. His second option would be to go to Logan Airport in Boston. Rent a car.

Delayed notices flashed on two flights headed to Boston. Looked as if flights into Providence were affected as well. The storm they'd been predicting must be worse than they originally thought.

One Boston flight was still on schedule. It was due to leave within the hour. Bear prayed there was a still a seat. He'd sit in the pilot's lap if he had to.

"Bear, I'm sorry." Diane tugged at his sleeve.

He shook loose. "Go home, Diane."

"If it's any consolation, I was feeling pretty guilty. I called FTD before our flight left Portland. I sent her a peace offering. The card said *Sorry*. Signed from you." She shrugged one shoulder. "I'm sure once you've explained what a bitch I am..."

That prickling sensation was back under his collar. "What are you talking about? What kind of peace offering?"

"I sent flowers. Come on. What woman can stay mad at the man she loves after he sends her a stunning bouquet of three dozen long-stemmed red roses?"

Chapter Twenty-Seven

Kay moved as if she were walking under water while the rest of the world was on fast forward. For the first hour after Bear left with Diane, she did nothing but circle Bell Harbor. The blur of happy tourist's faces only adding to the shock of what happened.

Had he been lying to her this whole time? Playing two women? Two coasts? Had Diane not shown up, would he have gone on lying? Let Kay move in with him?

"Likes having someone warming his bed..."

What was he telling Diane? Was he lying to her as well?

"Bear's told me such stories about all of you."

Was she just another colorful character he'd met here? Another worker at the inn he'd joke about not working weekends? A charming, quirky addition to his new life in Maine?

No, she was a charming, quirky idiot who made the mistake—again—of trusting the words that came out of a man's mouth. A shaft of pain through her chest stopped her in her tracks. This couldn't be happening again.

Not again, not Bear.

She was so sure this time. She'd been careful. Cautious. After Todd, she'd watched for all the signs, the little avoidances, the occasional trip up, when he couldn't quite remember one lie from another, body language…another naked woman in the bed.

Kay slapped a hand over her eyes. No. There had been nothing to warn her off handing Bear her heart on a silver platter. She had no one to blame but herself.

She still had the letter from Madeline Sullivan crushed in her fist. Bear had been in such a hurry, he hadn't even read it before he scribbled his signature at the bottom. Kay let out a sob. See, it was easy to get away with a lie. She'd done it too. It was amazing how easy it had been. It had rolled off her tongue and she hadn't batted an eye.

But she was an amateur compared to the rest of them. Todd, Claire, Bear. How did they do it? Maybe after a while you just believed all your lies. Perhaps that was the biggest lie of all—the one you convinced yourself was the truth.

She tore the letter in half. Tears flooded her eyes as she tore it again, and again. There was no way she was going to head down that dark, potholed road. The truth would always scream through the chaos for her. It was the only way she could survive.

Bear wasn't her future. The truth was, he wasn't even her present. She really couldn't blame him. She was the one who wanted a relationship with no strings. Wasn't that the agreement?

He was a job. A job where she forgot the rules about getting involved with clients. A summer's folly. She'd been foolish and naïve to see it as anything more. The summer might not be over, but the game was.

She had work to do. A painting to finish. As hard as it was going to be to step into the lobby, she had a professional responsibility to her client—Mr. Barrett

Coulter.

Then what? Hell, she was practically all packed, thanks to her mother. Another wave of pain settled on her. Claire was sick. Dying? Kay couldn't pretend that wasn't happening either.

She did a slow turn there on the sidewalk. Bell Harbor. It had always been her soft place to land. Perhaps this was the biggest lie of them all. There was no soft place. Only children believed pretty pink fantasies. Life was hard. Her heart had the scars to prove it.

The phone rang again.

It had started not long after Kay had worked up the nerve to come back into the inn. She didn't answer it. Her cell rang a moment later. She turned it off. Part of her wanted to unplug the inn's phone, but each time it rang, it only solidified her resolve.

She wasn't leaving until the mural was done, even if she had to work straight through until morning. The last addition before the final wash was placing the new into the old. The inn's new owner…and his dog, resting in the shade of the inn's front porch.

Over the last few weeks, Kay had taken several candid pictures with her phone of Bear to work with. Looking at them now, remembering when she took them—the afternoon at the lighthouse, one of him talking to Skippy, and one from yesterday.

She'd taken it in the penthouse, where the fading light of day had fallen across his face. It hurt her heart to look at it.

The phone rang again, and Kay choked back the tears threatening to wash her out to sea. She added the paint she needed to her palette.

The image came like water from the end of her brush. Bear lounging on one of the long benches that lined the porch. Dressed in dashing period costume, he sat casually. One arm draped along the back of the bench. Legs crossed in a relaxed pose.

Shadow sat at his feet. His eyes bright and attentive. His tongue lolling out one side as it had the habit of doing when he was happy.

It was as if Kay blinked, and there they were. A touch of highlight showing the gleam of Shadow's coat and it was done. She stood there, brush poised, searching for any small touch she had missed or anything more she needed to add.

But there was nothing more to add, only one tiny thing to erase.

Starting at the far end, she began the final wash with a wide brush in one hand and a wiping rag in the other. Brushing on, wiping off, she left it only slightly darker at the edges The whole process took less than two hours, but the effect was even more stunning than she had anticipated. It aged the painting. Softened the brightness. Mellowed the color. Stepping back, it truly appeared that the mural had been painted a hundred years ago.

It looked amazing.

Kay swallowed the sudden lump in her throat. Had she finished this one day earlier, she would have rushed to Bear and pulled him into the lobby to show him. He would have loved it. Said so before saying how much he loved her. Lifted her in those strong arms of his and spun her around in the excited way he celebrated each room as it was finished.

But there was no celebrating. The inn was silent.

Even the phone had stopped ringing.

Kay added a touch of thinner to a dab of classic red. Lying on her belly, she took her liner brush and swept in her signature on the bottom right corner of the far wall.

Time to pack up and leave.

With all her brushes cleaned and sorted, and the paint stored in bins, Kay folded up the last of the drop cloths.

"Special Kay? You in here?" Walter pushed into the lobby, followed closely by Shadow.

The dog rushed her, then past her. He must be looking for Bear.

"There you are. You had the lot of us worried." He picked up the inn's phone and listened before hanging it up again. "Don't you know how to answer a phone?"

She ignored him. "I was finishing the mural. What do you think?"

Some of the bluster faded from Walter as he did a slow turn. "Oh, baby girl… You've outdone yourself on this one."

"Thanks." She crossed her arms over her chest and held tight.

Walter narrowed his eyes at her and cocked his head. "Bear's been trying to reach you, Honey. Called the house in quite the state looking for you. What's going on?"

Kay was saved from answering by the return of Shadow. He sniffed the bins of paint, danced around her, sniffed some more. She tried to pet him, but he kept dodging her. "He's hyper. Did you feed him too many cookies again?"

"Naw, I think he's sensing the storm they say's

coming. It's all those damn fools on the Weather Channel got to talk about. Say it's gonna be a cocka, but I don't believe it." Walter grabbed for Shadow's collar. "Sit, boy, relax 'fore you wear a hole in the floor." The dog obeyed but sat panting. "He's been twitchy and whiney for the last hour or so. Probably worried about where Bear's gotten to."

Kay added the last drop cloth to the bin of supplies. "He's probably landing in Los Angeles by now." She rubbed a hand over her forehead and studied the floor. "Um…the next time you talk to him, let him know I'll send him a final bill in a week or so. I don't know where he should send the check, so—"

"Next time I talk to him? Why ain't *you* talking to him?"

"It's complicated." Kay planted her hands on her hips.

"Like ex-wife complicated?"

"I really don't want to discuss it."

"What do you think is going on? You don't believe he's gone back with her, do ya?"

Kay swept the room with a hand. "Do you see him here?"

"One thing's got nothing to do with the other."

"Walter." Kay shook her head. "I know you like Bear, and somehow you thought he and I would end up together, but…"

"But what? The man's crazy about you."

She met his gaze. "That's not exactly what his ex-wife is telling me."

"And who you gonna believe? The man you obviously have feelings for or some woman you just met?"

"She's not *some woman*, Walter." Kay sighed "She's his wife."

"Ex," Walter emphasized.

"She's not convinced of that."

"Who cares what she says? I've seen the way he looks at you. The way you both be moony eyed for one another."

"You know how great my judgment is where men are concerned. Seems I was wrong again." She couldn't fight the tears that had been threatening for hours. She swiped an angry hand at her cheeks.

"That's bullshit, and you know it." Walter scowled at her. "I love you, Special Kay, like you're my own. I know you've had a tough road, but…enough is enough. You're so used to people failing you. You're waiting to jump up and say, *See! I told you, you're just like everyone else*. Well, folks ain't perfect. Life ain't perfect. But if you're going to walk around expecting people to hurt you, guess what you're going to get? Hurt. Loving someone is all about trusting. Trusting they have your back. That they have your heart. Doesn't mean they won't screw up. It means there's something stronger to hang on to when the water gets too deep."

By now, Kay couldn't fight the flood of tears. "I'm not waiting for people to fail me, they just do."

Walter shook his head. "Because then it's easy for you to bail."

Kay caught a sob. "Well, maybe no one has been worth the fight."

Walter closed the distance between them. He pulled a folded bandana out of his rear pocket and mopped at her face. "Maybe not, but what if you're wrong?" He spoke to her gently. "What if you ran before you knew the whole story? What if you took off on something wonderful?" He rubbed her arm until she met his gaze. "Your heart has been broken for so long, baby girl. Don't you think it's about time you gave someone a chance to put the pieces back together?"

Kay buried her face into his chest. Shadow whined at her feet.

"I just want to see you happy, Special Kay. Both of you." He hugged her tight. "Before you run off, just think about what I said." He pulled back and tipped her chin. "I may be an old curmudgeon, but I've been in love with the same woman for thirty years. It hasn't always been smooth sailing, but it sure as hell's been worth it."

Walter handed her his handkerchief before kissing her forehead and gathering Shadow to leave. Kay pulled a deep shaky breath and blew her nose. He was right. She was too quick to believe the worst. Bear had only been kind and loving. If he hadn't told her about Diane, perhaps it was truly because there was nothing to tell.

She looked around the lobby again. Secretly, she was glad Bear wasn't around to witness her meltdown. It was foolish. Surely, if Bear Coulter was planning to move back to California to be with Diane, Kay would have seen some sign of it long before now.

"Kay Winston?"

She spun around. A delivery man stood just inside the door with a clipboard and a long white box tied with a wide blue ribbon. She dabbed quick at her eyes, sniffed, and tucked her hair behind an ear.

"Yes, I'm Kay Winston. I'm sorry, I didn't hear

you come in."

"These are for you. I just need a signature."

She quickly scribbled her name where he indicated and took the box from his hands. "Thank you."

"Enjoy." With a quick wave, he was gone.

A small white envelope sat tucked into the ribbon. Placing the box on the desk, Kay opened the card. *"Sorry, Bear."*

Fresh tears threatened. She'd been so unfair to doubt him. She should be the one apologizing.

Kay tugged on the ribbon and lifted the lid. The rich smell cut through the disbelief screaming in her brain.

Roses. Oh, God… He sent her roses.

Chapter Twenty-Eight

Bear pulled his wallet out of his rear pocket and slipped out his credit card. "I need a ticket on the next flight to Portland, Maine, or Boston. I'll take whatever you have."

"I'm sorry, sir, but all the flights into Portland are cancelled until further notice due to inclement weather. Boston has issued an alert. We're to hold some of those later flights on delay until they are cleared."

"What about the 4:19 to Boston?"

She tapped into her computer. "Seems they're going to try and get that one out." She checked the screen. "Unfortunately the flight is full, but I can put you on the standby list."

Bear nodded. "Fine, put me on the list. I'll take my chances. What gate?"

"D15. If you can't get on that flight, your gate attendant can go over your options." The agent leaned over the counter. "But if I were you," she whispered, "I'd try to find a hotel room. Anybody heading to New England is going to be looking for a bed tonight. Sorry."

Bear took off running. He had to make that flight.

People packed into the gate. He was fifth on the wait list. Bear didn't bother to plead his case to the gate agent. It would be a waste of time. Scanning the waiting area, he spotted a lone man. Business traveler by the look. Laptop, wrinkled suit. Bear approached him.

"Sir, I'll give you six hundred dollars for your seat on this flight."

The man glanced up from his computer. "Fuck off."

"I'm serious. I have to get on this plane."

The man snorted. "Yeah, so do I."

"Eight hundred." Bear held out his wallet.

The man narrowed his gaze and smirked. "Fifteen hundred."

"Shit, I don't carry that kind of cash on me. I was lying about the eight."

"Then good luck getting to Boston." He laughed as he closed his computer and slipped it into a battered leather briefcase.

The call came over the speaker that they were loading first class and premier members. Bear scrambled to open his wallet. "Fine, fifteen hundred. Listen, I have six hundred and..." He counted. "...forty-seven bucks. Here's my business card and my credit card. I promise I'm good for it. As soon as I reach Boston, I'll wire you the rest of the money."

"Like I believe that." The man shook his head and pushed past him.

Bear called after him. "This credit card has a three-thousand-dollar cap. If you don't have your money in forty-eight hours, go nuts."

That stopped him. The man turned and narrowed his gaze. "What makes you think I won't go nuts anyway?"

"I trust you."

The man snorted. "Good way to get screwed."

"I have to get on this plane." Bear pushed the bills

at him. "Please."

He looked past the money, giving Bear a head to toe sweep. "How do I know you're not a terrorist?"

"Really?" Frustration surged through Bear. "What terrorist hands out his business card?

"Lemme guess, this has something to do with a dame."

Bear held his hands up in surrender. "Guilty."

The loud speaker informed them they were now boarding families with small children and anyone needing assistance.

He was running out of time. "Come on. Do it for romance."

The man shook his head while he grabbed the handle on his carry-on bag and headed toward the gate. "I have three ex-wives."

"Then do it for...hell, I don't know..." Bear noticed a familiar logo on the man's luggage tag. "The Red Sox. Do it for the Red Sox. Bet with the money you could get some great seats at Fenway."

Ten minutes later, Bear was clicking the seat belt and making sure his tray table was secured.

He'd given up calling the inn. Either Kay wasn't there, or she couldn't hear the phone. He gave Walter a quick call, but he hadn't seen Kay. Walter did promise to check over at the inn for her.

Only when the wheels of the plane left the tarmac, did Bear begin to relax. They'd get into Boston by seven. It would be late by the time he reached Bell Harbor, but he'd have this whole mess settled and be back in Kay's arms before midnight.

About forty-five minutes into their flight, the pilot made an announcement. "Attention, ladies and gentlemen, this is your captain speaking. We've been getting some bad news out of Boston, folks. Seems tropical storm Daphne headed up the coast has turned into hurricane Daphne with sustained winds near seventy miles an hour. ATC has directed us to divert this flight to Hartford. We may encounter a bit of turbulence between here and there, so I'm turning on the seat belt sign as a precaution."

"Wait." Bear questioned the woman seated next to him. "Did he say Hartford?"

"He sure did."

"How the hell are we getting to Boston?"

As if to answer his question, the next announcement was from their flight attendant. "Ladies and gentlemen, we are sorry for the inconvenience, but be assured there will be gate agents waiting when we land in Hartford who will assist with overnight accommodations and alternative arrangements to get you all to your final destinations. In the meantime, sit back and relax. If we have any further updates, we'll be sure to bring them to you. As the captain has instructed, please return to your seats and observe the fasten seat belt signs. Thank you."

Passengers grumbled throughout the plane as seat belts clicked back into place.

"What does that mean exactly?" asked Bear to no one in particular.

"Means we're spending the night in Connecticut, courtesy of this fine airline." The woman next to him shrugged. "They'll either fly us out first thing tomorrow, or if the storm moves off, they'll probably stuff us all into buses and drive us to Boston tonight." She leaned back and closed her eyes. "I don't know about you, but I'm up for another night of room service with someone else picking up the tab."

Bear dodged the crowd gathered around the promised gate agents and headed straight for the car rental counter. "I need a car." Thank goodness he had another credit card. At this rate, he'd lay money on Steve Griffin, aka Mr. Red Sox, reaching his final destination before him and using his other card to "go nuts." Bear set the second card along with his license on the counter.

"Well, let's see. It's been a busy evening. What type of vehicle were you interested in?"

Bear gave the man his best defensemen stare. "Four wheels and a gas pedal."

The rental agent gave him a tight little smile. "I see." He tapped the keyboard in front of him rapidly, shooting nervous glances toward his computer screen and then back to Bear. He tugged at his collar. "I have nothing in midsize...or economy class..."

"Anything. I'll take anything you've got."

More tapping. The man behind the counter started to sweat. "I do have two luxury cars due back later this evening."

"How much later?"

"Well, hard to say. We close at eleven."

Bear scrubbed at his jaw. Frustration had turned it into granite. Holding his anger in check, he joked. "Let me guess, you have a brother Tom who sells mattresses?"

"Excuse me, sir?"

"Nothing." Bear gripped the edge of the counter. "I'm done listening to what you don't have. What *do* you have? Something that's actually sitting in your lot.

I see keys over there—" He gestured to the counter behind the man. "What are those for? I'll take one of those."

"Well…those aren't—"

"What. Do. You. Have?"

Bear secured yet another seatbelt. Had anger, worry, and complete frustration not been raging through him, he'd be laughing. Hysterically. Until white-coated attendants dragged him off to a rubber room.

Glancing over his shoulder, he shook his head as he jammed the key into the ignition of the eighteen-passenger transit van. All he needed now was some choir group going on a church picnic singing *Kum ba yah* in the back.

His phone was officially dead. Even if he had his charger; A, he hadn't packed the car adapter for it, and B, even if he had, his luggage was now flying toward Los Angeles with his certifiable ex-wife.

Bear pulled out onto the highway heading north. A light rain had begun to fall. It took him ten minutes just to find the windshield wiper switch. The vehicle handled like a refrigerator box, and the front end pulled to the left. The whole van shimmied at speeds over fifty miles an hour, but the good news was the brakes worked. He'd almost stood this beast on its nose the first time he stepped on the pedal.

Didn't matter. What mattered was getting to Bell Harbor, finding Kay, and trying to convince her that breaking her heart was not what he had planned for today. All he could think about was three dozen red roses like three dozen fists hitting her. He couldn't imagine what she must be thinking.

He pushed hard on the accelerator until the front

end began to dance. He had to get there. The sun was setting behind rain-filled clouds. Bear flipped on his headlights and focused on the road. It was going to be a long ride.

"Dammit," Bear shouted at the traffic in front of him.

Now he couldn't get that stupid *Kum ba yah* song out of his head!

Chapter Twenty-Nine

Kay wedged in the last box and struggled to get the hatch door to secure. The wind had picked up. It moaned through the tops of the pines as they bent under a pewter sky.

Only thing left for her to do was coax Hope into the carrier, load her in the last spot on the passenger seat, and point her overstuffed car west. Some cat treats, a long feather, and some catnip should work.

After that, her road was clear—and empty. She didn't have a clue as to where she was heading. Back to Stoddard? Somewhere new? She just had to be gone from Bell Harbor. It didn't matter where she went. She'd figure it out on the way.

Each time she stopped long enough to think, the memory of opening the white box…the smell of those roses. Grabbing them by the fistfuls and throwing them to the floor. How many had he sent? She didn't count. The box seemed bottomless, and she couldn't see through the tears and the hurt. Even Todd hadn't been so cruel.

Tears threatened again, but Kay doubted she had any more left to shed. She laid cool fingers over her eyes. No more.

A car pulling into the graveled pad behind her startled Kay. The familiar silver BMW came to a stop.

"I see you're still running." Claire jerked her chin

in the direction of Kay's car as she slid from the driver's seat.

Now that Kay knew the truth about her mother's illness, she could clearly see the signs. She was thinner, paler. Claire tugged her cardigan tight against the rising winds.

Kay shrugged. "It's easier this way."

"Sometimes." She shivered. "Could we go inside? It's freezing."

Kay hesitated. Part of her didn't want another show down with her mother. She'd already been through the emotional wringer, but there was something in her mother's manner. "If you've come here to gloat…"

"No. Don't you think it's time we talked?" Claire didn't wait for an answer before heading toward the stairs. "I need a hot cup of tea, and you look like you could use one yourself."

"Did Dottie send you?" Kay followed in her wake.

"No. I wanted to come." In the kitchen, it was Claire who filled the kettle and put it on the stove. "There are things I need to say to you, and I'd appreciate it if you'd give me a chance and just listen."

Kay was hit by another wave of sadness that their relationship had been reduced to this. Things could have been so different between them.

"Do I have a choice?"

"No, you do not." She pointed to a chair. "Sit." Claire pulled two cups from the cupboard. "I promise I'll make it short and sweet."

Kay sat. Claire busied herself with finding teabags, sugar, spoons. Kay waited. She could still hear the wind and couldn't help but compare the building of the storm outside to what might be building in this kitchen.

Claire didn't speak again until they were both dunking their teabags by their paper tags in steaming cups of water. "So, you're all packed up ready to go. Where are you headed?"

"Does it matter?" Kay stirred her tea.

"It matters to me. I'd like to know where to find you." She met Kay surprised gaze. "Don't look so shocked. I'm not a monster, you know. I do care. I may not have been a great mother, but I always knew where you were, and how you were doing." Claire opened her arms wide. "Why do you think I'm here?"

"To sell the cottage." Kay sat back and crossed her arms over her chest.

"Yes, and no. I wanted to see you."

Kay dropped her arms and refocused on her mug. "I don't believe you."

"Well, it's true whether you believe it or not," Claire snapped, then she seemed to catch herself. "Dottie told you…about my health issues. And, well, I've been forced to take a step back and look at things from a new perspective."

"Dottie didn't tell me anything other than you were sick. Per your instructions." Kay pointed an accusing finger at her mother.

"Kay…I've never been one of those women who shares every small, intimate detail of their lives with everyone from the bagboy at the Shop n' Save to the Pope."

"I'm hardly the bagboy at the Shop n' Save. Telling your daughter you might be dying isn't a small detail, Mother."

"It's not as if we have the kind of relationship where I could pick up the phone and say, Hey, Honey, I

241

have cancer."

The C word sucked the air from Kay's lungs. She suspected, of course, but a tiny corner of her brain prayed she was wrong. "H-how bad it is?"

"Bad enough. I've had the surgery. They ran new scans. Next week I meet with my doctors, and we'll discuss the results and further treatment options from there."

"You could have told me." Kay's voice sounded small.

"I could have. Maybe I was…afraid."

"Claire Winston, afraid? You're the toughest woman I know. You're not afraid of anything."

"I'm afraid of this." Claire frowned into her cup. "You were so angry. For so long. And rightly so. I didn't know how to tell you. I wanted to think, in time, I could fix things. That maybe I wouldn't have to tell anyone."

"I'm sure Charles—"

"Charles was destroyed by the news. He always played the stoic, tough man, but when the doctors told him my prognosis, he refused to believe them. Spent months researching holistic medicines and new experimental treatments, but in the end, he couldn't deal with it." Claire sipped her tea. "He left me a few weeks ago."

"Bastard! How could he?"

"Don't." Claire held up a hand to stop her. "No matter your opinion, he's still a decent man. Weak. Frightened. But he gave me a great life."

"In exchange for your daughter," Kay countered.

"I was weak and frightened too, back then," Claire rushed to explain. "I don't expect you to understand, but I grew up poor. The poorest of the poor. Do you know I never had a pair of new shoes until I met Charles? I always wore hand-me-downs. Never my own. New shoes, still in the box with tissue in the toes. I think I cried the first time I wore them."

Claire moved to take Kay's hand but stopped and pulled back. "I didn't want that for you. Scratching for every penny. Yes, I made mistakes, but you never went to bed hungry. You were always dressed in clothes without patches and had a roof over your head. It was a lot more than I had growing up."

"Until Charles kicked me out." Kay couldn't keep the bitterness out of her voice.

"I should have fought him harder, I know."

"You didn't fight him at all."

"But look at you. You've made it despite us. I'm not the tough one, you are. You're strong. So much stronger than I've ever been. And so talented. Your mural at the inn blew me away. Your future is set, and after I'm gone, you'll be a wealthy young woman. I named you beneficiary on my life insurance."

Kay stared at her. "I don't want your money. I want my mother."

"I'm right here." Claire reached out again, and this time, laid a hand on Kay's arm.

"But for how long?"

"Long enough." She held Kay's gaze for a long moment. "Just let me know where I can find you."

Kay chewed at her lip. This was all too much. She'd spent so many years being angry, fighting to get away from her mother when she would have given anything to have her in her life. Here she was asking for nothing more than a bit of peace between them. Dottie was right. If she didn't try to mend their relationship before it was too late, she'd regret it forever.

Kay laid a hand over her mother's chilled fingers. "You'll know where I am, I promise."

"Good." Claire pulled some papers from her purse. "Then I have just one more loose end. I need a dollar."

"I don't understand."

"You owe me a dollar."

"Why did you lose a bet with Dottie that you couldn't get me to stay?"

"No. The terms of the contract state I've sold you the cottage for the sum total of one dollar."

Kay jerked as if she'd been slapped. "You're selling the cottage...to me?"

"Yes. I want you to have it." She pulled out a pen. "This place was always going to be yours. You've loved it all these years. Sign here and here and hand over that dollar."

"I-I don't know what to say."

"Say thank you." Claire held out the pen. "We're never going to have the Hallmark mother-daughter relationship. I think too much water has passed under the bridge, but it doesn't mean I don't love you. It doesn't mean I'm not proud of the talented woman you've become. The cottage isn't a bribe. It's the one thing that is truly mine to give you. I want to know you'll always have a roof over your head. Stay. Go. Keep it. Sell it. It's your decision now." She watched Kay sign and gathered the pages and put them back in her purse. Standing, she slipped the strap of her purse over her shoulder.

"I have just one more question." Claire jerked her chin toward the cove. "What about him?"

Kay stood and tugged at the hem of her T-shirt. There was no need in asking who the him was. "It's over."

"Dottie tells me you love this man, and the way he defended you this morning, I'd say he loves you, too."

Kay gave a quick shake to her head. "You'd be wrong."

"I'm sorry." Claire did something then she hadn't done in close to fifteen years. She hugged her daughter.

After Claire left with a promise to call after she'd talked to her doctors, Kay followed the sound of the surf to stand on the back edge of the beach. She needed time to think. With the storm in the gulf, and the tide on the way in, the waves were impressive. Crashing, foaming, churning as one pushed and another pulled.

Kay was experiencing the same thing. The push and the pull. The realization she'd found her mother again, only to be facing the prospect of losing her for good.

And now the cottage was hers, the same moment everything falls apart? She couldn't possibly stay. Not now. Not and be reminded of Bear everywhere she turned. It wasn't even the point house being there.

This place was where they met. Where they first kissed. First made love. Everything was too fresh and raw to even dream of staying here. Maybe in time she could come back. After some distance, she may gain the perspective she'd need to return. They say time heals.

Fat drops of rain polka dotted the stones at her feet. She needed to find Hope before it was too late. The storm was here. In more ways than one. It was her cue to leave.

Kay turned, then stopped. Over the roar of the waves, she swore she heard barking. In the growing dark, she must have imagined it. But then, she heard it again.

Shadow?

Out of the corner of her eye, she saw him. Racing, frantic. He still wore his leash. She looked back up the breakwater. Was Walter with him?

The dog headed straight for the point house through the spray of waves hitting the rocks. Was he alone? It wasn't safe for him to be running around out there. Kay could hear him barking over the wind and surf.

Sea water wet the bottoms of her jeans and filled her shoes as she dashed to catch him. She kept looking over her shoulder. Any minute Walter was sure to appear. The icy rain fell harder now.

"Shadow! Come here, boy!" If he heard, he wasn't acknowledging. He continued to bark and circle outside Bear's house.

By the time Kay reached him and got a firm hold on his leash, the rain was blowing at them sideways. It was growing darker by the minute. The breakwater rushed along the tops of the stones. It would be stupid to try and head back that way. In the dark, she'd end up breaking her neck or getting swept out to sea. Or both.

Shadow continued to tug and bark. The dog was going to strangle himself. "Easy, boy. Settle down. Let me think."

They had to get out of the rain and the wind. Kay tried the door to Bear's house, in vain. Of course it was locked. Wait, there was a spare key. In a rock that doesn't look like a rock.

"God, help me." She pushed the hair out of her eyes and turned her back to the force of the wind. "Shadow, where the hell is the damn rock?"

Chapter Thirty

The van handled like a kite in these winds. Thank goodness Bear was the only fool stupid enough to be on the roads in this weather. He'd lost track of the number of times he been blown into another lane.

Bell Harbor looked like a ghost town by the time he rolled into the parking area of the inn. Wind-driven rain obscured the end of the docks. Shop signs swung. The town had lost power. Traffic lights did little but sway violently on their wires. The emergency generator at the inn had automatically switched on, lighting the stairways and exits.

Hoping against rational thought, Bear called out as he entered the inn. "Kay? Are you here? Anyone? Kay?" He flipped on the lighting in the lobby to grab his own car keys. His worst fear greeted him.

Roses...three dozen goddamn roses littered the floor. "Son of a bitch..." He closed his eyes to the shaft of guilt and anger rushing through him. "Oh, Kay, I'm so sorry," he shouted at the ceiling. He ran a hand over his face.

Bear noticed something more. The taping was gone. All Kay's supplies cleared away. The mural had its final antiquing. His gaze flew to the wall behind the desk. There was his likeness along with Shadow, just as she'd described her idea of including them. She'd finished it. The effect was amazing.

His boots crushed roses into the tiled floor as he made a slow circle to take in the richness of the simple finishing technique. A disturbing thought pierced through his brain. If she was done with the mural, there'd be no reason for her to stay. Not after Diane's lies and these damn flowers. He kicked at the stems.

Something else caught Bear's eye. "No…" The word rushed from him as if he'd been punched. He moved closer to the wall, praying he was wrong. He wasn't. The lovers…he and Kay…in the rocks. They'd been painted over. Seamlessly, as if they had never been there.

Pushing back out into the tempest of the storm, Bear rushed to his car. He plugged his cell phone onto the charger, and it sprang to life with a flurry of message notifications. If any of them were from Diane, he would throw it into the street. No, there were four messages, all from Walter.

"Bear, call me as soon as you get this. Doesn't matter what time it is. We got us a situation here."

The rest of the messages were about the same if not increasingly more panicky. *"Bear, where the hell are you?"*

Bear was out of his car and running toward Polka Dots. A single light burned in the apartment upstairs. Walter's generator growled in the back. If Kay was hurt, he'd never forgive himself. He pounded on the back door until Walter answered the door.

"Dammit, son, I've been trying to reach you for plum near five hours. What the hell are you doing back here in the middle of a hurricane? You're supposed to be in LA?"

"I have to find Kay. Is she all right? Have you seen

her?"

"She cleared out hours ago. Probably over in New Hampshire by now. She was some upset when I saw her earlier. Claire said she was all packed and fixin' to leave before the storm hit."

Bear grabbed Walter's arm. "So she's okay?"

"'Spect so. Storm ain't so bad west o' here. It's Shadow. Blasted dog. He's why I've been callin' ya half the night."

"What about him? Is he sick?"

"Took off. Leash an' all. Near tore the arm off me."

"You lost my dog in a hurricane?"

Walter tossed up his hand. "He just bolted. Like somebody shoved a rocket up his arse. He'd been acting squirrelly since you left."

"What do you mean?"

"Squirrelly." Walter stretched out the word as if saying it slower would somehow clarify its meaning. "Think he might have been sensing the storm coming. Took off before it hit. I've been looking for him all over town ever since."

Bear planted his hands on his hip and studied the tops of his shoes. "Shit."

"Well, like I said, he skedaddled just before dark. The rain hadn't even started yet, so if he's tucked in somewhere out of the storm. He may just hole up there until this mess passes."

"He's not at the inn. I just came from there."

"He sure as hell ain't. I've been back there looking a dozen times." Walter ran a hand over his head. "I sure am sorry, Bear."

"Wasn't your fault."

"Was the damnedest thing. I said, 'Come on, ya mangy mutt, let's head home,' and the next second he was gone."

Bear knew at once where he went. But, if he was on the point in this storm…There was no time to explain. "I have to go." Bear thumped Walter's shoulder.

He pulled a long yellow rain slicker off a hook by the back door and tossed it at Bear. "If you're gonna try to run through a hurricane, you'll need this. Radio's saying the storm taking a turn to the north, but we're still in for some beatin'. Watch yourself."

"Thanks, Walter."

Bear drove at breakneck speed dodging fallen branches and debris in the road. He had to get to the cove. Without the streetlights, the back roads were treacherous. His headlight beams barely reached into the murk.

Adrenaline pumped through him. If Kay was safe, even if she was God knows where in New Hampshire, he'd find her. He wouldn't rest until then. But Shadow was in real trouble here.

Walter had said the magic word. Home. Shadow only knew one home. It was a game. When Bear said "home," the dog ran there like he was shot out of a cannon.

The question was, did he make it out there before the storm lowered its fist into the cove? Was he trapped out there wet and cold battling the elements? There weren't many places to hide and ride it out. If the waves got too high…

He wouldn't think about that. Bear punched down on the accelerator.

He swerved to miss a shattered limb stretched across the road. Almost there. Just around the next corner.

Speeding past the upper lot right before his turn, his headlights caught a side reflector in the dark. Bear slammed his foot on the breaks and spun into the graveled area. "Kay!"

He grabbed a flashlight from the glove compartment and leapt out of his car. The batteries were old and gave a weak light, but it was something. Bear pulled the wide, yellow hood of Walter's rain gear over his head. It may make him look like a frozen fish-stick spokesman, but he was grateful for the little protection it afforded.

Waving the light over Kay's car confirmed what Walter said. She was packed. For the first time since Chicago, he had something to thank hurricane Daphne for accomplishing. Kay was still here.

He hurried down the slick stone stairs and pounded on the back door. "Kay!" There were no lights visible inside. No candles, or lanterns. Bear held the flashlight under his chin to locate Kay's key on his key ring.

"Kay?" Bear pushed through the living room and took the stairs two at a time. "Kay? Are you up here?" He checked both bedrooms. They were both empty. The beds were stripped. Everything had been set for her to leave.

Where the hell was she?

Opening the back to the deck door brought a renewed rush of wind and rain into the cottage. Bear ducked his head and scanned the deck. His light was fading. He gave it a sharp knock to brighten the pitiful beam.

As he did, two round disks reflected in the dark. Kay's cat was huddled tight into the corner of the deck against the wide posts. Now he knew Kay was here somewhere. She wouldn't have left Hope behind.

In one quick move, Bear scooped up the cat and cradled him to his chest. "Where is she?" The panicked kitten yowled. "That doesn't help me. Aren't you supposed to give me some hope? Isn't that your name?" He opened the deck door again, and the cat scrambled out of his grasp in favor of the safety inside.

Stepping out onto the beach moments later was like landing on a hostile planet. The cottage was protected somewhat, but the cove was taking the full force of Daphne's beating. Bear leaned into the wind and pushed forward.

The tide should have made its turn. A few hours ago, he'd have been washed away, but the waves were still too high. The driving rain and seawater stung at his eyes. Churning water covered a portion of the breakwater spanning a strip maybe fifteen feet across where the stones followed the curve of the beach before rising to the point.

As each crashing wave began its ebb, Bear could see more of the stones, but how deep was the over spill? Two feet? Four? Without the wave swell?

Beyond he could see the point house. Any sane man would wait for the tide to recede. Wait for daylight. Wait for the f-ing Coast Guard.

His clothing was already frozen to his skin, but when he dashed into the icy waves, the shock to his system had him screaming obscenities into the wind. As if to scream back, the sea raised a watery fist and slammed into him.

Chapter Thirty-One

Shoving his way into the point house, Bear nearly wept when he saw them. *Thank you, God. Thank you, God.* He gripped the edge of his counter to steady the sudden stagger in his legs.

Shadow rushed him, head down, whining. His whole body wagged. Bear bent and pulled the dog against his leg and wrapped an arm around the dog's neck. Shadow pressed into him.

"Oh my God, Walter! Thank goodness. How—"

Bear stood and pushed back the hood of the rain slicker. "It's me."

"Bear." His name fell from her lips in a gasp. "What? How did you…"

Blood rushed in his ears. Adrenaline still pumped through his veins. He wanted nothing more than to cross the room, drag her into his arms, and kiss her senseless. He'd never been so relieved to see anyone in his life.

"She had me 'til we reached Chicago. The second I found out what Diane was up to, I headed back." His breath still came in short pants. "Would have been here h-hours ago. Hurricane Daphne had other ideas."

"You're soaked. How did you get out here? The tide's cut us off." She took a step closer. "Don't tell me you braved those waves?"

"I had to find you." Shadow was now sitting on his

foot, gazing up at him. Bear stroked the dog's throat. His tail thumped the floor "And him. Walter told me he'd taken off. I knew he'd head here, but I thought…" The words damned his throat. "They said you were gone. Then when I saw your car, and I couldn't find you…the cat wasn't talking…"

"You swam for me?"

"I had to get out here. Make sure you were okay. If anything happened to you, I don't know what I would have done."

"You swam for me." The firelight caught the tears in her eyes.

Every fiber of his being needed to touch her. He took a single step closer. "I saw the mural, Kay. You erased the lovers. Erased us. And those *fucking* roses. I could have killed Diane when I found out she sent them and what she said to you. None of it—*none* of it was true. You have to believe me. I'm so sorry."

Kay stood shaking her head with an incredulous look on her face.

A greater chill than he had just endured spread through him. *Please say something. Anything.* "Kay Winston, I swear, if you don't tell me you forgive me and let me kiss you in the next ten damn seconds—"

She flew into his arms, and he crushed his mouth to hers. His arms caught her. Locked her to him. Hours of desperation and fear crashed down on him harder than the waves outside. He didn't care what it took, what he had to do, he was not losing her. Not now. Not ever.

Holding her face in his frozen hands, he wiped away her tears with his thumb. "I never wanted to hurt you. I was trying so hard to keep all of *that*"—he used one hand to gesture pushing Diane and California back—"keep all the craziness from you. It's why I left to start a new life here."

Kay kissed his cheeks. "I didn't want to believe what Diane was saying, but then the flowers... The card...I'm sorry. I never should have doubted you."

"I hadn't been totally straight with you, and it blew up in my lap. I should have told you what was going on long before then. But everything she told me was a lie. Every bit of it. Diane played us both."

"She still loves you."

He gave a bitter laugh as he pictured Diane's florid face as she screeched after him in Chicago. How had he ever had feelings for her? Had she changed so much from the girl he married, or was it him? "Don't worry. It's over."

"That's not what she thinks."

"Oh, she does now. It was a very short, intense scene in the middle of Chicago, O'Hare. She got the message." He kissed Kay again, and all else fell away. The anger, the panic, the fear of losing her. She was safe in his arms where he wanted to keep her forever. There was just one more truth she needed to know.

"You're drenched." Kay ran her hands over his chest. "Come get warm. I managed to find the fireplace and some matches in the dark, but I've been so scared. This storm is crazy. Shadow and I have been huddled together here praying the house doesn't get swept away."

"Not a chance. We're bolted to the rocks. And those windows are storm rated." The fire would wait. Bear didn't want another moment to pass with any more hurdles between them. He'd lost his flashlight somewhere between the cottage and the point. "I have some emergency candles in the kitchen. There's one more thing I have to tell you, show you, but I need light."

"You need to get warm and dry first."

"No. It can't wait another minute. I've already waited too long." Bear lit one of the short, white candles, dripped its hot wax, and secured it and two others to saucers to protect their hands. He handed one to Kay. "Follow me."

He pushed into the dark of the master bedroom. The storm was louder here as the room had two full walls of windows.

Kay moved closer. "Storm rated and bolted to the rocks?"

Bear set the candles on the long, low dresser. The wide mirror mounted behind helped reflect the light and washed the room in a soft glow.

"We're safe." He took advantage and gathered her close. Breathed in the sweet smell of her. Shiver as the warmth of her body penetrated his icy clothes. "This isn't how this was supposed to go. I had it all planned. Dinner. Wine."

"All to get me into your bedroom?"

He smiled into her hair. "Yes, and no." He'd practiced this speech a hundred times over the last few weeks. And now they were here, and all those carefully chosen words eluded him.

"Do you believe in fate?"

Kay shrugged. "I'm not sure."

"I do. I'm a firm believer now. It was fate that I met you, Kay. I was supposed to come here to Bell Harbor, find you, and fall in love with you." Bear took a deep breath and released her. "Look."

Kay followed the direction of his outstretched hand and gave a small gasp. "M-my painting. You? You were the buyer in Boston?" She looked at him with wide eyes.

Bear nodded. "Had I told you I loved you before I met you, knew you before I'd laid eyes on you, you'd have thought I was some creepy stalker art-fan guy. Hell, I would have. But I think everything happens for a reason. Being here. Choosing here. It was all so I could have you in my life.

"I took one look at that painting and fell in love. It was perfect. As if the artist painted it for me. *You* painted this for me. My point. *Our point.*

"I didn't care what it cost. I wasn't letting some woman stick it in her camp because it matched the new slipcovers. I would have paid ten times as much to have it. It was always mine.

"Then there you were. You stepped into the sunshine out onto the beach. A day later, you walked into my inn. I put two and two together about the painting not long after I saw your portfolio. I knew I'd seen your work before. It was crazy. How was I supposed to tell you without it all sounding crazy?"

Bear took her hands. "Fate brought me to Bell Harbor. Because you were here. I was supposed to find you. It sounds insane, I know, but there it is." He kissed the back of her fingers. "I love you. I've always loved you, and now I finally found you."

Kay looked back at her painting. "I don't know what to say."

"Say you believe me." In the flicker of candlelight, Kay turned back to look at him. Silvery tracks shimmered down her cheeks. "Dear God, don't cry."

"I do believe you." Kay reached out and placed a hand on his chest. "I'm not used to anyone loving me like you do. I never thought I'd ever have it or that I'd ever feel this way." She pulled in a shuddering breath. "I've been running for so long, but I've always come back to Bell Harbor. It's why I painted that. It's where I feel I belong."

"You do belong here, with me. I'm just sorry it took me so long to get here."

****

Kay rolled over in the wide bed only to find the space where Bear had slept empty. She raised up on an elbow and marveled at the stunning room in the light of the new day.

Daphne still churned a dull green sea but had moved far enough off the coast to allow the rising sun to creep below its clouds and bring the promise of calmer skies. Two banks of windows running along the eastern and northern walls of Bear's sleek, modern bedroom made it feel as if you'd get your feet wet should you step off the rug. The view swept clear to Ireland.

From where she lay, she could see the lighthouse out on the farthest rock. Standing as it had for hundreds of years. She turned her head to see its framed twin upon the wall. It still amazed her that Bear had been the one to buy it from the Bruce Gallery. Call it fate, serendipity, destiny…if she was seeking a sign that Bear was indeed who she was meant to be with…

She swung her legs off the side of the bed and surveyed the scattering of clothes. The storm had nothing on them last night in the way of intensity. They'd made love well past dawn. Her body still thrummed with a well-sated hum.

"Where do you think you're going?" Bear stood in the doorway with a black lacquered tray. "Get back into bed."

"I was coming to find you. Where did you disappear to?"

"I'm pleased to report we are no longer an island. The tide has receded, and the breakwater still stands."

At one point last night, Bear explained he'd found Hope in the middle of his search for her, and she was safe. "I should go to the cottage. Check on Hope."

"Shadow and I checked on the cottage. You've lost a couple branches, but everything looks okay." He set the tray aside while he added his clothing to the chaos on the floor.

Kay's breath still caught at the sight of him. With or without his clothes, he truly was the most beautiful man she'd ever seen. She cleared her throat and struggled to remember what they'd been talking about.

"Hope," she blurted.

"Hope is fine. You may have to give her a bit more food later. Shadow helped her finish her breakfast, but he paid for it. She's a feisty one. Puffed up and danced under his nose before she batted at him. Put him square in his place. I doubt he'll be stealing her food again."

Bear picked up the tray and joined Kay in bed.

The smell of fresh coffee made her sigh. Seeing the rest of the tray, she gave him a coy look. "You brought me pie?"

"Haven't you ever eaten blueberry pie for breakfast?" He broke off a piece of crust and fed it to her, giving her a wicked smile before his gaze turned more serious. Bear moved the folded napkin to one side revealing a small blue velvet box

"It's not Dottie's recipe, but I was hoping it would bring me luck." He cracked open the lid and held it out to her. Inside cushioned in snowy white satin sat the most perfect diamond ring. "There's only one thing I want to wish for."

Epilogue

"Where are you?" Bear's voice reached through Kay's phone.

"I just got out of Girard's glass class." She slipped into the warmth of her car. The fall air was still heavy with the last of the Indian summer heat. "He didn't care if it was a long weekend, he kept us late pulling stringers for our paperweight lesson."

"I can't wait for you to get here. How's Mom?"

"She's doing okay. The doctors at Dartmouth are amazing. Her treatments are going well. They're cautiously optimistic. I'm heading back to the apartment to pick her up now, and then we're heading over."

"Hurry." The low huskiness in his voice rumbled clear to her knees.

"Are you sure you want to do this?"

"Honey, I've been sure about this since the day I met you."

"But you've an inn full of people."

"Who are almost as excited as I am that there's going to be a wedding here this weekend."

Kay couldn't help the rush of bubbly nerves to rush through her as well. It had all come together so quickly. Almost as if their Labor Day wedding was fated to happen. "I love you for doing all this."

"Just remember that when we've been married

thirty years, and I'm still leaving the cap off the toothpaste."

It was to be a tiny affair held on the back patio of the inn. "It means a lot to Mom, too."

"She wanted to see her daughter married."

A lump caught in Kay's throat. Her mother's health was stable for now, but Claire Eustice Fenton Winston was determined to see her daughter happily wed. According to her, "The sooner the better."

She and Kay had come together after the storm. As if it had somehow blown some of the discord from their relationship. They talked. Set aside some of the hurt and anger. There were still some conversational landmines between them, but at least now they both tried to avoid them.

Kay moved into the point house after deciding Bear was right all along. It was stunning. Her treasured cottage became her full-time studio until it was time to head back to Stoddard. But instead of renting a place close to the school, Kay made the decision to find an apartment farther north, with two bedrooms, close to one of the finest hospitals in the Northeast. Claire wasn't the worst roommate she'd ever had. Kay wanted to be there to help her mother, and the commute to Stoddard wasn't bad at all.

Not that Claire allowed her to *take care* of anything. It just made Kay happy to be there should the need arise.

"Are you sure you want Shadow to be the ring bearer?" The question pulled her back to the wedding plans. Walter and Dottie were standing up for them. Claire was walking Kay down the aisle.

"Yes, I have his bow tie all packed. If I could just

convince Hope to be a flower girl, it would be perfect."

"I can't wait to see you in your wedding gown." Bear's voice did the caramelly thing that made her thighs ache.

"I can't wait for you to take it off me."

"And don't worry, the florist has been warned. The entire town of Bell Harbor, Maine, has been scrubbed. This wedding is rose free."

Who knew Shadow would be so allergic to lilies?

A word about the author...

Lisa is an artist/writer living in her dream house nestled among the lakes in New England. She loves getting lost in a steamy book, finding the perfect pair of sexy shoes, and hearing the laughter of her men. Being an estrogen island in a sea of testosterone makes her queen. She believes in ghosts, silver linings, the power of a man in a tuxedo, and happy endings.

Thank you for purchasing
this publication of The Wild Rose Press, Inc.

If you enjoyed the story, we would appreciate your
letting others know by leaving a review.

For other wonderful stories,
please visit our on-line bookstore at
www.thewildrosepress.com.

For questions or more information
contact us at
info@thewildrosepress.com.

The Wild Rose Press, Inc.
www.thewildrosepress.com

Stay current with The Wild Rose Press, Inc.

Like us on Facebook

https://www.facebook.com/TheWildRosePress

And Follow us on Twitter
https://twitter.com/WildRosePress